The End and Then

Hannah Bird

THE END AND THEN

Editor & Formatter: Lea Ann Schafer

Cover Design: Y'all, That Graphic

Published in the United States.

NOTE FROM THE AUTHOR:

I have compiled a list of content warnings below. If you don't feel you need them, I would suggest not reading to avoid spoilers.

Mistreatment by a parent, stepparent sexual abuse, mentions of child pornography assault, depression, PTSD, religious trauma, and pastoral misconduct.

Dedication

To my big sisters,
for their relentless strength and enduring hope.
The healthy cycle begins with us.

Chapter One

"Let me introduce you to my baby."

Zoey turns and gestures broadly to the dimly lit room lined with dark wooden booths on the right and a bar running the length of the wall to my left. "Well, technically it was Gary's baby first, but I'm making the payments now, so it's mine by adoption."

I smile because this is exactly the kind of place she and I would have frequented in college, and it reminds me a little of the pubs we'd duck into to escape the rain during our summer in London before senior year. "Where did Gary retire to?"

She smirks and points to the ceiling. "The apartment upstairs," she says, chuckling. "The deal was that he'd sell the bar to me at a price I could afford, but he'd stay rent-free in the apartment till he dies."

"Sounds like he's just guaranteeing he can haunt you afterward," I say, laughing. It really is an impressive place, and I can see where Zoey has added touches of her personality. Namely in the potted plants that seem to fill every visible corner and the black-and-white tile she laid herself in the entryway. I wince internally remembering the many FaceTime calls I suffered through to help select that damn tile.

Zoey blows the blonde curl that has fallen from her bun off her face and places her hands on her hips. "He already haunts me. You'll see, he's here every day at five o'clock sharp for his supper."

"But I'm a friendly ghost!" a gravelly voice rumbles from behind me. I startle and turn, my hand over my heart. I'm met with a man equal to me in height, bald and sporting the kind of beer belly that comes from years of sampling a little too much of what he was selling. "You must be Eden. I've heard so much about you," he says, extending a hand.

"Good things, I hope," I reply, clasping his hand in a firm shake. He has the lightest eyes I've ever seen, nearly gray, but they hold a mischief when he regards me that makes him feel like an old friend rather than a stranger I've just met. It probably helps that he resembles a mall Santa with his trimmed white beard.

"Not a single good thing, I'm afraid to say." He appears morose as he delivers this news, and he nudges Zoey to play along. She rolls her eyes and grimaces at him, but I can tell by the upturned corner of her lips that she likes his pestering. I'm relieved she has him here, looking out for her so far from the rest of her family. "Well, ladies, I'm going to head next door and see Rose for my coffee. Would you two like anything?"

"No thanks, Gary. Eden just got into town after driving through the night from Tennessee," she says, looping her arm through mine. "We're going to bother Chase for some assistance unpacking her U-Haul, and then I'd guess she's going straight to sleep."

Gary blows out a whistle and looks me up and down. I can only imagine I look as bedraggled as I feel. At some point in the night my hair fell partially from its ponytail holder, and I've been wearing the same white T-shirt and running shorts since I started loading the trailer yesterday. I probably should have slept before driving but sleep is hard to come by lately and I needed to leave before I lost my nerve.

"Tell that man I said he better not let you ladies lift a finger or he'll be hearing from me," he threatens playfully. "I'll be seeing you around then, Eden?"

I look from Zoey to him and wink. "Yes. I'll try not to smell so bad next time."

He gives me a deep belly laugh in reply as he turns and makes his way down the street toward what I assume is the coffee shop. Zoey locks up the doors behind us and looks at what I am now realizing is objectively a terrible parking job on my part.

"Still haven't mastered the art of the parallel park, huh, Eden?" Zoey says, cringing. In my defense, my CR-V is definitely in the lines. It's the U-Haul that is hanging out into the street. Luckily it is before eight on a Saturday morning, and Loveless doesn't seem to have woken up yet. I wonder, not for the first time, what sad person settled this town surrounded by all the beauty the Colorado Rockies have to offer and thought Loveless seemed like the perfect name. He and I would probably have been friends.

She walks over to the neighboring business and bangs on the glass of the front door. Taylor's Landing Outfitters looks closed, but the door pushes open with the chime of a bell. I see a man likely in his late twenties poke his head out, brushing back shaggy brunette waves with his fingers. He's sporting two days' worth of shadow on a jawline I can appreciate even from here. "What's up, Zo?"

"Chase, this is Eden." She gestures toward me standing by the door to her bar. I unfold my arms to offer him a wave. "My friend that I told you about. She just made it to town, and we need some help unloading her boxes. Think you could lend a hand?"

He grins at me, and I'm met with chestnut-colored eyes that elicit a warmth in my stomach I discourage by looking at my hands. "Yeah, we won't open for another hour anyway and, with that trailer blocking the street, wouldn't have much luck getting customers," he says playfully. His voice is unlike any I've heard before, with a rasp just coarse and deep enough that I feel it all the way down to my toes. I blush at the comment on my parking skills.

"Listen, it's the first time I've ever hauled anything!" I explain. I don't know why I care what he thinks. I don't, I decide. He and Zoey share a laugh at my expense, but he turns and locks the door to his shop behind him.

"Chase, why don't you just drive Eden over to my place?" Zoey suggests. "That way you can back it into my driveway, and we don't risk the lives of any pedestrians along the way. I can give you a ride back afterward."

I start to object to having a stranger in my car with me, but he speaks up before I can. "No problem. Does this mean my beer tonight is free?"

"There's a Coors Light with your name on it," Zoey says over her shoulder, jingling her keys at us as she walks the same direction Gary went. She passes 8th & Main Roasters and turns the corner toward what I assume is a parking lot behind the buildings. The downtown area is set up like the one in our hometown, a main street lined with old brick buildings that share walls with one another.

I turn back to Chase, and he's half smiling at me as he strides toward the driver's side of my car. "Keys in the ignition, Eden?" I nod and climb into the passenger seat. He groans as he tries to squeeze his long legs into the space I've left between the seat and the pedals. "Jeez, I know you're short, but do you really want to take an airbag to the face?" He grabs the bar under the seat and slides it all the way back.

He's lucky I'm not an easily offended person given all this teasing within five minutes of being introduced. As it stands, I kind of like that he's not doing the forced politeness that so often accompanies meeting new people. It makes him feel familiar.

"I'm not even that short. Five-foot-four is average for women," I explain. "It's just all in my torso, so my legs can't reach." I shrug my shoulders and turn to look out the window. I don't know why him being in my space feels so overwhelming, but it does. I catch the scent of pine trees and soap coming from him as the air-conditioning kicks on and moves the air around us. My stomach feels like it is doing cartwheels.

He backs us out onto the street after Zoey passes, and then begins to follow her toward her house. I wonder how often he goes there. She's never brought him up in our daily phone calls, and she always mentions guys she is seeing. He seems to know the way even without looking as she turns ahead of us. I swallow against the pang of unfounded jealousy as it swells in my throat.

"So, Eden, I don't think I've ever met anyone with that name before." He says it casually, just trying to make this car ride less awkward for both of us, I imagine. I like the way my name sounds when he says it, and I normally don't like my name very much.

"My mom found God sometime between when my sister and I were born. She got Ella; I got Eden," I say in a rehearsed tone, an explanation I've given often in my life. It has always made me laugh to see how differently my mother named us, Ella after a character in the romance novels she loves. "She named me after the garden that Adam and Eve got kicked out of for sinning."

She hates it when I phrase it that way. "*I named you after the most perfect place that ever existed, where there was no want and no suffering,"* she'd say.

"If it was so perfect," I'd tell her, *"why did they want to leave?"*

She never really had a great response to that.

Chase looks at me out of the corner of his eye as he flips his blinker to turn down a tree-lined street a few blocks from the bar. "Do you believe in all of that?" There's no hint of judgment in his voice. He just seems genuinely curious.

"I used to," I reply simply, purposefully trying to leave any trace of bitterness from my voice. This isn't a conversation I really want to have with a stranger, albeit a gorgeous one, after twenty-four hours with no sleep and a lifetime of pent-up frustration.

I see his jaw tighten and then release as he watches Zoey pull into what I assume is her driveway. I've only ever seen pictures of the house since she bought it last fall, but it's even more adorable in person. The sage-green Craftsman is tucked behind a few mature trees at the end of the quiet street. There are picture windows lining the small porch accented by white columns, and her green thumb has lent itself to flower baskets hung along the railing. I feel pride swell in my chest for the life she has created for herself here.

I also feel the breath whoosh out of my lungs as Chase grips the back of my headrest and checks the side mirrors to reverse expertly up to the garage door. His black T-shirt pulls up over his bicep to reveal the edges of a tattoo the design of which I can't quite make out without staring more obviously than my subtle side-eye will allow. He catches my gaze as he turns back to place the car in park, and his eyes crinkle at the corners when a soft smile tugs at the corners of his mouth. The minute he is stopped, I push my door open and hop out, letting the late spring air hit my face and calm me down.

He looks confused at my urgency but shrugs it off as he opens his side and climbs out. Zoey walks over, smiling as she gestures to the windows above the garage. "You've got your own mother-in-law suite up there with a separate entrance and a kitchenette. Laundry is in the main house, and your key works on both locks," she explains as she holds out the silver chain with a pink tag added to it that has my name written in her perfect script. "Lead the way." She points at the exterior staircase that climbs the side of the garage up to a white door on the back of the second story.

"There's a joke somewhere in there about me being your mother, but I'm too tired to make it," I say, grabbing the key from her as she laughs. There was a time not long ago when I was the responsible one keeping her alive. My how the tables have turned.

"I think putting a roof over your head establishes me as the official mom friend," Zoey says, pursing her smile into a matter-of-fact pout.

"How quickly you forget the nights of me spoon-feeding Pedialyte to you on the bathroom floor," I call behind me as I lead the way up the stairs. I hear Chase snort, and Zoey reaches back to swat him.

The key turns easily, and I open the door to a cozy living space that doubles as the bedroom of the studio apartment. There's a bed in the front of the room between the windows that overlook the driveway, and I can see the mountains in the distance beyond the town. She has a love seat arranged in the middle of the room facing a coffee table I remember her dad having built for us in college and the tv stand to match.

In the back of the open floor plan, I see a kitchenette with a little bar table that seats two and a door that I assume leads to the restroom. "You weren't kidding about me not needing much. This is perfect, Zo!"

She shrugs modestly. "I was going to just rent it out to some college student anyway, so I'd much rather have you here. What's mine is yours. Your wall backs up against my spare bedroom. Mine is on the bottom floor, opposite side of the house, so I won't even hear your activities," she explains with a wriggling of her shoulders that inflames my cheeks so badly I'm sure they match my hair. Chase laughs and points at the door.

"I'll go get started with the boxes then," he says as he takes his leave.

Zoey turns to look at me and nods her head toward the direction he went. "Eh?" she says suggestively, with her signature raised eyebrows and blue eyes twinkling mischievously.

"He's really handsome, ten out of ten. How come you didn't tell me you were seeing someone?" I ask, realizing she wants my opinion on her newest fling. I'm not even disappointed. Not much, anyway.

Zoey cackles. "Not for me, Eden, for you. He's not my type. Too nice."

I hear his footsteps on the top stair just before he turns into the doorway, easily carrying the heaviest box I've packed. "Ouch, Zo, hurtful," he says jokingly. I die a little inside thinking he heard the first part of what she was saying. "I'll be sure to tell Aaron you only flirt with him because he's an ass."

Zoey pretends to toss her hair flippantly even though it's still knotted on top of her head. "I only flirt with him because he *has* an ass. There's a difference." She turns to walk out the door to assist in the unpacking effort. Chase rolls his eyes and laughs.

He hefts the box up when he begins to lose his grip. "Jeez, Eden, what do you have in here? Rocks?"

"It's my collection of special edition Shirley Temple VHS tapes," I deadpan.

An eyebrow perks up. "Really?"

"No," I say, shaking my head. "They're just books."

He chuckles at the joke, though the only part I made up was that I brought the movies. My collection is real; it's just in a closet at my parents' house, unable to be retrieved.

"Where would you like me to put them?" he asks, amusement still sparkling in his dark eyes.

"Along the wall is fine. I'll unpack everything tonight," I say, turning and following Zoey's lead down the stairs. I don't want to think about his twinkling eyes or how good it felt to make him laugh. I suddenly very much wish I'd at least had a shower before my sixteen-hour drive.

Between the three of us, we get everything unloaded in half an hour. I sold my furniture before the move and donated a lot to Goodwill. I'm sure to the two ladies at the receiving lane for donations I must've looked like a woman on the run from something. I wonder if the story they created in their heads for me was better than the one that is my life. I wonder if it was less sad.

Chase nods toward me from the doorway. "I'm sure I'll be seeing you at the bar. Have Zoey call me if you need help returning the U-Haul." He then turns and heads down the stairs. Zoey starts to follow behind him but stops, pivoting to face me. I'm leaning against the kitchen counter, finally feeling in every bone how tired I am. I can see in her eyes she wants to talk, but she can probably see in mine that I do not. Instead, she closes the space between us and wraps her arms around me.

I have not been held in months, and the contact of someone I trust is almost enough to break me. There are so few of those people in the world now. She brings a hand to my hair, and I feel like a child rather than a grown woman. Tears are burning behind my eyes, and I do not want to cry anymore, not in front of her. I just want to be alone. She pulls away when she feels me stiffen but holds on to my elbows until I look her in the eyes.

"I'll be back this evening, but call me if you need anything before then," she says kindly. "I'm so sorry for why you are here, but Eden, I'm so glad you are." With that she leaves, closing the door behind her. I hear the car crank and retreat from the driveway, and then it is just me and my thoughts. I no longer want to be alone.

I grab my box of toiletries that I kept in my back seat and go to the restroom, shutting myself in. She's stocked it with towels and toilet paper, and the walls are painted a lilac I can only assume is left over from the previous owner. Zoey detests purple. I turn the water on and let it warm as steam begins to fill the room. I regard myself in the mirror, trying to see myself as they must have seen me. Against my pale skin, the bags under my eyes look like bruises. My broad shoulders sag from having held my head up for too many hours. I've always thought my athletic body type made me look strong, but right now I look fragile. Eventually my reflection is lost to the fog.

I open the cabinet and remove three towels. I place two on the toilet seat for easy reach when I'm done showering. The other I unfold and kneel down to shove it into the crack under the bathroom door. When I am satisfied that it is fully covered, the shaking in my hands subsides and I begin to undress for my shower. *You are safe,* I tell myself. *No one can see you.*

The shower is so hot it burns my skin, but it unfurls the tightness in my back from hours of sitting in a car. I wash away the grime of the past day and let the water pressure lull me to relaxation. Like Zoey suggested, I try to forget why I am here and just be grateful that I am.

I dress in the oversize T-shirt I packed in the same box as my toiletries. It is soft and worn threadbare from years of being used as a comfort item when I was little. My mother tells the story of how I'd rub the hem between my thumbs when I nursed, and then how I'd bury my face in the material to survive my first sleepovers away from home. The scent of my mother would calm me then. At some point it became mine, and when I found it in the bottom of my drawer while packing, it still comforted me despite everything.

I curl up in the white linen comforter Zoey has made the bed with after relocating the five unnecessary decorative pillows to their rightful place on the floor. I'm grateful for exhaustion as it seeps through every inch of my body, leaving even my toes feeling heavy. When I close my eyes, sleep immediately washes over me. For once I do not dream. I'm grateful for this small blessing.

Chapter Two

I wipe the glob of sauce from my chin unceremoniously and forget to feel self-conscious about it because I'm eating the best burger that has ever graced my taste buds.

"Santi, what on earth have you done to me?" I groan, getting a laugh from Zoey's head chef and my new favorite coworker. The thin patties are dripping a green liquid onto my hands, and there appears to be shredded pork on my burger as well. The spices are so indulgent I find myself licking my fingers when the meal is gone.

"Colorado green chili," he explains, grabbing my now empty plate and heading toward the back corner of the kitchen. He rinses it clean of debris before dropping it into the three-compartment sink to soak. "Wait till you try it on loaded fries," he teases.

His pitch-black hair is close-cropped and graying at the temples. His skin is the color of sun-drenched sand, and his hands move deftly as he slices the tomatoes on his chopping board. These two quipped answers are the most words he's spoken to me in the hour we've been readying the bar to open, but I don't mind his quiet demeanor. He listens intently when I speak and does not say more than is necessary in return. I can respect that.

"Next time, for sure," I say wistfully, standing and tying my black bar apron around my waist. My stomach aches from being crammed so full of food. "As it stands you might have to roll me out of here before any customers arrive."

When I push through the saloon doors to leave the kitchen, Zoey is walking out of the office door on the opposite end of the bar. She pulls her black-framed glasses off, polishing the lenses with her chambray blouse as she laughs. She only sheds the contacts when she's been staring at a computer for too long. "I told you this place will make you gain ten pounds."

I pull open the dishwasher below the counter, releasing a billowing cloud of steam into my face, which will inevitably add a halo of frizz to my board-straight auburn hair. I start stacking the highball glasses along the bar mat, drying them as I go. "I thought everyone out here was a fitness guru," I admit.

Zoey scoffs at that. "That's for the people who don't have to spend their days locked inside." She helps me finish stocking the garnishes and wipes her hands on the towel tucked into my back pocket. "Which reminds me, now that you're here, I finally have someone to share the paperwork with."

I nod in agreement as I listen to her reiterate the plan that brought me here in the first place, quitting my job leading the catering department at a Marriott in Nashville to come be her bar manager. Inventory and ordering are the tedious but necessary parts of the job. Bartending is my favorite, though, because I'm able to listen in on conversations people wouldn't normally have in front of strangers. When Maddie, the regular bartender, takes Mondays and Thursdays off to attend classes at the local college, I'll be covering for her.

I unlock the door ahead of a Monday lunch rush that I imagine will hit Santi worse than myself as Zoey moves about the room watering her various plants. "Zo, any reason why there isn't a name on the building?"

She grimaces as she pokes her finger into the soil of a snake plant, checking if it's thirsty. "Yeah, pretty much everyone in town calls it Gary's Place and will continue to do so for the next fifty years, I'm sure," she says, tipping her watering can back when she is satisfied. "But he said I could change it when I bought it, so I took down the sign a few months ago."

"When does the new one go up?" I ask, shooting Coke from the soda gun into a glass for myself.

She stands up straight and puts a hand on her hip, clearly frustrated with herself. "When I eventually decide on a new name."

"*No Name's* it is, then." Zoey rolls her eyes at me but seems to mentally consider the possibility before writing it off as the joke I intended it to be. She turns toward the door as we both hear it open, and I watch her switch into hospitality mode like the donning of a mask. She brushes her blonde curls back behind her ears, straightens her glasses, and plants a broad smile on her delicate face.

"Have a seat anywhere you like. I'll grab you some menus!" she says sweetly to the middle-aged couple that have just walked in. I swear she's speaking two octaves above her normal pitch.

The rest of the afternoon goes like that, Zoey waiting tables while I pour the occasional beer and take orders from those sitting solo at the bar. It feels like the five years since graduation never passed, and yet they have. The lunch rush finally dies down and Zoey leaves to grab more buns from the store so we are able to make it until the truck delivers tomorrow morning.

I glance up from my loaded fries to see Gary shedding his light coat despite the unseasonably warm day. I flick my wrist to light up my watch. "Five o'clock on the dot, right on time, Gary."

He chuckles at me as he takes a seat at the bar and reaches over to grab himself a fry. "I've been told women like a punctual man," he says while chewing. I'm sure my expression is a dead giveaway that I'm not a fan of sharing my food, but if it is, Gary doesn't seem to care.

"We also like a little mystery," I reply. "You could start with concealing your food while you eat it."

Gary lets out a bark of laughter. "You are just like Zoey," he muses. "All bark, no bite." He reaches for another fry, and I lift the plate onto the bar so he doesn't risk dripping on the glasses I just stacked. I resign myself to the fact that this is now *our* snack rather than just my own.

Santi walks by us toward the bathroom. "Oh no, she bit me once, hurt like a bitch," he deadpans. One look at Gary's shocked expression mirroring my own and I succumb to a fit of giggles.

"So, Gary," I say when I'm able to breathe again. "Letting a twenty-seven-year-old buy the bar you've owned forever. How did that happen?"

He wipes his mouth after swallowing the last fry. "Well, my late wife, Wendy, and I were never able to have kids of our own. Since Zoey came to work for me, it's been like having the daughter we always wanted, and it's nice to keep the business in the family."

I smile at that, pouring him a Sprite before taking our empty plate and turning to walk through the saloon doors. Santi heads me off on his return from the restroom and takes the plate with him, tossing over his shoulder, "Two daughters are better than one!"

Gary grins and raises his Sprite to toast me. "That they are," he says, nodding in my direction.

I duck my head, suddenly fascinated with my hands as Zoey walks back through the door, the subject quickly changing to how they never have enough of the good buns at Safeway. Gary grunts his agreement, and Santi grabs the bags from her, fielding Gary's request for his regular, whatever that may be. Santi seems to know because he doesn't ask for details, just nods at Gary before disappearing to the back.

He finishes his dinner and wishes all of us a good night before exiting onto the street. The door is caught before it can close, and I have to fight the thrill that goes down my spine when I make eye contact with Chase as he walks in. Behind him trail two other guys, but I can't seem to look away from him. I'm focused on the way his face is now highlighted with a fresh tan from a day spent in the sun. He has a black ball cap flipped backward on his head that holds the hair out of his face. The freckles on his nose have darkened, giving him a boyish charm I wish I didn't notice.

He smiles as he walks toward me, but before he can speak, the man behind him does.

"Zo, I heard you think I have a nice ass!" the man shouts to her. She's slicing limes on my left and drops the knife and her jaw as she glares at Chase. Chase, looking sheepish, backhands the other man in the chest. He's shorter than Chase and built with lean muscle like an MMA fighter. He's Black with a set of striking jade-colored eyes, good-looking the same way Zoey's frat-boy hookups were in college.

"Man, I told you that in confidence," Chase says through gritted teeth.

"I told *you* that in confidence!" Zoey exclaims, hand planted firmly on her hip.

"Bros before hoes, Zo," the man replies jokingly. Zoey mocks offense, moving her hand from her hip to her heart.

"I know you aren't calling me a hoe, Aaron," she says threateningly, but there is a smile playing on her lips. She enjoys this game. I have never seen anyone play it better than her. I'm convinced she invented this game.

"Uh-oh, Zo, someone told him about your past life," I tease, elbowing her in the ribs.

"I don't know what you're talking about," she sings, but she winks at Aaron suggestively. He smirks at her before turning his gaze on me, stepping to Chase's side as he extends a hand across the bar.

"Hello, I'm Aaron Moore, a perfect gentleman with a great ass," he jokes. I laugh, shaking his hand while pretending to check him out.

I shrug. "I'm Eden Ross and I've seen better." Chase and their other friend howl with laughter while Aaron sticks out his lower lip in a pout. I pour a Coors Light from the draft and place it on a napkin in front of Chase while Aaron continues to chat with Zoey. He peeks up at me with a smile.

"You remembered," he says, voice warm and rough like tires on a sun-kissed gravel road. I offer him a pinched smile because now that he is this close, I can see his eyes aren't just brown, they are the color of honey, and I don't trust my face not to give away my thoughts. I turn to their other friend, tall like Chase but with long blond hair he has tied into a knot at the base of his neck and a mustache that doesn't seem to be ironic. He introduces himself as Zander and orders an IPA. His baby face underneath all that hair makes me ask for his ID, which gets the others going again. Zander's cheeks and forehead are a rosy pink in the same places Chase has tanned, and it makes his slate-gray eyes stand out like ice.

"So where'd you guys hike today?" Zoey asks, pouring a can of ginger ale over the whiskey shot she's prepared for Aaron.

"Bierstadt," Zander answers, taking a seat while the other guys follow his lead. His coastal accent does nothing to detract from his hippie appearance. "Too early for any of the other four-teeners."

"Fourteeners?" I ask, vaguely remembering the term but not being certain of its meaning.

"Mountain peaks taller than 14,000 feet," Chase explains. "Colorado has a lot of them, but May is a little early for any of the challenging ones." He tosses the beer back, and I force myself to look away from his throat as he swallows.

Zoey smiles and squeezes my shoulders. "Eden loves to hike. You guys should take her sometime."

Chase's eyebrows rise and the other two nod appreciatively toward me while sipping their drinks.

"I love hiking in *Tennessee*," I explain. "Our mountains are molehills. Ignore her." Would I love to hike something that impressive? Absolutely. Do I want to embarrass myself in front of this beautiful man and his friends? Absolutely not.

"We can start small, let you get used to the altitude," Chase offers kindly. "You'll be hiking the big boys in no time." I nod to acknowledge his olive branch, appreciative that he is helping me save some face. The conversation switches to how hungry they are, and Zoey takes their orders while I replace the now empty round of drinks.

I tend to the handful of other customers as the guys inhale their dinners. I'm half listening to an older woman tell me all about her plans for a summer garden, but my mind is focused elsewhere. I force myself not to check if Chase is looking at me, but I find myself standing a little straighter than usual. I smooth my hair down as the lady goes on. I only allow myself to steal a glance when Zoey walks that way from across the room.

Aaron places his hand on Zoey's lower back as she collects their empty plates, and he whispers something into her ear that makes her laugh. He then turns and announces his exhaustion to the group, stretching his arms out and giving an exaggerated yawn. He slaps Chase and Zander on their shoulders before heading out the door.

Zoey returns from the back sans plates and looks around at the few remaining patrons before checking her phone for the time. "You've got this, right, Eden?" she asks innocently. "I've had a super long day. You can probably close early with how slow it's been."

I don't even look at her, instead locking eyes with Chase as I bite my lip to catch the grin that is itching to spread across my face. The sides of his eyes crinkle, but he keeps the rest of his expression blank. "Yeah, go home and get some rest. Santi and I are good."

She thanks me and heads to grab her purse from the office, rubbing her neck like it has a kink. She waves over her shoulder as she walks out the door, and I pretend not to see the skip in her step. When I glance over at Chase again, we share a knowing look. While so much has changed, some things are still very much the same.

I finish counting the deposit out and lock the envelope in our safe in the office. Santi exits the kitchen, headphones still tucked into his ears and his chef's coat draped over his shoulder. He gave me a free concert the whole time I was closing, singing loudly in Spanish while he washed up the remaining dishes. He doesn't comment on it, so neither do I.

When I lock the door behind us, I begin walking in the direction of Zoey's house, the opposite way from the parking lot Santi is heading toward. "Eden, do you need a ride home?" he calls out from behind me.

I spin on my heel to face him, waving my hand to show it isn't a big deal. "I'm good, Santi, thanks. It's only a twenty-five-minute walk, and I like the exercise." He nods and then continues on his way, disappearing around the corner into the night.

I pull my phone from my pocket and click through to my list of contacts, selecting the silly picture of Ella from my favorites. The phone rings once, and then her familiar voice comes on the other line.

"Eden! I was wondering when you were planning on calling me," she says with exasperation. "You moved to Colorado? What the hell is in Colorado?"

Even her chastising me is a source of comfort. "Zoey's in Colorado. She has a restaurant out here, and I'm running the bar for her." It's brisk out tonight, and I didn't bring a jacket to work with me. The days feel like summer is here, but the nights still hold on to that spring chill.

"If you needed a change of scenery, why didn't you come to Texas to live with me? You know we have a spare room." The hurt is evident in her voice. I know she wishes I would just let her take care of me.

I didn't want to be close enough that you'd try to fix me, I think. "I thought Mom was supposed to move in with you?"

"That was the plan, but she called a couple weeks ago and said she just couldn't move right now, they needed her at the church too much. Apparently Pastor What's-His-Face can't live without his bookkeeper."

I hear thunder rumble uncomfortably close, but I'm halfway home so I hope it will hold off. "Well then where is she staying?"

"Still in the house. I think she moved into your old room," Ella says, her voice softer now. "I don't know, Eden. I try to ask how she's doing, but I think it's hard for her to talk about it."

"I know how that feels," I mumble. Though I've always been more outspoken than our mother in a conversational sense,

I inherited her distaste for discussing the hard things out loud. Ella verbally processes everything on our behalf.

I feel the first drop of rain on my shoulder when I'm still a few blocks away from our street. The second is close behind it, and before I know it the bottom drops out and it's storming in earnest. I quicken my pace as a white Silverado pulls up next to the sidewalk and the window rolls down.

"Do you need a ride?" Chase yells, trying to be heard over the rain.

"Who is that?" Ella asks in my ear, concern elevating her pitch.

"It's a friend, El," I explain, getting wetter with every second that passes.

"You've been there less than a week; you can't possibly have made any friends!" She is an eternal skeptic, and seeds of doubt are her favorite to plant. The longer I let this conversation go on, the more we both get watered. "He could be a murderer!"

"Are you going to murder me?" I yell back to him. My white blouse is soaked through, and I admire his ability to maintain eye contact in spite of that fact.

"No!" he yells back, chuckling. "Get in the truck!"

I run around to the passenger side and swing open the door. "You heard that, El? Not a murderer. Talk to you later!" I hang up the phone as I climb in, stopping her protests before I lose my nerve. "You're my hero, even if you murder me," I tell him, slumping into the seat as he pulls away from the curb.

He laughs and it warms me from the inside out. "That your sister?" he asks, eyes trained on the road. My soaked shirt is so transparent the birthmark next to my belly button can be seen through the material.

"Yes, she's very protective of me," I explain. The car is messy but not unclean, three empty coffee mugs clambering around the floorboards as he slowly navigates the drive. It is now raining so hard even his windshield wipers aren't enough to clear his view.

"Are you two very close?" He chances a glance in my direction, eyes flickering down to my chest before he turns to face forward again, sitting up straighter. He clears his throat, and I mentally pat him on the back for exhibiting such manners.

"As close as we can be since she's fifteen years older and lives in Texas with two teenage children." I shrug. She likes to say I was her test baby before she had any real ones. Even after she went to college, she'd visit me often and bring me to her dorm for sleepovers. She married Jarrett the same year our mom married Mark. When they moved to chase his dream job, I was devastated. "What about you, any siblings?"

Chase flips the blinker as he finally approaches my street. A flash of lightning illuminates his face, and I see him shake his head and grin. "Nah, my parents achieved perfection with me on the first try; no need to risk their luck with a second."

"An only child, that makes perfect sense." He rolls into my driveway and cuts the lights, but it's still raining so I don't immediately reach for the door.

"What is that supposed to mean?" he asks, trying to sound indignant. He finally allows himself to look in my direction for more than two seconds. His gaze travels down my body, and there is a nearly imperceptible struggle on his face as he drags his attention back upward.

"You just come across very self-assured," I say, tilting my head and smirking when he looks again at my cleavage. "Very *mature*." The emphasis catches his attention, his eyes locking with mine. He doesn't look embarrassed to have been caught.

"Anyone looks that way next to Aaron," he jokes, but the smile falls from his face and a more sober expression replaces it. "I had my wild days when I was younger. When my dad died a few years ago, I had to step it up for Mom and the business he worked so hard to build."

Grief turns his eyes nearly black, and I am overwhelmed with the urge to hold him. I have to remind myself that he is practically a stranger, even if it doesn't feel that way. I settle for patting his hand where it rests on the gearshift. "I'm very sorry, Chase." It is a different kind of loss than mine, one I cannot imagine, but I feel the aching nonetheless.

"Thanks, Eden," he says, looking at the hand I've just touched. The rain slows and stops as the silence stretches in the car. I realize I have overstayed my welcome. I open the door and fall with as much grace as I can muster down to the ground.

"I'm sorry for bringing that up," I say, turning to look at him. His expression has softened to one of tenderness.

"Don't be; it's okay," he says, shaking his head. "I like talking about him, remembering him. It gets easier with time."

I nod, but all I can imagine is a bandage that has been ripped off so many times the adhesive no longer hurts as much. I wish I were the kind of person who knew what to say in these moments, but all I can think to say is, "Well, thank you for the rescue."

His eyes crinkle at the edges as I close the door, and he waves before backing out and driving away.

Chapter Three

I balance my laptop on a few of my larger paperbacks before flipping it open and clicking on the Zoom bookmark. I smooth my hair nervously, pulling long strands out between my fingers. When I log into the meeting a couple minutes early, Stephen's already there waiting for me.

"Good morning, Eden. How's it going?" He jostles his camera as he shifts in his seat. The angle is unflattering; I'm currently staring at two of his chins as he looks down his nose at the screen. His wire-rimmed glasses bounce the light back at me and he scratches his salt-and-pepper goatee as he finally settles the computer on his desk.

"I'm doing okay, Stephen. A little tired, but good."

He nods sympathetically, having listened to my complaints about sleep for months now. His eyebrows furrow in confusion when he catches a glimpse of the half-unpacked box of dishware on my kitchen counter.

"Where are you at today?" he asks. Nothing slips by him.

"I moved to Colorado a few days ago," I reply, ringing my hands in my lap. "You remember my friend Zoey's been asking me to come out here."

"I remember you've been telling her no for months. What changed your mind?" He asks it gently, the way he asks everything. He doesn't show surprise although he must feel it. He knows by now I don't make rash decisions. Moving twelve-hundred miles since our last session two weeks ago probably qualifies as rash.

"I found a letter," I mumble. "In my mailbox. Hadn't been mailed, he'd just left it there." I clasp my hands tighter to fight the tremble as the memory of his scrawl on the unstamped envelope passes through my mind.

"Did you read it?" he asks, pushing his glasses up the bridge of his nose. I can see the concern for me on his face. I can also see the understanding.

"No, I didn't," I lie. Whether he catches this or not, I'm unsure, but he lets it slide for now. The letter is somewhere in a soybean field in Kansas, but the words it contained are burned into my brain.

"Well, okay, Eden," Stephen says, shifting from one uncomfortable subject to another like it's his job. "I'd like to start with your trauma narrative now if you don't mind. That way we have time at the end to decompress a little before I let you go."

I nod.

"Remember, you can stop at any time," he assures me. "You can tell me as much or as little as you'd like. Today I just want you to focus on the days leading up to the event. What you did, how you felt, anything that feels relevant."

I nod again, pulling my notebook into my lap to look at the notes I have written since our last session.

"Are you ready?"

No. I nod once more. It seems it's all I know how to do.

"Go ahead, then," he says softly, encouraging me.

There are tears in my eyes already, and they blur my vision to where I cannot read what I have written. I close the notebook and hold it to my chest instead for strength. My eyelids squeeze shut so I do not have to see him watching me, and I remember it all out loud the way he taught me.

It's snowing when I arrive at my parents' house. It never snows in Alabama on Christmas. I imagine waking up tomorrow morning with the fields I grew up playing in blanketed in white. Mama must be so excited.

I walk through the door with my bag slung over my shoulder. It's a two-hour drive from Nashville to Ardmore, just over the border. I'm excited that I've managed to get the holiday off. In the hotel business that almost never happens. Mama runs to hug me before I've even managed to shut out the cold. It is so good to see her.

"Baby, can you believe it's snowing?" she says, ushering me in with one hand and shutting the door behind me with the other. "We're going to have a white Christmas!"

She's shorter than me, barely over five feet tall. Her red waves are graying more each time I see her, the same way a new line frames her smile from all the laughing she does. My mother is the happiest person I know.

I set my bag in what was once my childhood bedroom, the only room with a colorful wall in the house. Mark, my stepfather, insisted on keeping things beige to preserve resale value. But Mama snuck the gallon can of blush paint in one weekend when he was out of town. "Every little girl needs a pink room," *she'd said. I had eaten popsicles the way some people chain-smoke cigarettes, back-to-back till my mouth turned blue. She painted my walls while she sang every Elvis Presley song she knew, in a key all her own.*

. . .

The memory makes me smile even as I feel the tears roll down my cheeks. I do not open my eyes. I swallow around the lump in my throat, and I keep going.

"We waited for you to decorate the tree," Mama says, handing me a cup of hot chocolate. The Claymation Rudolph movie is playing on TV, just like always. Every sentimental moment from our lives is spread around us in tins of ornaments. She tells me the story of each one as she hangs them on the tree.

"This one was from your first Christmas," she says, eyes glossed over as she remembers. She's cradling a ceramic ornament with a baby sleeping in the curve of a crescent moon. It's heavy, so it always has to go on the thickest branch. That was also our first Christmas after she left my father. I don't remember it, of course, but she loves to talk about her first Christmas with just us girls. It's a badge of honor for her, after finding the courage to leave him.

I never knew the man. My mother and Ella didn't really speak about him to me, not until I was older. Aside from comments about me inheriting his angled chin or making a face just like his when I was angry, he wasn't a topic of conversation. After Mom remarried and Ella moved away, details slowly slipped through. He was abusive, both emotionally and physically. She left him when I was just a few months old, not willing to raise a second child in that environment.

"This one Ella made when she went to that crafting camp the year before you were born." Mama holds up a letter E carved from wood, dangling from a red ribbon. Ella has always been more artistic than me. I can plan, but Ella can dream.

Mark enters the living room from their master bedroom. He's already dressed in his Christmas pajamas, decked out in red flannel pants and a matching shirt. Gray chest hair pokes out from the gaping collar where he's left the top button undone, the same color as the fuzz on his balding head and his bushy mustache. "There's my girl! You made it!" He wraps me in a big hug, his large belly jostling the mug of hot chocolate in my hand.

Mama holds up two turtledoves dangling from a golden hook.

"From the year we got married," she swoons. Mark towers over her, but he bends down to kiss her lips, grabbing her free hand and pulling her in for a pseudo-dance. They really just sway back and forth. Mama is a wonderful dancer, but Mark has never been able to keep up.

"When I found the Juliet to my Romeo," he grumbles through the kiss. Mama pulls back, laughing.

"You know I hate that name," she chastises. She does hate that name. In my whole life she's corrected every bank teller, school principal, or DMV worker who dared read her name out loud. It's Julie, she always insisted. Only Mark has ever called her Juliet and lived to tell the tale.

The first time he called her that in front of me, my seven-year-old self thought he was superman. She hadn't even bristled. She bloomed.

Just like Mama, my grandmother was a romantic. So much so that she'd married five times before the age of forty. She died before I was born, but I love to hear stories about her travels. Grandma could never stay in one place for too long. The story goes that she saw Romeo and Juliet performed in a theater somewhere in Kentucky while pregnant with my mother, and Mama kicked her so hard when Juliet professed her love that Grandma knew she had to use the name.

Mark attempts to spin her, but he's grabbed the wrong hand this time. When he lifts her arm up to give her a place to duck under, the turtledoves fly through the air. The sound of shattering glass does not compare to the pain in Mama's gasp as she realizes *what has happened. I jump out of my seat, startled. Hot liquid splashes from my mug onto my arm and then the carpet.*

"Oh, Juliet, I'm so sorry. I didn't mean to do that." Mark tries to hug her to him, but she pulls away as she replaces the sadness on her face with stoicism. I can still see it though. She can mask so much but never the bright green eyes we share. They will always tell the truth.

I grab the dustpan from under the sink, and she kneels on the floor next to me as I sweep the pieces up. Mama grabs a lone wing and rolls it over between her thumb and index finger. I see the trembling in her lower lip, but she lets out a deep breath as she sets the piece among the others.

"I'm so sorry, honey. We'll get another one," he offers weakly. He extends an arm to help her off the floor. She takes it, along with one last look at the contents of the dustpan before I walk into the kitchen to throw them away. She pats Mark on the shoulder, redirecting his comforting back to him.

"It's not your fault, Mark," she murmurs. "I shouldn't have been so clumsy." With that one sentence, she takes the blame away from him and places it on herself. Just like always.

I open my eyes to find Stephen staring at me thoughtfully, mulling over something I've said. I use the edge of my sleeve to wipe the tears from under my eyes and clear my throat of the thickness holding my breath hostage.

"I think I'd like to be done for today," I say, my voice sounding foreign in my own ears.

"You did a wonderful job." He sounds proud. I don't know why; I haven't even gotten to the parts that really hurt.

"I don't know why I have to do this," I tell him. "Talking about it doesn't change anything. It doesn't fix what happened."

"You're right," he says honestly. He scratches his goatee

again, thinking before he continues. "It doesn't change what happened. But the more you say the words, the less they will hurt coming out. You own what happened to you, and there is power in telling your story, Eden."

I nod politely so he will let me end the call. We agree to talk more in two weeks, and I even manage to smile at him before I close the laptop. I stand and walk to my bed, catching a glimpse of Zoey returning from a walk with a coffee in hand. She meets my stare and waves me to come over, but I shake my head and close the blinds before I have to see her disappointment.

I curl up under the blanket, covering my head completely. The sobs rock through my body like waves crashing against a jagged cliff. I try to remind myself to breathe. I wish for my mother's arms around me. I curse Stephen under my breath. I do not feel powerful at all.

Chapter Four

The craziest part of surviving something tragic is how some days you feel completely normal. Some mornings I wake up and the sky is so blue it hurts my eyes in the best way and my heart feels as light as a feather in my chest. The pain is so distant I almost don't remember its name and that I am anchored to it. My existence is so effortless on these days that I forget to question it for once.

Then someone says a phrase offhand that strikes a nerve, or I dream I am walking through a memory I can no longer relive, or a vicious thought intrudes my otherwise average day and suddenly I am flayed open. Exposed like a raw nerve where even the gentlest touch feels like a cheese grater on my emotions. The simplest tasks feel insurmountable and irrelevant.

I'm fighting this internal battle the whole time I try to enter our invoicing into the system. To avoid another unnecessary outdoor shower, I've been driving the short distance to work. This morning as I drove in, a strange scraping noise accompanied me. My first thought was, *Something is wrong with my car; I need to call Mark.* And then I realized that was no longer an option. After that, even when I realized it was just a tree limb that had gotten caught in my undercarriage and was dragging along the road, I couldn't shake those feelings from my mind. Now here I sit, something as simple as the sound of the keys clicking as I type almost driving me to madness.

"Eden, can you help me out here?" Maddie calls out. I've left a crack in the office door while I'm working, and I tilt my head to tune into the low hum of conversation taking place on the other side. It doesn't sound particularly busy, not enough for a second bartender to be needed. But in the short time I have worked with Maddie, I've learned she's not high on the autonomy scale.

"Ed*en*," she groans. I hate the way she makes my name into two separate words.

I close out of our invoicing system and push back from the desk, wiping the annoyance from my face before I pull open the door. She has the keg fridge open underneath one of the taps and is looking at me with her brown eyes opened wide in desperation. She's barely a hundred pounds soaking wet, with a patchwork of tattoos on her arms that remind me of a child's sticker book. Her combat boots and black ripped jeans combined with the dark eyeliner and nose ring are like the Paramore era of my teens coming back to haunt me.

I scan across the room to see Zoey preoccupied in a conversation with a group of backpackers. When my gaze flicks back to Maddie, she's pulled the keg halfway from its hiding place and can't seem to move it any further.

I close the distance between us and lean over to offer my assistance. Maddie lets go completely once I grab hold, and she steps back with a huff. "Oh, thank God, I've been trying to change this thing for ten minutes," she says, massaging her thin arms. I'm bracing the steel barrel against my thigh, and when I glance up at the gentlemen waiting at the bar for their beers, they give me a look that says, *Took you long enough.*

I blow a bang out of my face in frustration, but I keep my expression polite. "No problem, Maddie." Am I too young to be thinking *damn kids these days*? "Can you go grab the replacement please? There's a keg dolly in the fridge you can use."

She nods, turning on her heel and strutting into the kitchen. Hopefully Santi sees what she's doing and offers to help. I straighten my back and hoist the barrel out. They aren't nearly as heavy when they are empty, so I don't know what all the fuss was about. She hadn't even made it to the hard part yet.

Santi rolls back through the double doors with the new keg on the dolly. Maddie is traipsing behind him, happy to have suckered yet another one of us into doing her job for her. He catches my eye and stops whistling, blowing what air remains in his lungs out and shrugging. Together we lift the new drum into the refrigerator while Maddie leaves to talk to the tan woman at the end of the bar with cropped brunette waves just brushing against her chin and a small, upturned nose on her angular face. Maddie pops the top off a beer bottle and slides it to the woman, twirling a strand of dyed-silver hair flirtatiously.

I thank Santi and he wordlessly turns and retreats back to his sanctuary.

"Sorry, guys, let me get this hooked up and we'll have your beers right out." I grunt, tracing my hands along the tubing that will lead me to the tap. I tilt the keg back onto my knee and pull out the nozzle, nestling it into the mouth of the keg. The handle is slick with condensation, and I lose my grip as I turn it.

It happens so fast I don't even have a chance to shield my face. The air pressure blasts me with pale ale in every orifice on the front of my body. It fills my eyes, ears, even my nose, and all I can smell is hops. I'm coughing and sputtering as the men across from me let out wails of laughter. Zoey gets to me before

Maddie even turns from where she's leaning against the bar. The keg is lifted off my leg, and Zoey reestablishes the connection, making sure it is secure before shutting the fridge door.

My cheeks are in flames, the heat traveling down my chest and up behind my ears. It was a rookie mistake, and I can't believe I did it with an audience. Beer is dripping off my nose and fingertips. The feeling of wet fabric against my arms and torso is sickening. Luckily I seem to have somehow spared my jeans save for a little splattering. At least I don't look like I wet my pants.

I stand up straight and make eye contact with Zoey. Her lips are pressed tightly together as she makes a heroic effort to look concerned rather than amused. Mascara is running into my eyes, which burn with the intrusion. I look like an alcoholic clown, I'd venture to guess. Laughter bubbles over her lips, and she slaps a hand against her mouth to trap it.

"I think I'm going to just head home early," I say. I work to maintain my composure in front of the men at the bar. I am both annoyed and mortified, but I'll be damned if it's going to show.

"Nonsense, just run next door. Chase has extra sample clothes from brands all the time. I'm sure he can spare a shirt," Zoey says. She has switched into fix-it mode in order to distract herself from how ridiculous I look. She grabs a stack of rags from the sanitizer tub and rings them out, tossing them to Maddie, who finally seems to have registered that she should be helping.

"I am not going to see Chase"—I gesture to my cling-film shirt and melting makeup—"*like this!*"

Zoey *pfffts* at me. "Well, I have plans tonight, remember? You said you'd watch the bar. Someone has to make sure the place doesn't burn down, and Santi's got enough tickets on his hands that he can't be babysitting." She looks pointedly at Maddie. "So unfortunately you're going to have to suck it up."

I glare at Maddie over her shoulder. Before I can even ask

the question, Zoey answers it. "She's young, and you're a perfectionist. Lighten up."

I know she's right and I'm just being a bitch. I take the paper towels she offers me to wipe my face free of the sticky substance. The smell is all-encompassing; I legitimately reek. She's got her hand on her hip again, and I know this is a battle I will not win. Instead of giving her the pleasure of agreeing, I just pivot and walk toward the entrance before I lose my nerve.

It's my first time seeing the inside of Taylor's Landing. The door chimes to announce my arrival and then softly closes behind me. It smells so strongly of wood and tobacco in here, I almost can't smell the beer anymore. Or I've just gotten used to the aroma. There are racks of outdoor clothing for both men and women, and the walls are lined with camping grills, shoes, and anything else one might need to take a hike in the nearby mountains. The floorboards creak under my step, comprised of the same oak wood that panels the walls, giving it the feel of a log cabin.

Aside from a young couple perusing the CamelBak section, the only other customer is a ten-foot-tall taxidermied grizzly bear wearing a hat and sunglasses. A sign is propped in its hand that reads: *You've Landed at Taylor's!*

Chase appears from a hallway tucked behind the counter. My skin feels like it is covered in pins and needles when he looks up at me. No matter how many times I see him, it never stops shocking me how beautiful he is. Men shouldn't be allowed to be so beautiful.

He lets out a long whistle. "What happened to you?" I can tell he wants to laugh, but he doesn't want to offend. He's wearing a baby-blue T-shirt that makes his olive skin even darker in contrast. He's freshly shaven for the first time since I've known him, and I notice he has a small cleft in his chin. I'm overwhelmed with the urge to press my lips against it before reality comes spinning back to me and I remember why I am here.

"There was an incident while changing a keg," I explain, attempting to make fun of myself before he can. "You should see the other guy."

He comes around the counter to me, chuckling. For some reason I don't bristle when he laughs. Instead I feel the anger unfurl in my chest, dissipating in his presence. He doesn't stop walking until he is inches away from me, and then he reaches forward, running a finger from my collarbone up to my neck, causing a shiver to run down my spine. He then takes that finger into his mouth, licking the beer off it. Goose bumps rise across my arms and legs, and the air gets trapped in my lungs. He rests one arm on the counter and leans into it. "Eden, *why* are you always wet around me?"

It's a good thing I'm unable to breathe, because otherwise I would choke. My mouth opens to speak, but no words will come out. He bursts into laughter when he sees the expression on my face. My gaze shoots across the room to the couple, who continue on with their conversation without missing a beat. They clearly didn't hear what he just said.

He follows my gaze, smirking when he says, "Don't worry, Geronimo thinks my jokes are hilarious."

"Geronimo?"

"The bear." He points in case I'm blind and have somehow missed the giant creature. "And before you get upset, I didn't shoot him. He's a hand-me-down.

"How can I help you, Eden?" he asks, facing me once more, residual laughter still lighting up his eyes.

I jolt at the sound of my name, suddenly regaining feeling in my extremities and the ability to speak. "Um, I can't go home and change because Maddie will be all alone and she's mildly incompetent, and Zoey said you might have some sample shirts here that I could borrow. It's totally okay if not though, I can buy one, I'm not saying you have to give me anything for free, it's just..." I cut myself off. I'm rambling. It's not like me to ramble. I think I just said more words in that response than I ever have to him collectively.

His eyes are wrinkling at the corners, and I remind myself to be offended later that this is all so amusing to him when I'm so light-headed I can barely stand. He turns without comment and goes into the back room, returning with a green L.L.Bean tee. He holds it out to me with an eyebrow cocked. "It's the same color as your eyes."

I grab the shirt from his hands and look down at it, wishing the blushing would subside so I could face him. This is all Zoey's fault. For hiring Maddie and for making me babysit her. For working in this dumb town in her dumb bar next door to this dumb man. What an idiot.

I realize I'm just referring to myself, so I mutter a thanks and turn to leave, hoping to lick my wounded pride in private. He clears his throat, so I turn around. The intensity is finally fading from his stare. He grabs a fire starter from the display on the counter, rolling it in his hands. I'd almost guess he looks a little nervous, though I can't imagine why.

"Instead of paying me for the shirt, how about you let me take you on that hike sometime?" I start to object but he holds a hand up. "Nothing too intense your first time. I'll go easy on you," he assures me.

I shift my weight from one foot to another, a war transpiring between my hormones and my better senses that say I am not in a place for this to work.

He notices my hesitation and presses on. "I know the bar is closed on Sundays, right? Aaron can cover for me. We could go tomorrow. Or next weekend."

Looking at him, I want so badly to be the girl who can just

say yes. I want to forget everything that has brought me to this point and just go for the hike with the charming guy next door. I wish I could let myself take that leap of faith, because I have no doubt he's capable of catching me. It's all the baggage I'd carry with me that keeps me from jumping.

"I just don't think it's a good idea, Chase, I'm sorry," I say, regretting it the whole time. He quickly recovers, but not before I see the shadow that falls across his face.

"I totally understand," he says, though I know he couldn't possibly. The way his throat tightens around his voice tugs at something within me, desperate for him to understand that it isn't his fault. That I'm just a mess he shouldn't waste his time on. "No need to repay me for the shirt."

I bite down on my lower lip, watching his eyes zero in on the motion before flickering away.

"I want to, believe me. It's just bad timing."

My words do more than balm the wound. Hope comes alight in his expression, and I immediately regret that I've let myself speak them aloud.

"Well, Eden, good news is I'm a patient man." The mischievous glint in his eyes cuts off my ability to say anything, let alone to argue.

I turn and retreat before I backtrack any further. I desperately need some fresh air. As the door swings to a close behind me, I call out, "Thanks again for the shirt!" I see him wave in response just before he disappears behind the window display. When I walk into the bar, Zoey is passing me to leave for the night. There's a bounce in her step that I'd have more questions about if I weren't still dizzy from my encounter. She glances at the blouse in my hands before squeezing my arm.

"See, that wasn't so bad," she says. "He even gave you a nice one!"

"It matches my eyes," I reply absentmindedly.

A small crease forms between her eyebrows, but she doesn't comment. I head into the office to change, Maddie barely looking up to acknowledge my return. My head emerges through the neckhole of the shirt, and I catch a glimpse of myself in the small mirror Zoey has mounted on the wall. My skin is flushed and eyes wide open. My reflection begs a question, though I don't know which side it is for or against.

What the hell were you thinking?

Chapter Five

All the windows are open along Zoey's front porch. As I make my way up the steps, I am hit by the smell of baked cinnamon rather than the chemical scent I had expected to find. When I open the front door, my eyes are immediately drawn to the sticky buns cooling on her kitchen island. She has the sliding glass door that leads to her backyard opened wide, allowing the breeze to flow through.

"Wow, no wonder Chase won't shut up about you!" an unfamiliar voice says. I trace down the source to a woman with ash-brown hair clipped loosely at the nape of her neck and a baby carrier strapped to her body. She's regarding me with amusement from inside the dining room, licking her fingers to clear them of caramel. She turns to Zoey, who is lining the baseboard edges with blue painter's tape. "She's so pretty!"

Zoey glances up and smiles in my direction. I'm still stuck on the comment about Chase when she stands and wipes her hands on her overall legs. "Hey, Eden, this is Rose. She and her husband own 8th & Main."

Rose grins at me and turns to her side, revealing a plump infant sporting a bright yellow bow in her fuzzy hair and an angry expression. "And this is Cleo," Rose says. "Don't mind her; she just inherited my resting bitch face." Cleo regards me with her mother's big hazel eyes under a furrowed brow. She doesn't appear to be impressed.

"I'm so glad you're here now to help her with this stuff," Rose continues. "I make a much better supervisor than I do a laborer."

I laugh as I carry the bags of paintbrushes Zoey instructed me to buy into her dining room. The furniture has all been exiled and a tarp draped over the hardwood floor. A bold navy is awaiting me in the can she has set aside for detail work. Zoey has no qualms when it comes to making a statement with her decor, but she also has no patience for windowsills and edging.

"I made sticky buns if you want any!" Rose says. "They are"—she kisses her fingertips and blows them out—"chef's kiss." A dimple appears in her right cheek. She is probably the most adorable person I've ever met.

I drop the brushes and speed walk over to the island, peeling a cinnamon roll piled high with brown sugar–coated pecans out of the pan. I take one bite and have to contain a moan at the burst of flavor. If I were a superhero, baked goods would be my kryptonite.

"Rose, you are my new favorite person," I sigh.

She giggles, bouncing Cleo back and forth in an attempt to soothe her as she's begun to fuss. "Santi said you told him the same thing, so I'm beginning to think you just like whoever is feeding you."

Zoey cracks up as she shovels a piece of a bun into her mouth. "Like a dog," she says around her bite of food.

I roll my eyes at both of them. "Jeez, first Chase and now Santi; is nothing sacred?" I say, carving out another bite. I'm not fishing, I tell myself. Just making conversation. Unfortunately she doesn't take the bait.

"I catch everyone before they've had their morning coffee," she says matter-of-factly. "They're vulnerable."

"And she preys on vulnerability," Zoey says. "Like a woman who started a diet two days ago."

"As if you needed one," Rose replies. Cleo has fallen asleep now, and her cheeks have squished her lips into a puckered pout. I don't even honor Zoey with a response. After years of telling her how much I envy her curves, she knows how I feel about her fad diets.

It is no wonder men have always flocked to her. She carries extra weight in her butt and chest, giving her the perfect hour-glass figure. Between that and her unencumbered confidence, she's like a drug to them. I would kill to have a body like hers rather than one that tapers from the shoulders down to narrow hips. If it weren't for my breasts, I would feel like a teenage boy.

I wash my hands in the kitchen sink and then return to the dining room, laying out my brushes and stretching a rubber band around the small paint can so I have a place to wipe the excess from the bristles. I begin with the large window frame that Zoey has already taped off.

"So, how's Julie doing?" Zoey asks. She's covering the wall in broad strokes with a roller while Rose supervises from her vantage point in the kitchen, careful not to have the baby too close to the fumes. I let out a quiet sigh of breath I didn't know I was holding.

"Um, I assume as good as she can be." I roll my bottom lip between my teeth. "She hasn't been talking to anyone much." I try to engage with my mom. I sent a text upon my arrival letting her know I got here safely, something she demanded I do in any previous travels. This time, instead of her usual barrage of questions, she simply replied, *Love you.*

Zoey pauses mid-wall and looks at me with an odd expression. One of confusion and something else I can't place. "That's so odd. You and your mom talked every day in college."

She's right. Even after I graduated and was working full-time, Mom would call me just to chat while I commuted to work each day. After having a child at home for the better part of her life, life as an empty nester hit her hard. But after Christmas the phone calls grew strained and uncomfortable. Recently they've gone from infrequent to nonexistent. Neither of us is able to comfort the other from the depths of our own grief.

"What happened?" Rose asks unabashedly. I'd be impressed if I weren't so taken off guard. I shrug and return to my trim work. It's not that I don't trust her. I just don't even have the words for myself, let alone anyone else. Zoey looks from me over to Rose, who holds her hands up to show she's innocent. "Sorry, I didn't mean to overstep."

"You're fine," I say quietly. There's a beat of awkward silence before Zoey does what she does best and interrupts it.

"Eden's got daddy issues," she explains.

It takes a moment for the shock of that statement to hit me, and when it does, I nearly drop my brush. The room grows so quiet it is a physical sensation. Rose's eyes are huge as she braces for whatever is coming, and Zoey looks at me as if she's daring me to disagree.

The absolute absurdity of what she has just said overwhelms any sadness she might have triggered, and I find myself laughing so hard I cannot breathe. I am lying flat on my back wheezing in between guffaws. Zoey is bent over in a fit of hysterics. Rose looks like she doesn't know whether to join in or call someone to take us to an asylum.

"That is the *understatement* of the year!" I exclaim when oxygen finally makes its way into my lungs. Cleo is awake again and watching us with pure disdain. It feels so good to laugh, the aching in my stomach a sensation I barely recognize. Zoey has always had this ability to take the heaviness out of a situation, like I am a trapped toddler and she's the mom with super strength to lift the car off me.

Rose's phone rings and she pulls it from her back pocket, half turning from us and holding it to one ear, index finger pressed to the other to drown us out. I look at Zoey and stick my tongue out at her from my place on the floor. She blows a kiss back to me and I giggle.

"Ladies, I'm sorry; that was Mitchell. He's got a flat, and the jack is in my car." She gathers her purse but not the remaining sticky buns, I'm relieved to notice. "It was so nice to meet you, Eden, I'll be seeing you both!" I sit up and watch through the window as she saunters to her car and gently removes Cleo from her carrier. She clips the baby into her car seat and kisses her on her forehead. Cleo is all smiles for her mother.

"I'm sorry, that was probably not the best first impression I could've made," I say. This is exactly why I avoid talking about things if I can help it. I don't want to make people uncomfortable. The shame I feel now eats away at my core.

"Don't be!" Zoey reassures me. "Mitchell works in construction and gets a nail in a tire a week. I guarantee you that was a legitimate excuse." She sounds genuine, and Zoey isn't one to bullshit. Still, I can't help but feel a tad like a cloud that has brought rain to their parade.

"And besides," she adds, a shadow falling over her face, "Rose is just as fucked up as the rest of us. She just carries it very well."

I look back out to watch Rose walk around the front of her red Kia and climb into the driver's side. She catches my gaze as she looks up to check her mirrors, and a soft smile passes over her lips as she waves goodbye. She backs out and disappears down the street. I wonder what burden she has to bear, and how she learned to look so good doing it.

"What do you think Chase said to her about me?" I ask, trying to sound unaffected. I dip my brush in the paint can one too many times, repeatedly draining the excess before dipping it again. The jig is up.

"Why do you care?" Zoey's eyebrows are perched high on her forehead, and she's smirking at me. I notice some blue paint has dripped into her blonde ponytail, but I don't mention it out of spite.

"Just curious." I finish the window frame and move on to the far corner of the room. I climb onto the stepladder she's brought in so I can start at the top and move downward. She huffs out a breath of air in annoyance. "Okay, *look*, I'm emotionally unavailable but I'm not blind!"

"I knew it," she says, jabbing her paint roller at me. The victorious look on her face passes, and her mouth sets in a resolute line. "He's a good man, Eden. You could do much worse."

I turn back so she doesn't see how much that statement affects me. I've dated infrequently over the years, but aside from one ill-fated relationship with a man that had a lot of growing up to do right after college, nothing has ever been serious. I wasn't confident I had a lot to offer a man like Chase before, but now I am even less certain. I feel like a wrecking ball that leaves nothing but destruction in her wake.

"So how are things going with Aaron?" I ask, turning to look at her as she stops painting, and a spark lights up her eyes. Her love of gossiping about her conquests overtakes her commitment to being my love guru. Just like that, I'm in the clear.

She launches into a long-winded exposé, explaining how they met when he started helping Chase out at his store a couple nights a week in addition to his teaching job. How he'd come over to the bar and grab two sodas in to-go cups, just to see her and flirt. Then they began sneaking around, but she urges me not to tell anyone. It's nothing serious, she assures me.

45

I bite my tongue, not wanting to burst her bubble by informing her that they've been about as subtle as the stress pimple forming on my nose. Zoey doesn't make a habit of letting the men she dates get close, and I'm afraid bringing her obvious feelings for Aaron to her attention will have her running scared. He may be a flirt, but there's something to be said for the way he looks at her. Less like a conquest and more like a prize.

Midafternoon we break out a bottle of wine as we complete the finishing touches. I take a sip from my glass of chardonnay as Zoey slowly peels back the lines of tape, revealing crisp borders professionals would be lucky to accomplish. I help her eyeball the placement of two golden-framed drawings of the silhouette of a woman. We hammer them into studs and mount the pictures. On wobbly legs, we move the furniture back into the room, and when it is all complete, we stand back and admire our work. Between my meticulousness and her whimsy, the room has turned out exactly the way she planned.

"It's perfect," she says. It really is. Where I have always been drawn to minimalist decor and whitewashed color palettes, Zoey has never feared color and statement pieces. For that very reason, our apartment in college was a live-in Anthropologie window display.

"You could've been an interior designer if you'd wanted to," I reply. As she slowly adds her touch to each room in the house, the resulting look is cozy yet inspiring. It could be on the cover of a magazine.

"Maybe." She tilts her head to the side, ever the critic of her own work, before she turns to me and smiles. She holds out her wineglass, and I clink mine against it. "But I much prefer helping people drown their sorrows."

I wrap my arm around her waist, the double entendre not lost on me. "I'll drink to that."

Chapter Six

I pour coconut rum and blueberry vodka into a short glass filled with ice before adding a splash of pineapple and lime juice. Gary and Zoey watch with perked eyebrows as I pull a stick of red rock candy from the plastic sleeve I picked up before work and use it to stir the cocktail. A rub of an orange peel around the rim completes the drink and I drop it in for additional garnish.

"I call it the Rocket Pop," I say, setting the glass between them on the counter. It reminds me of spending the night at Zoey's house as a kid, when the ice cream truck would roll through her subdivision, and I'd order the iconic red, white, and blue popsicle. Gary's nose wrinkles at the same time Zoey shrugs appreciatively and pulls the drink her way for a sip.

"Leave it to you to find a way to add a snack to a cocktail," she says, smacking her tongue against the roof of her mouth. "It's really good."

"That's just so much sugar!" Gary says, but he grabs the glass from Zoey and takes a swig. Once it hits his taste buds, his suspicious eyes widen at me, and he purses his lips. "Okay, maybe you do know a thing or two."

I laugh. "I'm going to take that as the compliment it wasn't. Bear in mind, people ordering cocktails usually like sweet drinks. The boring people order beer."

He grumbles in response while Zoey adds the cocktail to the list we've been prepping for our summer menu. Maddie actually came up with the idea of an ice cream theme. The orange creamsicle shot whose recipe she suggested has disappeared, and all that remains is a frothy film on the shot glasses I placed in front of my two taste testers. I reach for the candy stir stick, watching as the red color bleeds out of the sugar into the beverage. I take a bite out of the end, alcohol mixing with the sweetness just the way I hoped it would.

"Drinking on the job?"

The familiar rasp triggers every alarm my senses have, and I nearly choke on the candy in response. Chase reaches around Gary to grab the cocktail and take a sip, eyeing me the whole time. I'd be lying if I said I didn't feel a tad relieved when he sets it down and nods his approval.

"It's research," Zoey replies, flipping her list toward him for his inspection. He leans forward, squinting to read her neat script. "Not as tasty as those self-heating meals you made us sample last fall, but it'll do."

"Hey, the chili wasn't that bad," he says, raising his hands innocently. The motion pulls his gray T-shirt taut against his shoulders, which I pretend not to notice.

Gary levels his gaze with mine, a look of warning passing from him to me. "It was pretty bad for my toilet."

It's enough to shock me out of my nerves, and I mock gag behind the counter while Zoey smacks Gary's shoulder and Chase cackles behind him.

"You're disgusting," I say, shaking my head. Gary shrugs, unashamed.

"Just thought you should have all the facts before he tries to sucker you in next," he replies.

I begin returning the various bottles to their rightful places on the display shelves behind the bar, very aware of Chase's eyes on me as I move. When I let myself glance up at him, there's a grin spreading across his face. I shake my head but can't help the matching expression that tugs at my lips.

"Did you come here to order lunch?" Zoey asks, interrupting our silent standoff. "Or just to critique our work?"

His gaze doesn't break from mine as he replies. "I actually came to see if this is a better time."

My hand freezes around the neck of the rum. Gary and Zoey follow his gaze to me, their faces carrying twin expressions of confusion. I shake my head nearly imperceptibly at him, unable to speak. I feel like a deer locked in a stare down with a semitruck barreling toward me. This does nothing to deter his foot from the gas pedal. He keeps watching me, the edges of his eyes crinkling.

"It's literally been a week," I say.

"For what?" Zoey asks, her voice overpowering mine.

Though I know he heard me, Chase finally breaks his gaze away from mine to answer Zoey. "Oh, I invited Eden on a hike last weekend. She said it wasn't a good time, so I just wanted to check if now was better."

His face is the picture of innocence. I see the gears immediately begin to turn in that mastermind head of hers while Gary putters, still trying to catch up with what conversation we're having and how it so quickly changed from MREs and their effects on his bathroom habits.

Before I can protest, Zoey says, "Oh, it's a perfect time!"

"I was thinking the same thing," Chase says, smiling at me like, *See?*

"You guys are being ridiculous," I say. Zoey knows better

than anyone why it is *not* the perfect time. A silent war transpires between the two of us, but she's always been a better fighter.

"I really think it's in your best interest to just do it because he will continue to be this upbeat and annoying until you go," Gary says, finally up to speed on the conversation. Chase laughs but shrugs at the accurate assessment.

"He's very enthusiastic about the outdoors. He even got me to go hiking," Zoey adds. My jaw nearly slaps the floor, I'm so impressed. Aside from a brief stint with horseback riding lessons because "the outfits are cute," Zoey has never been the outdoorsy type. Even as kids, her version of playing outside was sitting in the lawn chair next to my mother and sunbathing, heart-shaped sunglasses resting on her head. "Besides, it'd be good to get your mind off things."

A current flows through the group as they assess what she might mean by this. She catches her slipup, adding after a brief pause, "You know, with moving and the new job and all."

"It just so happens that I don't like a man who can't take no for an answer," I say pointedly, eyebrow perched.

"I can take no for an answer," Chase assures me.

"Yeah, right," Zoey snorts. Gary pretends to smooth out his mustache, but it's really just his sly way of covering a smirk.

I grab a glass from the stack in front of me and rub at the water spots with my rag. He's really trying, I'll give him that. I don't know why he bothers. He's like a kid in a store with his eye on a toy, made all the more alluring by the fact his parents said he couldn't have it. Once he realizes there's less to me than meets the eye, he'll let it go, and I can go back to suffering in private.

"So what do you say?" Chase asks. He leans on his elbows, resting his chin on his knuckles and batting eyelashes at me that are too dark and long for his own good. He buzzes with a captivating energy, a light brighter than I've seen in months. I feel like a moth flying too close to a bug zapper, the magnet of his smile drawing me in even as I know it will only get me burned.

The hope in his expression, along with the expectant stares coming from the two other traitors, is enough to turn the tides against my better judgment. After all, what's one more scar when you're already covered?

"Fine, I'll go." My voice sounds much more confident than I feel. Eager, even. I'm vaguely aware that my heart skips a beat, and I have the distinct feeling that I've just jumped off a precipice I'll likely never be able to climb my way back up.

He nods, smiling and shoving his hands into his pockets. His dark hair is cut into a fade on the sides, but the top is longer, and a thick wave falls onto his forehead. It crosses my mind that he looks like Elvis. My mother would be so proud.

"Perfect, I'll pick you up bright and early next Sunday," he says, triumphant. Gary goes back to picking at the tacos in front of him, oblivious to the underlying tone to what has just transpired. Zoey's cheeks twitch in her valiant effort to hold back a smile, very much aware of what she's aided and abetted.

"I'll try to be dry this time," I say. An immediate internal cringe follows my weird reference to a joke he's probably forgotten, and my gaze falls to the list of recipes in front of me, spots of water causing the ink to bleed. Chase rests a palm flat on the counter, drawing my attention upward.

His face is sober of the humor from before, and the sudden change stills the turmoil in my stomach. An expression I can't read causes those caramel eyes to harden, his mouth set in a determined line. "Thank you. You won't regret it."

Somehow he's read my mind, and I just nod because it catches me so off guard. Despite everything in me screaming otherwise, I cling to his words, desperately hoping they are true.

Chapter Seven

Sometimes therapy feels less like a conversation and more like taking a beating.

Because of this, and the raging headache I have from way too much caffeine and self-contemplation, I pop a couple Advil before subjecting myself to more torture.

Stephen watches me as I return into frame. He's used to me interrupting our sessions to grab a snack or a pill, depending on how the day is going. He sees that there is not a bag of chips nor a cookie in my hand and assumes the worst. Correctly.

"Does this mean you're ready to tell me more about that night?" he asks. He has patiently listened for the past fifteen minutes as I've droned on about Maddie's antics at the bar. I've carefully curated my stories not to include the nights Chase stops by, checking to make sure I haven't chickened out from our hike. I spend so much time talking to Stephen about the negative parts of my life, that it feels like if I mention something that has the potential to be good, the poison might bleed into it.

"I am." I gulp. I have never had the best memory, holding onto ideas rather than concrete facts. But for whatever reason, likely some curse placed on me for wavering in my belief of the

God of the universe, I remember every detail of that night. Even the days that followed, although they are hazy by nature of my mental state at the time, feel visceral to me in recollection.

"Go ahead, Eden." He peeks at the notes on his desk, eyebrows furrowed. "What happened after the turtledoves?"

"If he was worth having, he'd see how wonderful of a woman you are," Mark says. My shoulders slump as I roll out the pie dough. Pieces of it are sticking to my knife when I try to slice ribbons to lattice braid the top layer. It's not cold enough. I drop the knife, frustrated at the pie for having the audacity to be difficult when I'm in the middle of complaining to my stepdad about my unsuccessful dating life.

"I know that," I reply. "I just don't know what's wrong with me. We only went on two dates. How is that enough time to know he didn't want me?" I shove the pie crust in the fridge, hoping this will do the trick. The scraps of dough on the counter find their way into my mouth rather than the trash can.

"Didn't you call Juliet after the first date and say he ate with his mouth open and- how did you put it? Mansplained everything to you?" Mark has a point, and I giggle at the reminder. It's not that I particularly wanted to continue seeing Landon, I just don't appreciate being dumped. Especially when I was the catch in that situation.

"What's worse," Mama says, re-entering the room from her shower. "He mansplained things incorrectly. Didn't he try to tell you that your name wasn't from the Bible and was in fact just a feminine spelling of Aiden?" She scrunches her curls with a raggedy blue towel, the same one she used to wrap me in as a child to scrub me dry. My mother is nothing if not sentimental.

Mark groans and I laugh in earnest, relieved to see Mama seems to have recovered from the ornament fiasco. I know how deeply she cares for the memories tied to her possessions. This house is a museum to mine and Ella's childhoods, despite the fact that my sister never lived here. From framed photos on every wall to the knickknacks overflowing from my mother's bookshelves, every detail of our lives has been enshrined. If I look really closely at the doorframe leading to the kitchen, I can still faintly see the marks from my height through the years. Mark finally won the argument to paint those over last year. Beige, of course.

When the pie crust has cooled enough, I try again, this time cutting through it smoothly. Mark reaches over the island where I am working and snags himself a ribbon of dough. He drops it into his mouth in one fell swoop before I can even protest.

"You two are one and the same," Mama comments. She makes a tsk-tsk at us before retreating to the living room where she can move on to her next favorite holiday film, Jack Frost.

"I better go stop her before she starts drooling over Michael Keaton." Mark puts on an expression of mock panic before swiping another dough slice and escaping to join her.

It wasn't always so easy between us. When it became clear he was going to be permanent rather than just another boyfriend, I rebelled. I hated him. I would tell him we were just fine on our own before he came along, and we didn't need a man in our lives. In reality I think I just didn't want to share my mom. Ella moved away and Mom was getting married, and I felt like collateral that got shuffled around in the aftermath.

But on the day of their wedding, after the vows were exchanged and pictures taken, it came time for the first dances. Mark took my mother's hand and lovingly escorted her out onto the dance floor. Anyone in a mile radius could see the adoration in his eyes. Her tea-length gown swayed as they rocked back and forth. He tried to dance, he really gave it his best shot, but the shuffle was always their signature move.

When the music faded, their DJ announced it was time for

the father-daughter dance. I scrunched my nose up, confused because my mother's father died when she was very young. I had no grandfather to speak of, so who was going to dance with her?

I felt a firm hand resting on my shoulder, and when I turned, there was Mark kneeling next to me. His face was kind and hesitant. He knew how I felt about him, but I could tell he was hopeful.

"Eden, could I have this dance?"

I picked at my white satin gloves, anxious but excited. Every year my elementary school hosted a father-daughter dance for Valentine's. Mama would always try to distract me, take me for ice cream, make it a big date night for her and me. But I mourned what I'd never had. What I would never have. A father to take me to the dance.

When I placed my hand in his, a smile grew across both of our faces, his hidden under his broom of a mustache. He hoisted me up into his arms and spun me around to the applause of everyone in the room. My mother cried on the sidelines, tears of joy for her little girl. My flower-girl dress billowed around me. I understood then how my mother must have felt. When Mark chose you, you were the most special person in the world.

Now I can hear them laughing in the next room, arguing over the remote. Though our bond has continued to ebb and flow through puberty and college and adulthood, above all else I am grateful for him. It is a relief to know my mom has someone here with her, someone who loves her.

I lay the lattice across my apple pie and place it in the preheated oven. I join them in the living room just as Jack Frost is magically brought to life as a snowman. I always forget how cheesy—and how good—these movies can be.

The movie finally ends, but instead of immediately moving on to the next in her marathon, Mama shuts off the television. "Well, Santa still has to wrap presents," she says. She holds one palm open to block Mark's view and points at him from behind it. "So I'm gonna need you to hit the hay, ma'am."

I groan and pull myself from the comfortable spot where I was dozing off just moments before. The oven beeps to signify my pie is ready, so I shuffle into the kitchen and remove it. I rest the dish on a cooling rack and shut off the oven.

"Well, do we think Santa can cover this up when he's done?" I ask, playing along for her sake.

"Eat the entire pie? Got it."

I jab a finger into Mark's chest. "If one piece of that pie is missing when Zoey's family joins us tomorrow for dinner, there will be hell to pay."

He puts up his hands in innocence while Mama chastises me for saying hell.

"Good night, Eden," she calls to me as she heads for the spare bedroom. It's where she keeps all the photos and memorabilia she cannot fit on the wall, and her extensive shoe collection. It's also where, as I discovered in the sixth grade, she stores our Christmas presents. I walk into my room opposite that one. As I reach for my door, I catch her eye and she looks at me with a mischievous grin. We shut our doors in unison, and I drag myself to bed.

I read once about a study that showed the chemical makeup for different types of tears. The article showed how tears of change and grief and even those from cutting onions look different under a microscope. All tears contain oils and enzymes. They contain salt water, which I taste now on my lips. Tears from emotion, the study found, had something a little extra. A hormone called leucine enkephalin. A hormone that acts as a painkiller.

As this silent torrent is flowing over my face, I wonder why it still hurts so badly. Stephen is quiet, holding space for me in this moment to speak if I would like to. To divulge how it is I am feeling. To let him in. As I've said before, I remember every aspect of that night. I remember how my mother worried her hands together the same way I do as I swept away the ornament. I remember the black speck of pepper that had lodged itself between Mark's front teeth. I remember the peace I felt in my soul as I laid down that night, listening to my mother shuffle through photo books and shoeboxes as she dug for the presents that were hidden across the hall. I remember being startled awake, not even realizing I was asleep.

I remember how everything shattered in the moments that followed.

"It won't always feel so overwhelming, Eden." Stephen leans forward as if this will bring him closer to me, make me listen and absorb what he is saying. "Sometimes, when a person breaks their bone, it starts to heal before it has been set in the right position. This only hurts the person in the long run, so the doctor has to re-break the bone in order to heal it properly. That's what you are doing when you recall the memories of that night through a therapeutic lens. You're setting it to heal properly, without any misconceptions in the way."

I look at him and nod, understanding that it is work that must be done even when I desperately want not to do it. I suffered through so much that night, but this hurts so much worse, reliving it without any of the blessed numbness of shock. "Healing," I manage to choke out on warbled breaths, "is fucking brutal."

He relaxes back into his chair, grimacing. "I know." He contemplates his response before continuing. "But the thing is, you either do the work now to heal, or you let it slowly eat you up inside. And that is a much worse fate, believe me."

It's not a comfort, but it is a challenge, and I'm nothing if not competitive.

"Eden, can I ask you a question?"

"I guess."

"I noticed you don't call Mark 'Dad,'" he says, studying me for any reaction.

"That's not a question," I say, hedging.

He gives me a hard stare before adding, "Why do you think that is? You grew up from such a young age with him; you seemed to have a bond."

He's genuinely curious, but as there always is when a therapist asks a question, I know there's an ulterior motive. I stare at the messy scrawl in my notebook, trying to put myself in those shoes again. To see him as I once did, rather than the monster he's become in my nightmares.

"It is so hard to separate what I know now from how I felt before," I begin. "I like to think maybe I suspected all along that something was off. But more likely, I'd already lost one father. Maybe as long as I refused to call him Dad, he couldn't do what my real one had done. He couldn't hurt our family like that."

Clearly I was mistaken.

Stephen scribbles in his notebook. I like to imagine what he writes in there. It's my own personal inside joke that despite his understanding persona, he secretly puts things like *bit of a whiner* when I complain about my circumstances. *Selfish bitch* when I vent that I deserve better than what life has given me. *Gross slob* when I wipe snot away from my face like I'm doing now.

"That was very good, Eden, nice self-evaluation." *Pretentious know-it-all*. I cover my mouth to suppress a giggle.

Once we've said our goodbyes, I bend over the sink and splash my face with cool water. I don't even have to look at myself to know that my pale skin has broken out in red blotches from all the crying. I grab a clip and twist my hair up, securing it on top of my head. Shorter pieces at the nape of my neck fall immediately, but at least this will help me cool down.

Three quick raps against my door cause me to startle. Zoey peers through the thin window bordering the doorframe. *I've got to get a curtain for that.* As soon as I turn the knob, she's pushing through, two coffees in hand from 8th & Main.

"Zo, I—"

She raises a hand to cut me off.

"Before you say anything, I'm not going to make you talk. I know you've been doing that for the last hour anyway." She shoves a warm cup into my hand, the scent of a vanilla spiced latte radiating from it. "But Noah Gundersen released a new album, and we don't have to be at the bar for a few hours, so we're going for a drive."

I roll my head back but allow myself to be dragged out of my home and down the stairs. We pile up in her car, and before we even roll out onto the street, we are enveloped in the warm embrace that is Noah's voice. We roam through town and the neighborhoods beyond. In the weeks since I've been here, aside from the occasional trip to Safeway, I haven't explored much beyond the brief commute from our house to Main Street and back. The mountains loom ever closer as we sit in awed silence, sipping our coffees and memorizing all the words.

Eventually we reach the end of the album, and on our return into town we resort to his older, more familiar tunes. Now we sing along, crooning the songs that have carried us through each season of life. It's not long before we're belting out the lyrics to "First Defeat," and suddenly we're seniors in high school again, traversing the back roads of our hometown after Topher Nichols broke Zoey's heart.

I look over at her, wind whipping wild golden curls around her face. She sings with so much passion you'd think she wrote the song herself. She smiles at me and grabs my hand from where it rests on my lap, squeezing it to remind me she is here. I know if I had to, I could find the strength to walk this journey on my own. But sitting here with my best friend, I am so grateful I don't have to. Zoey doesn't criticize me for not being far enough along. Instead she meets me where I'm at and pushes me gently forward.

Chapter Eight

"Those are your hiking boots?" Chase asks incredulously.

I look down at the outfit that I spent an embarrassing amount of time picking out. My lightweight tank top and khaki shorts seemed the most sensible choice given the forecasted heat wave. I'm lathered in sunscreen so thoroughly that I imagine I reek of coconut and SPF. The years-old backpack at my feet is worn but still functional enough to carry what I need. What it is failing to do is hide the sneakers I am sporting, which are apparently insufficient.

"I don't have boots, and you said it wasn't a hard hike, so this is what you get." It's six in the morning, and I barely slept due to the tumbleweeds of anxiety rolling around my stomach. I don't have enough coffee in my system to defend my decision to him well, and I hate that I care enough about what he thinks to even try.

He seems to consider this for a moment before deciding it isn't worth the battle. He picks up my backpack, throwing it over his shoulder before disappearing down the stairs. I follow his lead, laughing when he groans as if it is the heaviest thing he's ever lifted.

"What did you load this thing with? More Shirley Temple tapes?" he huffs. He tosses the pack into the back seat of his truck while I hoist myself into the cab.

"Water. Sunscreen. *Snacks*," I emphasize. He reverses out of the driveway, and I force myself to look out the passenger window this time rather than ogling his outstretched biceps. The sun is breaking over the mountain peaks and bathing the town in a buttery glow. He aims the truck in that direction and drives.

"So what is your ideal hiking snack, Eden?" He glances over at me, his cheeks awash in light even as his sunglasses shield his eyes. It's probably best if I don't let myself look at him too often; otherwise my conversational contributions will be minimal. I face forward and think about my answer.

"Well, today you are getting CLIF BARs and beef jerky because that is what I had around." Technically it's what Zoey had around when I raided her pantry yesterday. "But my all-time favorite would be trail mix minus the—"

"Raisins," he finishes my sentence.

"Oh my God, right?"

He laughs at my passionate response. "Yes, raisins are the fucking worst." We debate the different brands of trail mix for longer than is probably normal, finally settling on Target's Caramel Cashew. Sweet, salty, sans wrinkly grapes.

"What is your go-to hiking snack?" I ask, finally letting myself steal another glance. He has a different baseball cap on today, this time an army-green one with a yellow logo across the front that reads *Sitka*. His lips curve into a perfect Cupid's bow, framed by his five-o'clock shadow. The melodic reggae tune filling the cab fades out as he dials down the volume.

"It's not a snack technically, but a drink. I'm a sucker for a good lemonade. There's a restaurant in the next town over called the Raven that makes it fresh and bottles it for sale. Don't worry, I brought enough for both of us," he assures me. The fact that he thought to bring some for me brings a giddy smile to my face that I force away by biting my lower lip.

"So…" He points a finger at my side of the floorboard. "Those are for trail running, right?"

I must give him a strange look because he continues. "I sell them in my store."

Right.

"You a runner?" he asks, tossing a glance my way out of the corner of his eye that I just barely catch behind his glasses.

"You could say that. I ran cross-country in high school and then just for fun after that. I stopped a few months ago and haven't really gotten back into it." Running used to be where I would go to think, nothing to distract me but the beat of my feet against the ground. Turns out when you no longer want to think about your life, running is more like torture.

"What made you stop?"

"Just got busy with work, I guess." The real reasons are far too ugly to share on a first date. If that's even what this is. I kick myself for the umpteenth time for getting into this mess in the first place.

"Speaking of work." I silently thank whoever's listening that he's taken the opening I created and changed the topic. "Is managing a bar the dream job?"

"I'm a firm believer that a job is never the dream, the dream is the life you have outside of it," I say, chuckling. "That's why I got a business degree. Generic enough to work most places, and I'm good with numbers and planning."

He considers this for a moment, a slightly amused curve forming at the edge of his mouth. "It seems to be the dream for Zoey."

He's got me there. "Most definitely. Owning a restaurant has been number one on her bucket list since high school."

"What's on your list?" he asks.

I rub the scar on my wrist absentmindedly, tracing its crescent shape where it forms a parenthesis around the knobby bone. He waits patiently for an answer while he takes an exit from the highway, climbing our new road steadily higher.

"At one point I dreamed of running in the Boston Marathon," I admit, gaze flickering out the window. "Camping. Any kind of travel, I guess. Having a family."

I cough to cover the way my voice stumbles over that last word.

"You've never been *camping*?"

I shake my head.

"We'll have to fix that."

The idea of the two of us curled up in a tent somewhere causes my cheeks to grow warm. I shift the spotlight off me where it doesn't belong. "What about you?"

"Hike a mountain on every continent," he answers easily. He flips on the blinker to pull into an empty lot at the base of a dam.

"Except Antarctica," I correct him.

"*Especially* Antarctica," he says.

His door swings open first, and he gathers our bags so that I have both hands free to assist in my dismount. It is so tranquil here, the quiet only disturbed by running water and birds calling to one another. He passes my pack to me, and I strap it onto my back. It's not *that* heavy.

"This is why you have to get here early. Beat the tourists!" He locks up the truck and tosses the keys into his bag before buckling it around his chest. "It's a five-mile round-trip hike. Should be no problem for a cross-country woman like yourself."

I blow a raspberry at him but fall in line as he treks toward the trail. He wasn't kidding about the altitude up here. The air is thinner, making it feel sharp in my lungs. I send a prayer up to whoever is listening that I don't get altitude sickness in front of Chase.

The view is breathtaking. In every direction there are rolling hills speckled with boulders and a myriad of wildflowers. Douglas firs dot the vista. The mountain peaks in the distance are blanketed with white, so high the heat wave cannot reach them. I know now why he was worried about my shoes; the trail is not flattened dirt like the ones in Tennessee. We are navigating over a path comprised of crushed rocks with various levels of stability. When one shifts from the pressure of my step, I curse under my breath.

I focus on Chase's feet. His steps are sure, and he moves with an ease I admire. He seems completely in his element out here. If I'm honest with myself, I don't believe I've ever seen him *out* of his element. It's part of what draws me to him. If life is a series of choices, one after the other, then I have spent my entire existence uncertain I'm making the right ones. Chase is the opposite. He seems confident that if whatever selection he's made is incorrect, he will find a way to make it work anyway.

"Hey, Chase?" My voice is almost jolting after hiking to just the rhythm of our footsteps for so long.

He looks back over his shoulder at me. "She speaks!"

I roll my eyes before continuing. "Why Taylor's Landing?"

He slows so that he is walking beside me now as the path widens just a little. While a thrill courses through me at his closeness, I am also very aware that he now has an unobstructed view of my stumbling.

"Well, my last name is Taylor, for starters." He chuckles. I blush, wondering how much of an asshole it makes me that I've never even asked for his last name.

"I grew up out here." He gestures broadly around us. "And

about ninety percent of that time was spent with my dad. My mom is wonderful, but she's just not the outdoorsy type, you know?" The coarseness of his voice is so alluring, I have to force myself to focus on his words rather than the sound. I nod to acknowledge his rhetorical question.

"Anyway, so my dad and I have been hiking together my whole life, and our all-time favorite hike is Angel's Landing in Utah. It was our dream trail, and we finally did it the year I turned sixteen. That same year, the storefront next to Gary's came up for sale, and Dad had to have it." His face softens when he talks about his father. My heart aches for him, knowing how that story ends.

"He had always wanted to run an outdoors store, and I was old enough to work there after school to help him get it off the ground. We combined our name with that hike, hence Taylor's Landing."

"Where did the bear come in?"

"Geronimo?" He bursts out laughing, shaken from his reverie. "My uncle out in Montana gave him to my dad as a housewarming gift."

I picture Geronimo obscured with rolls upon rolls of gift wrap, strapped into some cowboy's truck bed and rolling down the highway. The mental image causes me to chuckle. I stop laughing when the trees thin out and a cerulean lake opens up before us. My feet forget how to move forward. The mountain cuts into the sky beyond the water, and fir trees pop up from the rocks lining the waterfront. The meadow we've been hiking through guides us down to a small shoreline littered with pebbles.

I now understand why Chase texted me last night, insisting I wear a bathing suit under my clothes.

He turns to me, grinning proudly at this reveal. "Hope you can swim," he says.

"Chase, this might be the most amazing thing I've ever seen in my life."

He reaches for my hand and pulls me downward. His calluses are rough against my palm. I'm completely distracted by his touch and stumble on a loose rock.

He whips his head around to check on me. "Be careful," he says. "No broken ankles needed on this trip." I glare at him and continue walking. There's an inexplicable sadness in my chest when he releases his grasp in order to pull off his pack.

Up close, every pebble can be seen through the crystal surface. I follow his lead and drop my backpack onto a nearby boulder. He brandishes two glass bottles embossed with the black outline of a bird. "Prepare yourself for an addiction," he warns.

The cap twists off easily, releasing a hiss of pressure. The bitter tartness of lemon is the first thing to strike my tongue, followed by a soothing kiss of sugar. I take another swig. It immediately transports me to summer days spent playing outside in the woods behind my house, our fridge always containing a pitcher when Mama would call me in for lunch. "Wow," is all I can say.

"Told you so." He then blows my mind once more, grabbing his shirt between the shoulders and pulling it over his head. The lemonade gets stuck in my throat, and my cheeks grow hot. My gaze is roving from his defined chest to the ridges of muscle forming an arrow on his abdomen that disappears into his waistband. I drag it back up to the half sleeve of black and gray ink covering his right bicep. I force myself to swallow.

"Clocks?" I manage to squeak out. Every kind is depicted on his arm. He lifts it up to give me a better view, and there I am met with a grandfather clock adorning the tender skin above his elbow. Beyond that, a digital clock with the time 12:14

displayed. A melting clock face wraps around the back of his tricep, and roman numerals are flying up toward his shoulder.

He shrugs, setting his hat and sunglasses on the rock next to our bags. He looks me in the eye and holds my gaze, his familiar intensity returning. "There's never as much time as you think."

I'm still digesting that when he turns and dives forward into the water, submerging himself. I nervously pull my tank top over my head and lay it down beside his things. I stuff my socks into my shoes and unbutton my shorts. As I slide them over my hips and down my thighs, Chase resurfaces, watching me intently.

I suck air through my teeth when my toes first dip into the water. "Holy *shit*," I hiss.

"Don't be such a baby," he jokes.

"This water is like ice!" I yell. I don't know how the fact that I'm literally on a mountain and this water is only here as the result of snow melting has just registered with my brain. A thousand needles are pricking every inch of my skin as I slowly move deeper into the lake. How he managed to do this so quickly is beyond me. He's now just a head bobbing in the water, laughing at my misfortune.

"I can help you get used to it," he teases, making grab hands at me.

"If you touch me, I will kill you," I threaten. I'm only half kidding. I am not a dive-right-in kind of girl. I'm the wade-till-your-body-is-numb kind.

He respects my wishes and instead watches me with an eyebrow raised in amusement. He runs a hand through his hair, slicking it back. His gaze is roaming down my body, and I'm suddenly very aware of my striped bikini and how much—or really how little—it covers up.

I'm not sure if I am trying to be brave by diving in or if it's actually cowardice to avoid him admiring my figure, but either way I submerge myself in the freezing water. Fireworks go off behind my eyes, and then, like magic, my body adjusts. When I resurface, it is the most alive I've ever felt. Chase leans back and lets himself float. I do the same, all at once cradled by this body of water and covered by a pale-blue sky that expands beyond my field of vision. With the water roaring in my ears, every sense has been taken over and I don't know where I end and everything else begins.

I can see why he loves it here. I feel so small and insignificant in the best possible way. If I am this microscopic in the eyes of the universe, then the pain I carry inside of me must be infinitesimal. I don't know what I believe happens when we die, at least not anymore. I don't think I ever did. But drifting in this alpine lake, I take a mental note and file it away to remind myself that if we each get to choose a heaven, this will be mine.

Hands press against my back, releasing me from the responsibility of floating. I'm surprised to find his touch feels so natural, so comforting. I tilt my face toward him, wishing I could taste the drop of water pooling in the bow of his upper lip. He slowly rotates, water flowing around me as we go.

"What do you believe in, Chase?" I let my eyes drift closed. The sun basking down on us lights my vision up red.

"Um, definitely Sasquatch, possibly the Loch Ness monster. That people should put their carts in the cart return after shopping. I know Megalodon existed at some point, but the jury's out on if he's still hanging around—"

I smack him in the chest to cut him off.

"No, like you asked me when we talked about my name," I explain, though we'll have to circle back to the Megalodon thing at some point. "Do you believe in all that stuff?"

I crack one eye open to peer up at him. He's weighing his response. I like that he always gives me a straight answer even when the questions are overly personal or ridiculous. He never shrugs them off just because he doesn't have an opinion at the ready.

"I was never really religious, to be honest." The frigid water is taking root in my body, causing me to shiver. "What about you? What changed your mind?"

"I guess as I got older, I just found it harder to believe there was someone controlling all of this that could possibly be considered good, given all the horrible things that happen to innocent people." My teeth are chattering slightly. He grips me tighter and lifts me out of the water completely. Before I can even open my eyes, I'm laid on a sun-warmed rock by the shore. Flecks of water from his hair shower me as he sprawls by my side.

"I can understand that." He props himself up on an elbow, turning to give me his full attention. His eyebrows are drawn together, but he doesn't seem to mind how serious I've made the conversation.

"What do you think happens when we die?" I ask quietly. I secretly hope maybe he knows the right answer. One that will give me some kind of comfort. The warmth from the stone is spreading through my body, relaxing me.

"I don't know." He says it simply, without fear. It seems crazy that the same thing that terrifies me can make him brave.

"Doesn't that scare you?" I shield my eyes so I can see him better.

"No, it just makes me want to live the best life I can while I'm here."

Somewhere inside me, something unravels that I didn't even know was tangled. Maybe he does have the right answer after all.

"I like the way you see the world," I say.

"I like the way you question it," he says. I smile at the strange compliment.

He reaches for a tendril of waterlogged hair, threading it between his fingers. "You know, in the bar I can hardly tell your hair is red at all. But right now the sun makes it look like a copper penny."

I want to tell him that the sunlight turns his eyes into pebbles of amber. I half expect that if I search hard enough, I'll find a prehistoric mosquito that has been trapped in there forever. I want to tell him this, but I can't because he rests his palm across my stomach, thumb stroking next to my belly button, and I forget what language I speak.

"That night in the rain, I couldn't tell if this was just an oddly placed tattoo or what."

I sit up on my elbows, watching his thumb caress my birthmark. "No tattoos for me," I say. "I've always wanted one, but my pain tolerance is too low."

His gaze levels with mine, a serious cloud shading his expression.

"I'll bet you're a lot stronger than you think."

Then I don't think. At all. Because his lips are covering mine, and they are warm and soothing and just as soft as I imagined they would be. He cradles my head with one hand and moves his other from my stomach to my hip, pulling me toward him. It is as though the sun is inside me now, and I am bursting into flames. His tongue presses softly into my mouth and I think I might let out a sigh, but I can't even summon the presence of mind to be embarrassed. He is everywhere and all at once.

He pulls back and rests his forehead against mine, his breathing a shaky breeze caressing my cheeks. When I am brave enough to look into his eyes, the amber is molten.

"I've been wanting to do that since the day I met you." He is lying, of course. I was a shaken, frumpy mess the day he met me. But the sentiment causes my heart to flip just the same. "Don't do that."

"What?" I ask, confused.

"You're doing that thing where you mentally disregard any compliment you're given."

"I don't know what you're talking about." I sit up, daring him to disagree. How can he read my mind so easily?

"You made the same face the day Gary told you your hair looked pretty. And it did, by the way. Gary never gives compliments. You should not look a gift horse in the mouth." He squares his shoulders, firm in his opinion.

"That expression never made any sense to me anyway," I huff, hoisting myself off the boulder. I'm not in the mood to be psychoanalyzed right now. Stephen pretty much fulfills my quota for that.

I realize immediately that I've made a grave miscalculation. Pain like lightning jolts from my ankle all the way to my hip, knocking the breath from my lungs. I look down at my landing, realizing my foot has slid into the crevice between two rocks at an unnatural angle. An ache radiates from it with every heartbeat, causing tears to form behind my eyes.

Chase jumps into action, lowering himself more carefully than I did onto the unstable ground before kneeling in front of me and lifting my injured foot into his lap. I suck in air and blow it out slowly, determined not to cry in front of him. He tests the range of motion for my ankle, pushing it in each direction until my hand on his shoulder squeezes in response.

"You want the good news or the good news?" He's looking up at me with a mischievous smile. I think I might've misheard him, but he continues.

"Good news is, it's not broken. I've broken both ankles and shattered my entire right arm, for reference. You wouldn't be able to move it like this if it were more than a sprain." He tenderly sets my foot on the ground before turning to our pile of gear on the opposite boulder. "Other good news is, you cannot walk out on that foot in shoes with no ankle support."

"Why is that good news?"

He shoves my smaller backpack into his and pulls on his shirt and shoes. "Because, Eden"—he thrusts my shorts and tank toward me—"it means I get to carry you."

Chapter Nine

Chase shuts his door and waltzes around to my side with an eagerness I admire. Two and a half miles with me and all my snacks on his back and not one complaint. I must be one hell of a kisser. When the door swings open, he positions himself with his back to me so it is easy to climb on.

"You think you can handle one more flight of stairs?" I ask. My legs lock around his waist as I throw my arms over his shoulders. From this position I've been able to inhale all the pine-scented soap my heart desires.

"Girl, I've trained my whole life for this." I giggle as he hoists me up. He climbs the stairs with ease and squats down so I can insert my key into the lock from over his shoulder. Once he crosses the threshold, he pulls a chair out from my table, depositing me backward into the seat.

"I know I've called you this before, and I don't want you to get a big head or anything"—I hold a finger up in warning—"but you're my hero."

He bows, grinning from ear to ear. He presses a quick kiss against my lips before retreating down the stairs to retrieve my bag. The way he does it so naturally, as if we've just been kissing each other forever, leaves my head spinning on my shoulders. It occurs to me that maybe I haven't made a huge mistake. Maybe this is exactly what I need.

When he returns, he unpacks two white chocolate macadamia CLIF BARs, passing one to me before tearing into his own. My stomach has been grumbling since the last half mile of our hike. It lets out a final triumphant gurgle as I swallow the first bite. He props my ankle on his knee from his seat opposite me, turning it over to examine the damage.

"The swelling is already going down. Probably best to stay off it as much as possible for the next few days and keep it elevated when you can. Should be healed in no time."

"Guess Gary's going to have to bartend for Maddie tomorrow." I laugh. His touch is gentle as he rubs a thumb against the arch of my foot, careful not to jostle my ankle.

"You guys really should hire another bartender." Our laughter fades as he rakes his eyes up my leg, over my hip, and to my chest before settling them on my mouth. Thoughts of how his lips feel pressed against mine fill my mind, and fire lights up my cheeks.

"Well, you want me to carry you to your bathroom so you can change out of the wet clothes?" He says it with a slight tinge of hope, like I might request his assistance for more than transportation.

"I got it. Can you just grab my pajamas off the bed and toss some underwear from my top drawer. *Without looking.* Just grab whatever you touch first."

He jumps up excitedly, grabbing my oversized tee and plaid shorts from where they rest on the bed before swinging open my top drawer, eyes definitely not closed. He digs for much longer than necessary despite my protests before finally producing a lacy red thong that is not intended for sleeping.

He dangles it in the air and raises his eyebrows at me suggestively.

"If you don't bring those to me right now and stop ogling, you'll never see my panties again."

He laughs and brings the bundle to my bathroom, setting it on the counter. "So, what you're saying is, I *do* get to see them again?" He is entirely too eager. I'd be flattered if I weren't so embarrassed.

"Maybe," I reply, bracing against him as I hobble the short distance from the table, careful not to place too much weight on my ankle. As I swing the door shut behind me, he's still cheering, "She said maybe!" as if someone will hear and congratulate him.

Once the door falls to a close and I turn the lock, a familiar dread begins to spread through my body. I pull a towel from where it is drying on the rack and kneel on my good leg, shoving it into the crack. A bead of sweat breaks out on my forehead, and my hands begin to shake. I try to take a deep breath as I reach for the hem of my shirt, but I am trembling too hard to move it higher. My lungs seem to reject the oxygen I offer them. My breathing becomes shallow and broken.

When the panic attacks began shortly after everything happened, Stephen talked to me about ways to manage the anxiety. He told me to think of anxiety as a separate entity from myself, a monster that just wants to bully me into submission. It is that monster consuming me now, overthrowing every rational part of my brain that assures it, *That man out there is a good man. He does not want to hurt me. I am safe. I am safe. I am safe.*

He can see you, the monster says. I add another towel to the pile on the floor. I turn the lights off so I cannot see my stricken expression in the mirror reflected back at me. Tiny breaths burst in and out of my tight lungs. I'm certain I'm going to be sick.

"Need some help in there, Eden?" Chase calls to me. The

monster fills my head with darkness. Chase wiggles the door-knob when I don't respond. I choke on a sob that tries to escape. The monster thinks it is protecting me when it rips open the door, causing Chase to jump back.

"You need to leave," I manage to force out with what little air is in my lungs. His face goes from confused to concerned, not understanding why there are tears pouring down my face nor why I am hunched over a pile of towels like a gremlin.

"What's wrong, Eden? Is it your ankle?" His face is one of compassion. He doesn't know what is broken, but he wants to fix it. The monster wants to do it on our own. He takes a step toward me with a hand outstretched. I escape around him into the kitchen.

"Please. Leave." I force out through gritted teeth. My head is swimming now. Once the panic takes hold, there is nothing I can do except ride the wave. I don't want him to see me like this. Why can't he understand?

He reaches for my arm, and I reel backward as if he will burn me. "*Leave*, Chase!" I shout.

I know I am hurting him. I'm hurting myself, too. But I don't know how to explain this to him. If I tell him about the monster, he'll think I am crazy. He probably already does.

He backs away from me reluctantly, shock and confusion clouding his dark eyes as he steps out onto the landing. I cannot even look at him as I slam the door in his face. I stumble into the kitchen, pain radiating from my ankle. I rip open my medicine drawer and uncap the orange bottle rattling with pills. I force myself to swallow one. I hate how this will make me feel. I hate how I feel already.

A short time later I am crumpled in my bed under the weight of pharmaceuticals and my own shame. My arms and legs feel like they are strapped with sandbags like the ones Mark and my mother used when they were learning to scuba dive. I hear a knock on the door through the haze, and I know it is Zoey. I know Chase must have gone to her for help. The shame multiplies tenfold.

What must he think of me? Why do I ruin everything I touch? When will there be nothing left for this trauma to take from me?

Zoey pushes open the door when I do not respond. I hear her but remain still, facing the wall instead of my friend. I keep my eyes closed tight. I barely wince when she says my name, softly, sadly, as though I am a breakable thing.

When I don't answer, she pads across the room. She leans over and assumes that I am asleep. She brushes the hair back from my face, and a sad sigh escapes her lips. I hear her set something on the bedside table, and then her footsteps retreat, the door clicking into place behind her.

I wait for what feels like eternity before I'm sure she will not return. Only then do I roll over to look at what she's brought to me. A sob rocks through my body when my gaze falls on a glass bottle embossed with the black outline of a bird.

Chapter Ten

I'm not sure which hurts worse right now: my scalp or my ankle. I peer down to where my foot is perched on one of Zoey's less expensive throw pillows and find the culprit. As the ice melts and shifts, the bag I've balanced on my ankle has drooped, and in doing so a corner has snuck out of the protective rag I wrapped it in. The ice presses against my sensitive skin with no barrier to protect me from its stinging bite.

I can't have leaned forward more than a millimeter, but Zoey yanks me back using the tendrils of hair in her fists as reins. My scalp. Definitely my scalp.

"Could you please sit still?" she grumbles. When she asked to braid my hair, I thought it would be relaxing. I should've known she'd approach it with the same tenacity as she does everything else.

"Can I just adjust my ice bag, please?"

She releases the breath she's been holding in a frustrated sigh, but she unhands my hair. I tuck the olive-green hand towel back under the bag of ice, and the relief is instantaneous. The plaits unravel as I massage my tender head.

Zoey flops back onto her velvet, emerald-green couch and

grabs the remote, clicking to dismiss the *Are you still watching?* prompt that has popped up. Of course we're still watching. We haven't moved in hours except to pee and refill our bowl of popcorn and peanut M&Ms.

"How excited was Gary to be back in the limelight tonight?" Zoey asks. She shoves another handful of popcorn into her mouth. I tilt my head back and open wide so she can drop two M&Ms inside. The salt from the popcorn has coated the hard shell, making my favorite candy better, if it were even possible.

"He was more excited that it meant he got to teach Zander the ropes," I say. I carefully lift myself up onto the couch, propping my ankle on the arm and giving it a break from the ice. My skin is angry from the cold, a blistering red to compliment the purple bruise on the joint.

"Why the sudden interest in bartending?" Zoey asks.

"Something about putting away extra money for the PCT through-hike he has planned for next year." Zander, I learned, is a guide for a local ATV tour company during the day. His willingness to help Maddie out on the busier weekend nights and occasionally covering her off days for me was a welcome offer. She nods and we watch the show in silence for a moment.

"What do you think about 'The Village' as a name for the bar?" she asks finally.

I snort against my will. "It sounds like that retirement community in Florida. Did you know they have the highest rate of STDs in the state?"

Before she can respond, my phone chimes from its place on the marble coffee table. Thinking it might be a problem at the bar, I reach for it. My face unlocks it before I can read the preview. When I click on the red notification on my texts, I wince.

Chase: I'm sorry for upsetting you. Can we please talk?

The uneasy, sick feeling returns to my stomach, and I immediately regret the last bite of chocolate now curdling in my gut. I hate that he blames himself for what happened, but I don't know how to make him understand. Not without folding my cards, showing how ugly my hand really is.

"Do you want to tell me what's going on between you two?" Zoey asks, her voice inquisitive yet gentle. She is very much one to pry, but I can tell she is trying to tread lightly. "Eden, you know how much I love Chase, but if he did something to hurt you—"

"God, no, Zoey!" I interrupt her. "He didn't do anything wrong. He's been a perfect gentleman. I just..." Even with my best friend, it's hard. I don't know how to explain it to her when I can't even explain it to myself. "Sometimes, the memories just feel so real, you know? Like they're actually happening all over again."

She pauses *The Good Place* and turns to face me. "Have you told him what happened?" Her eyebrows pull together in concern.

"No," I say, picking at a loose stitch in the blanket covering my lap. "I don't want to freak him out, you know?" The chenille thread pulls loose from my prying. It's soft as I roll it between my thumb and index finger.

Zoey's expression changes suddenly, anger flushing her cream skin and darkening her eyes to navy. "It's such bullshit," she spits out. I jump back from her slightly, shrinking in on myself. Of course, she's sick of hearing about this. I can't blame her. All I seem to offer our conversations lately are my problems.

She stands and paces to her kitchen, resting both palms flat against the granite countertop on the island. She tilts her head back and releases controlled breaths, trying to de-escalate her tension. I scramble with what to say but come up short. She finally looks over at me, her stormy gaze rimmed with red. An apologetic smile softens the tight set of her mouth.

"It's such bullshit that he is the one who did something wrong," she finally says. "And yet you are the one carrying the guilt of his actions."

The tension cable in my spine snaps, leaving my shoulders sagging.

"I'm sorry, Eden. I just hate to see you like this," she says when I don't respond. "I think I need a minute." She pushes off the counter and strides across the room, closing the door to her bedroom behind her with a soft *click*.

Before I can process what's just happened, my phone lights up again. This time it is my ringtone instead of a simple chirp that fills the room. My mother's face appears, jolting me out of my catatonic state. I swipe the phone up and slide my thumb across the screen, cutting it off mid-ring.

"Eden? You there?" she calls out into my surprised silence. My reaction to hearing her voice is visceral. Every cell in my body responds to that voice I know better than my own. Relief clears the fog in my head, and I'm finally able to speak.

"Mama, I'm here! It's so good to hear your voice!"

Zoey's door cracks open, and her head pokes through. *Julie?* she mouths at me. I nod excitedly.

"It's good to hear yours too, baby!" my mother responds. "I'm sorry I've been so bad about calling. I've gotten so out of practice from talking to anyone these days." She sounds smaller than I am used to, more fragile. I feel as though if I pried at her words, even gently, they'd splinter off into a thousand pieces.

Zoey pads across the room and rejoins me on the couch. The baby hairs framing her oval face are slick against her skin from where she's splashed herself with water. The redness around her eyes has subsided. If it weren't for the fact that her irises still look like a storm at sea, you'd barely be able to tell she was upset moments ago.

"Hi, Miss Julie!" she says, leaning into my phone's speaker. I have it perched between our heads so Mama can hear us clearly.

"Zoey!" Mama shouts in response. "Are you keeping our girl out of trouble?"

"You know better than that," Zoey replies. "I'm doing my best to keep her in it."

Mama laughs and it is music to my ears. On our last phone call before I moved, she'd been listless and unreachable. I realize how much guilt I've been carrying, feeling like I need to be there taking care of her even when being there is the one thing that would hurt me most. The only thing that allowed me to leave was the knowledge she would be moving to live with Ella, and when that didn't happen, the sense of having abandoned her grew nearly unbearable.

"Mama, what happened to going to Texas?" I ask. I hate to ruin the moment, but it has been nagging at me for too long not to. She hesitates for so long I think her signal must have failed. Finally her voice comes through the line, more distant than before.

"Oh, you know, Brother Richard would lose his head if it weren't attached. I couldn't leave him high and dry with no one to make sure the bills are paid and the lights stay on." I can tell she is deflecting. No one does it better than her. There is an elephant on the line with us that no one wants to address. Luckily Zoey is a natural-born zookeeper.

"What about Mark?" she asks. Mama always told me growing up that I should be more like Zoey, more brazen. I wonder if she's regretting that right about now.

"Well, Zo, he does his thing and I do mine." I suddenly wish my mother knew how to use FaceTime so I could look her in the eyes and ask her to blink twice if she's being coerced. I can't read her now, as out of practice as I am. Zoey glances up at me, nostrils flaring as if she's smelled something foul. The weather report in her eyes is calling for hurricanes.

"Have you talked to that lawyer your friend referred you to?" I ask. I feel like I am walking on a balance beam every time we talk these days. Underneath me are all the ugly futures I desperately want to avoid, and the things left unsaid are blocking my path, threatening to make me fall.

"Yeah, baby, I have." That's all she says in response. She sounds exhausted, like just this brief conversation with me will take her days to recover from. I don't know how that happened. I try so hard to shield her from the ugly parts of my healing, texting her more uplifting things like my thoughts about the most recent season of her favorite true crime series or a photo of what new cocktail Maddie and I have come up with for the week. I don't want her to worry about me. I wonder if Ella is telling her what I am not.

"Girls, I better go," she says. "I'm working the silent auction tonight raising money for the youth group to go to camp." I try to picture any of the old ladies in that church being associated with an event referred to as *silent,* but the absurdity of it prevents me from doing so. Zoey scoffs, clearly thinking the same, but she's gone to refill her water bottle so my mother cannot hear the disdain.

"Have fun, Mama. Maybe we can talk again later this week?" I try not to let worry paint my tone, but I imagine it does anyway. I am doing to her what Ella does to me, and I resent myself for it even as I double down. "Maybe sometime this summer you could come out to Colorado and see me?"

Another pregnant pause fills the space between me and my mother. I can hear the clamber of dishes as I imagine she is pulling them from the dishwasher, one after the other, drying them before putting each in its rightful place. I picture myself, there beside her, towel in hand. *Really, baby, it's okay.* She keeps drying them, keeps ignoring my outstretched hand. *I can do it just fine by myself.*

"Maybe so," she replies at last. I set down my towel. I hang up the phone.

Chapter Eleven

I've been sitting in my car for longer than I care to admit trying to gather the energy to limp into work. After a couple nights of sleeping on Zoey's couch to avoid hobbling up any stairs, my ankle has finally healed enough to carry me short distances. My back, however, may never forgive me.

Dense fog swirls in the air of the parking lot, obscuring my view of the wrought-iron staircases scaling the row of brick buildings. A light from Gary's apartment cuts through the haze. At this hour he's probably already on his second cup of Rose's coffee. It occurs to me that I have no clue what he does all day when he isn't eating at the bar or refilling at 8th & Main. I can't imagine him piled up at a computer desk playing solitaire like Zoey's grandfather used to when he would "supervise" us after school. All that caffeinated energy must go somewhere.

I'm about to go down a very dark mental road picturing Gary power walking around the park in leg warmers when my thoughts are interrupted by the low rumble of an engine. Chase's white Silverado rolls into the spot opposite mine. He cuts it off, his headlights leaving black spots in my vision in their absence. It takes a moment for them to clear, and by my fourth blink Chase is rounding the hood of my car, eyes trained on me. Nervous sparks go off in my chest.

He's wearing black running shorts and a red tank top with a logo so faded I cannot make it out. When he stops outside my door, peering in at me, I notice a sheen of sweat covering his skin. A drop rolls down his throat and pools in the hollow of his collarbone. He raps his fist softly against the glass. Muffled as it is through my window, I hear the words he is mouthing.

"Can we talk?"

I move to open the door, and this is all the invitation he needs. It swings away from my outstretched hand, and I'm left with that arm suspended in the air between us. Even fresh out of a morning workout, the scent of the outdoors and something uniquely him envelops me. I'm overwhelmed with the urge to embrace him, but my good sense gets behind the control panel of my brain and reminds me that this is not the time. My hand falls into my lap, as does my gaze.

Chase squats in front of me, ducking his head so he can look me in the eye. Concern is etched in the wrinkle between his eyebrows. Tension sets his jaw, a slow grind working his teeth together as he considers my mood. His hand hovers over mine before he thinks better of it and grabs the doorframe instead. Guilt causes a tinge at the base of my skull. It's my fault he's this nervous. He doesn't know what will trigger the reaction I had in my apartment, so he's handling me with kid gloves.

"Chase, I—"

"I'm so sorry, Eden—"

We both pause to let the other speak. Awkward laughter fills the space between us, and I feel the mood lift ever so slightly. I gesture for him to go on, my lips pressed tightly together so as not to interrupt. He smiles and cautiously pats my knee.

"Eden, I'm sorry I've pushed so much. I misread things between us, and that's on me. I just—"

"You didn't," I interject. So much for letting him speak.

His eyes go wide with hope. Instinct overrules the logic I thought was running my brain. Before I know it is happening, I see my thumb press gently between his furrowed brows, smoothing out the wrinkle in that soft skin. I'm already here, beyond the barrier I erected to protect myself, so I keep going. I trace the pattern of freckles down the bridge of his nose and across his cheek. Stubble scrapes against my palm as I cup his face before letting my hand slowly fall away.

"I don't understand." He says it softly, the rasp in his voice causing it to break.

"I don't either," I admit. "But Chase, it's not your fault. You didn't misread anything. I had an amazing day with you, the best day I've had in *so long*. I just—"

Why is this so hard? I feel like this is the first time I've ever tried to form coherent sentences, and my mind just can't keep up. He shakes his head slightly to show me he's not tracking.

"I moved here to get away from some things." A choppy breath slips out from between my teeth. "Sometimes it all just comes back. Without warning."

I know I am not making any sense. I groan in frustration and place my hands over my face.

"I'm not trying to be cryptic. I'm just not good at this."

The words are muffled by my fingers, which Chase gently pries open. That single wave of hair has fallen onto his forehead. I expect confusion and maybe even anger when I let my gaze settle on his face, but instead I am met with a gentle kind of understanding that causes a fault line in my heart to shift.

"Eden, you don't have to explain yourself to me," he says. "I told you, I'm in no rush."

His words feel so genuine that I almost regret the first

thought that crosses my mind. I've dated men who found out I came from a broken marriage and immediately puffed out their chest, determined they'd make up for all the men that came before. I don't sense those waves of bravado rolling off Chase's skin, but the fear still remains. I feel us pulling toward one another, mentally and physically, and I muster up the last warning I'm able to give. "Chase, you can't fix me."

He shakes his head gently. "You're not broken."

I don't correct him, even though he's wrong.

My face crumples as the tremors spread from my heart all the way to my fingertips where they are cupped in his grasp, pressed to his lips. When I don't pull away, he turns one of my arms over, pressing another kiss gently against my wrist. He traces a path of feather-light kisses up that arm, pausing only to roll up my sleeve before continuing on to my shoulder. His sweet breath is so close now it washes over me. He bridges the gap slowly, giving me time to pull away.

Instead I lean forward, covering his mouth with mine. He takes my lower lip between his teeth, tracing it gently with his tongue. My pulse is pounding out a rapid rhythm in my head. Just when I think it's all too much, that my heart might beat its way right out of my chest, Chase pulls back from the kiss. He lays his head against my collarbone, catching his breath.

"How is your ankle feeling?" he finally manages to ask, standing to put distance between us. I give a shuddering sigh, ripping my eyes away from his and down to the floorboard where my bum ankle sits in the cheap brace I made Zoey buy at the drugstore.

"It's fine, still sore if I'm on it for too long but I can manage."

A familiar grin spreads across his face.

"What?"

"Does the lady need to be carried?" he asks excitedly. I

moan, throwing my head back in mock exasperation. When I peek back up at him with a smile, his eyes are as dark as night.

"Eden, you can't make that noise around me. Not when I'm supposed to take it slow with you." His tone is terse. A breath stops short in my airway. I nod, a thrill running down my spine. He presses a fist against his jaw, popping his neck.

I grab my purse from the passenger seat and turn to sling my legs out of the car. He's there with his back to me, squatting low. The thin fabric of his gym shorts stretches taut against his muscular ass.

Aaron, eat your heart out.

"Hop on," he says. I swat his back with my purse.

"I'm not letting you carry me in!" I squeal. "People will make assumptions!"

"Oh, I'm counting on it," he says over his shoulder. "I want everyone in town talking about how Chase Taylor has his sights set on the mysterious new girl."

I roll my eyes but shift forward, wrapping my legs around his waist in a way that is becoming too familiar to me.

"'Mysterious' is *not* the word I'd use."

"But you are, Eden." He smiles over his shoulder at me, shutting my car door as he stands. "What you need to understand, though, is that I have watched my fair share of *Sherlock Holmes*, and I won't stop until I've cracked the case of what is going on in that beautiful head of yours."

I giggle into his neck, surprised to find myself hoping that he succeeds.

He marches us down the sidewalk and around the corner along the bustling main thoroughfare. Most of the stores don't open until later, but it is still a Friday morning. A man pushes his babbling toddler in a stroller down the sidewalk across the street. He passes in front of a hairdresser in a black apron flipping the sign in her door to *Open*. A woman in a smart gray suit opens the door to the law office a block away and lets her male companion enter ahead of her.

As always, the line for 8th & Main is out the door with people fetching their morning fix of caffeine. Both exterior walls of the shop are floor-to-ceiling windows, allowing all her patrons to steal glances at us as we pass, trying not to outright stare at the grown woman riding piggyback down to the bar. When we walk by the windows, I see Rose skirting around her assistant manager Jessie as she pops the lid onto a travel mug and passes it to a customer. She looks up, flashing me a smile and a thumbs-up as we pass. I bury my face against Chase's shoulder to cover my blush.

He deposits me on the stoop of the bar. The smile on his face is broad and pearly white against the backdrop of his olive skin. It feels like the whole world is lighting up just for me.

"Bet you didn't plan on getting a second workout this morning, huh?" I joke, fishing for the ring of keys in my purse.

"Are you kidding?" He pinches my arm affectionately. "You're tiny. Now, if you'll excuse me, I'm going to join that mob and secure my cup of that holy elixir. You want anything?"

"No, thanks, I've had my coffee for the day," I reply, swinging the door open and flipping the switch to illuminate the dark room. It's mood lighting, but it's better than nothing. "Plus, I need to get in and unlock the back door before Shawn arrives with the new delivery of kegs."

Chase's nostrils flare but his expression remains otherwise unchanged. "Just be careful around that guy, something about him makes my skin crawl."

I nod, knowing exactly what he means. "See you later?"

He smiles again, leaning over and scooping me up into his arms for a firm kiss that the audience in line next door will definitely appreciate. He follows it up with a soft one against my cheek, and the encore is his grumbled whisper in my ear. "Definitely."

I watch him walk away and catch myself sighing pathetically before letting the door fall to a close. I've barely hobbled across the room and am about to enter the kitchen when it rips back open.

"Saw that."

Gary's voice startles me, and when I turn to look at him, the saloon door I've pushed forward swings back and knocks me in the back. A sharp laugh escapes before he muffles it with a hand over his mouth. I huff at him and then continue with what I was doing, flipping the much brighter lights on in the kitchen and crossing the room at a snail's pace to turn off the alarm and push open the delivery door. A light rain has begun to fall, washing the fog away.

"Santi won't be here until later, and I've got bad news for you about my cooking abilities," I call over my shoulder. He's watching me from the threshold as I check the temperature on our fridges and freezers and update the logs attached. He uncrosses his arms, but the knowing smirk hasn't left his face.

"I don't have much of an appetite anyway; stomach's been bothering me the past few days." He holds the door open for me as I limp through. I finally hoist myself onto a bar chair and lift my foot into the stool opposite me, letting out a sigh of relief. Today will be good for paperwork and not much else.

"You wanna tell me what that was back there?" he says, jabbing a thumb over his shoulder toward the street. "I don't like being the last to know about things." It's a little hilarious to see a grown man so interested in gossiping.

"Why are you laughing, Eden? It's not funny! First, he breaks your ankle; then he's macking on you on my front porch! It's too much to keep up with for an old man." He dramatically wipes imaginary sweat from his brow and slumps into a seat just as Shawn calls out from the back room. I throw my legs back to the floor. So much for a moment of peace.

"First of all, my ankle isn't broken, just sprained." Before I retreat into the kitchen, I add a whisper-shout just low enough that Shawn can't hear. "And second, you're the first to know so keep it quiet, okay?"

Surprised excitement flashes across Gary's face before he seals his lips with an imaginary zipper and throws the key over his shoulder.

"What happened to you?" Shawn asks when I step into the room. He's rolling a full barrel into our fridge, depositing it and then loading an empty one for his return trip. I grab his clipboard from the counter and read over our invoice, signing my name when I see it is all correct.

"Twisted my ankle on a hike last weekend," I explain, handing his copy back as he passes.

"So, she's beauty but not grace," he replies. Shawn is a short and stout man, barely an inch taller than me. His hands are meaty and covered in tattooed letters so blown out they are impossible to read. The sweat beading at his brow and the wad of chewing tobacco protruding from his lip are nearly permanent fixtures at this point.

"Something like that," I say curtly.

He loads the last empty cylinder onto his dolly, stopping short of rolling it out the door. "Gotta be careful out there, honey. Wouldn't wanna damage any of the good bits." He makes a point to ogle my breasts before winking and continuing on to his truck.

I slam the door shut and flip the alarm back on, walking as quickly as I can out of the kitchen and over the padded bar mats to our office. Gary walks out of the restroom just as I've slumped into the desk chair. I try to smooth the wrinkles out of the invoice where I gripped it too tightly in my fist.

The light from my corner lamp reflects off Gary's bald head as he peeks in through the crack I've left in the door. "You just tell Chase I'll whoop his ass if he hurts one of my girls."

I've completely forgotten what we were talking about after Shawn's disgusting comment, so it takes me an extra second to react. The moment his statement registers, the fact that he thinks of me as one of his girls overshadows the ridiculous mental image of him attempting to hit, well, anyone. Let alone Chase. Speaking of ridiculous mental images of Gary, that reminds me.

"Gary, do you play solitaire?" He looks at me strangely, unsure how I've made this leap in conversation topic. "You know, when you aren't here or next door at Rose's, do you play solitaire? Or go for power walks?"

He throws his head back, howling with laughter. It subsides only after he grips his stomach and groans in pain. "Eden," he manages to huff out on the breath of a residual chuckle. "How old do you think I am?"

Chapter Twelve

"You have to shit *outside?*" Zoey asks, upper lip curled in disgust. This is the fourth time she's asked a clarifying question on the subject, but Zander continues to humor her. He sets the spray bottle of blue cleaning solution on the wooden counter, rolling his eyes at her in a rare-for-Zander display of agitation.

My ears don't know where to focus between their comical spat and the couple at the end of the bar in the midst of a breakup. I carry a jar of cherries over to the mini fridge under the counter in front of the two men, disappointed when their tense voices go silent on my approach. The initiator of the breakup slaps a bill down on the counter to cover their untouched glasses of wine, pulling at the arm of his partner who, from the little intel I've gathered, was cheating on his weekends away for work.

The cheater flashes me a desperate look, hazel eyes wide and pleading, as if I could do anything to save him. As if I *would*. I just raise my eyebrows and give a subtle shrug, letting him know it's time to face the music. His partner, who towers over him by nearly a foot but has a kind face that contradicts his sturdy exterior, turns and marches away. The cheater scrambles after him.

"Yeah, Zo, you do everything outside. It's kind of the point of a backpacking trip." Zander's signature dirty-blonde ponytail bobs back and forth as he shakes his head in mock disdain for her lack of knowledge.

"But you'll be alone for months! Who will you talk to?" she asks, sounding horrified.

"No one. That's the point of a *solo* backpacking trip." I can hear in his voice how much peace fills his mind at the very idea. It's what I like about working with Zander. He speaks when spoken to but doesn't go out of his way to fill any voids left by others. He and Santi provide a nice balance to Zoey's and Maddie's tendency to chatter.

I don't hear Zoey's reaction as I make my way to the back corner booth where an older couple is lingering, waiting to sign their check. I hand the man his credit card along with my pen and their receipt. He thanks me and scrawls his name. Something in the way she is resting her head on his shoulder, a soft smile highlighting the laugh lines enclosing her lips, reminds me so distinctly of my mother that for a moment I lose my train of thought and forget to say *you're welcome*. Instead I grab the paper and pen from his outstretched hand without a word and turn away from the confused look on his face.

He holds the door open for her as they leave, and then the bar is empty save for the three of us. Zoey heads into the kitchen to assist Santi with cleaning up, and Zander grabs the broom from the coat closet. My key turns smoothly, and the register pops open in front of me so I can begin to count our deposit for the night. Just as I finish the stack of ones, Chase saunters through the door.

"Five minutes to close, man, better make it quick!" Zander shouts from the back of the room. A smile spreads across my face as Chase straddles the barstool across from me, leaning over the counter so he is two inches away from my face.

"Would it be totally inappropriate if I planted one on you right now?" His eyes crinkle as he observes how his words affect me. I'm certain my ears are bright red and thankful they are covered by my hair.

"As a matter of fact, yes," I whisper.

He settles back into his chair, an unfamiliar grimace taking up residence on his face. Zander finishes sweeping under the booths and brings the full dustpan around to empty it into the trash can behind the bar.

"I'll take an old-fashioned," Chase says.

"Man, I told you we're closing! I've got an early rock-climbing session with Aaron tomorrow. I'm going home," Zander replies. Santi and Zoey funnel out from the kitchen, chef's coat slung over Santi's shoulder to symbolize his workday is done. Chase looks from them to me, eyebrow raised in question.

"You guys go on ahead. I'll lock it down once I close out his tab," I tell them. Santi moves wordlessly toward the door and Zander shrugs before following behind him, but Zoey doesn't miss the opportunity to wink at me from over Chase's shoulder.

"Don't keep our girl out too late," she warns, giving him a squeeze from behind before following the guys out the door. I watch as she flips the sign to *Closed* before shutting the door and disappearing into the night.

My gaze flicks back to Chase, and his is trained on me with a sad intensity I don't recognize from him. I take a moment to look him over and realize his shoulders are slumped and his hair more disheveled than usual. I don't know this version of Chase, and I proceed with caution.

"An old-fashioned? You never order liquor," I say.

"Just one of those nights, I guess." It's so unlike him to be ambiguous that it tilts me off my axis.

I drop a sugar cube into a whiskey glass and top it with a few dashes of bitters. An orange slice goes in with no comment, but when he sees me pick up a slice of peach next, his eyebrows screw together. "Just trust me," I say. He watches me as I muddle the fruit with the sugar, and then deposit an ice cube on top. I pour bourbon into the glass, garnishing with a couple of cherries and another slice of peach. He hasn't broken eye contact with me as I set the glass on a napkin in front of him and he takes his first sip.

"Wow," he says, eyes wide. "That's really good."

The compliment makes me smile. I pour a ginger ale into another glass of ice and offer it to him for a toast. His glass makes a soft *clink* against mine.

"Drink with me."

"I'm working, Chase," I scoff. He looks around at the empty room and then back at me with a dare in his eyes.

"Drink with me, Eden." Something about his demeanor and the half smile pulling up a corner of his mouth flips a switch deep inside of me. I pull the bottle of Grey Goose off the counter behind me and add a double shot to my glass of ginger ale. His smile spreads until it touches his eyes as I take another sip of my drink. "That's my girl."

I can't describe the feeling that sentence sends through me, but it goes all the way to my toes.

"You're different tonight," I finally say after silence has stretched between us for several minutes. He pats the seat next to him, inviting me to join. I set the bottles of whiskey and vodka on the counter, as well as a notepad to keep track of how much I owe Zoey. When I finally settle in beside him, he turns to face me and interlocks his knees with mine. The simple contact of his skin is enough to distract me completely.

He finishes the last of his drink, but when I stand to go make him another, he places a hand on my leg to hold me in place. He grabs the bottle of bourbon and tilts it over what remains of that first ice cube. "I can drink it straight," he says.

He leaves his hand there, rubbing his thumb along the curve of my inner thigh. Even through the material of my jeans, the sensation is enough to make me tremble. He looks at his hand, then up at me. My skin is on fire everywhere his eyes touch.

"How am I different?" he asks.

It takes a moment for his words to register in my brain that is slowly turning to mush. I pour another shot of vodka into my empty glass. I add two more tallies on my makeshift bill.

"I don't know." I don't want to say something that will break whatever trance we are in, but the thought is gnawing at the edge of my consciousness. "You seem almost sad."

My suspicions are confirmed when his gaze drops to his drink. He swirls the glass in his hand, that lone sliver of ice slowly disappearing into liquid. I want so badly to lean forward and wrap my arms around him, pull him against me and protect him from whatever is hurting him. I have to remember that I can't even protect myself, so why would I think I could be of any help to Chase?

When he finally drags his gaze back up to mine, his eyes are glassy. The sheen makes them appear almost black. I never knew until I met him how expressive brown eyes could be. How mesmerizing.

"Are you close with your father?" he asks. The question hits so close to a target he doesn't know I have that it takes me a moment to right myself mentally.

"Which one?" Mama isn't the only one capable of deflecting. He just raises his eyebrows but doesn't rescue me from my obligation to expand on that answer. I pour another shot. Strike another tally. There's no burn as I swallow this time.

"Well, my mother left my biological dad when I was a baby. I have no clue where he is or if he's even still living," I explain. His thumb moves in slow circles on my thigh. He moves imperceptibly closer. The edges of my thoughts are becoming fuzzy. I have to reach further into my mind to access them.

"She married my stepfather when I was seven," I continue. The way he is watching me, I feel something shift inside of me. The urge to tell him the truth of what has happened to me comes bubbling up to the surface. I can feel the words buzzing on my lips. *It would be so easy*, I think. *He would know exactly what to say.*

"Would you like to dance, Eden?"

All the bubbles pop and disperse. Like a soda, the urge to share goes flat. My secrets shrink back from the light.

"I am a terrible dancer," I lie. I am my mother's daughter. I love to dance, love to feel the rhythm move through my body until there is no discernible place where the music ends and I begin. But the vodka has settled in my veins, and I fear if I step off this stool, my feet will not carry me with grace.

"Humor me." He lifts his hand from my thigh and stands, offering it to me palm up. I take it, if only to maintain the contact between us that I miss as soon as he moves. The radio is playing low, not enough to cover the shuffling of our feet as he pulls me so close to him I can barely breathe. He laces an arm around my waist and holds my hand gently beside us. We move in circles around the empty room, his steps surprisingly sure despite the whiskey he's consumed. He keeps me steady as my legs predictably stumble from the slight buzz I've given myself.

"Eden, I know this is all so soon," he says, his breath a whisper against my ear. My cheek is pressed against his, so he cannot see the panic in my eyes as I jump to conclusions. He pulls back to look at me, and my cover is blown. He smiles softly and uses our laced fingers to smooth the hair back behind my ear. "I just think that—"

"Don't, Chase," I choke, unable to look him in the eye. "I can't."

"Why not?" His voice is low, the rasp almost turning it to a soft growl. I stop moving, locked in this embrace with him in the middle of the room.

"I am so supremely fucked up I cannot even begin to explain it," I say, more honest with liquid courage pumping through my veins. "I am an absolute mess of a person, Chase, and if you get too close, that mess will get all over you."

He considers this for as long as it takes my heart to beat three times. I know this because I count each one, in rapid succession, until he takes away my ability to focus. He releases my hand and cups my jaw, gently tilting my head back so I am forced to face him, stripped of any of my defenses.

"I am ready to get dirty, Eden."

There is nothing left to count—my heartbeats stop altogether.

He closes what little distance is left between us and presses a soft kiss against my lips. He is testing the waters, seeing if they are safe. Before I know what I am doing, we are drowning. I take his lip between my teeth, slip my tongue into his mouth. His hand moves from my lower back down until he takes my ass in one firm grip. His other joins its partner, and soon I am being lifted, legs wrapping around his waist in a way that is familiar and yet completely different from each time he has carried me before.

I am pressed so tightly against him I can feel every breath that fills his lungs in quick gasps between kisses. He sets me on a barstool and snakes a hand under my shirt. The glorious heat of his palm against my spine makes me arch my back, desperately trying to find any way to be closer to him than we already are. I squeeze my thighs around his waist, pulling him so tightly against me that I can feel exactly what effect this is having on him.

He pulls back and I am breathing so hard you'd think I ran a marathon. Or hiked a fourteener.

"I need to get you out of here," he says, every word a struggle. My senses return to me enough to do some calculations.

"We can't drive, Chase." He's likely had too much to risk it, and I definitely have.

"Luckily I live next door." He grabs my purse from its place on the end of the counter and rejoins me where I am still sitting, confused, at the bar.

"No, silly, you *work* next door." Did I just call Chase *silly?* Definitely too drunk to drive.

He smirks at me and hands me my purse, which I sling over my shoulder. "I have an apartment above the store, just like Gary."

"Well, that's convenient."

He chuckles and loops an arm around my waist, kissing my neck before lifting me onto my feet. I'm not sure if it's the vodka or him that is causing the light-headedness. He pinches my chin and holds my gaze for five whole heartbeats before kissing me once more, deeply, until I see stars.

"You are so beautiful," he says when he finally pulls back. Okay, so the head spinning is definitely on him.

Chapter Thirteen

"Careful," he warns. It's the second time I've tripped in our short climb up the iron staircase that's more like a fire escape than an entrance in my opinion. I giggle but try to tread more cautiously as I finish the last of our ascent.

He turns the key and pushes the chipping black door inward. It opens into a hallway that is as dark as the night we are escaping from. When he closes the door behind us, I am suspended in that darkness for a moment until he walks ahead of me, and I hear a soft *click* followed by muted lamplight illuminating the space around me.

I now realize I am standing outside the entrance to his kitchen, finished with materials that suggest it's been updated recently. A pearlescent quartz countertop stands out in stark contrast to the black cabinets finished with sleek brass hardware. I look past the pony wall dividing it from the rest of the space, admiring the exposed brick and vaulted ceilings. The living room stretches to the front of the narrow building and is finished off with two windows facing the main street. There is a door next to his leather couch that sits slightly ajar. I try to imagine what Chase's bedroom must look like.

Based on the fire burning in his eyes, I'm about to find out.

He takes my hand and leads me through the living room and to that door, pushing it open and allowing the lamplight to pour in. He flips the light on in the adjoining bathroom, and finally I am able to see the space in all its glory.

On every wall there are framed photos and memorabilia stacked on floating shelves from Chase's adventures. There is a large map above his dresser of the United States, with each national park indicated with a little symbol that can be scratched off as they are visited. He has more than half of the map complete.

A black frame reclines on his side table, containing a photo of a younger Chase next to a middle-aged man that has to be his father. The two hold one another in a half-embrace with their other arms outstretched to the sky. They are surrounded by red rock and an endless canyon. The joy on their faces is palpable.

My gaze settles finally on the king-size bed filling the majority of the room. The space is slightly messy with pieces of clothing abandoned randomly in places on the floor, but the bed is made, and his pine-scented soap lingers in the air.

He takes my hand and backs slowly toward the bed, pulling me along with him. My heart is bouncing around inside my chest like it's trapped in a pinball machine. He falls backward onto the mattress and pulls me with him. I land on his chest, but he quickly rolls me over so that he is balanced on top of me, arms encircling me underneath him. He settles into the cradle of my thighs like the space was made just for him.

"It's been too long since I've kissed you," he says, stopping my giggle with a kiss so intense my heart stills, falling between the pinball levers. Point for Chase.

His hand caresses my arm, then my side. He grabs my waist

and presses harder against me, a desperation creeping into his measured movements. He trails kisses along my jaw, down until he is pulling my earlobe into a soft bite, his hot breath on my neck causing me to drag my hands down his back in response. This pulls a moan from deep inside him, and soon he is lifting my shirt from my waist up so slowly I almost cry out with impatience. When he stops kissing me while he lifts it over my head, the ache for him to return becomes a sharp lump in my throat.

His T-shirt flies over his head, and then he is back, this time with his hot skin flush against mine. The light smattering of his chest hair pricks against my stomach. I can feel the muscles in his back shifting beneath my touch as he moves to kiss my neck. And then my collarbone. And then the soft flesh of my breast where it threatens to spill out of my lace bra. He moves beyond my reach when he leans down and places a kiss on the dark skin of my birthmark. My lungs squeeze tight in response.

He reaches a hand around my back and deftly unclasps my bra. His eyes hold mine steady as he sits back, sliding first one strap and then the other over my shoulders. He pulls it away slowly, and when I am bare before him, he lets his gaze fall to my breasts, and all the air whooshes out of his lungs.

In an instant, a quiet cold creeps over my body. The butterflies in my stomach turn into knives, and I think for a moment that I might be sick. My desperation for Chase vanishes, and I am suddenly filled with panic, my mind screaming that we are exposed. We need to be covered. *He can see me.*

I squeeze my eyes shut, trying to block out the feeling of terror taking over my body. Every inch of me begins to tremble. I don't want this moment to be ruined. I don't want to be the reason that it is.

Chase must feel me shaking because he stills over me, and then he is not over me at all. His weight lifts and my thighs miss him as soon as he is gone. I hear his footsteps pad across the room and a door open. The distinct sound of hangers clicking against one another. Then a soft fabric settles over my chest. I chance a peek and see he has laid a T-shirt of his over top of me. All I see of him is his back as he disappears into the living room. I pull his shirt over my head, and his scent is all around me, comforting me despite the fact that I don't deserve it.

When he comes back into the room, his expression is unreadable. He sets a glass of water on the bedside table beside the photo of him and his father and holds out three pink pills in his hand.

"Ibuprofen. If you take it now, it'll help with your headache in the morning."

I take them from him and then swallow them with a swig of water. He cuts the lights in the bathroom and climbs into the bed beside me, scooting the covers out from under our bodies and then over us. In the dark I can hear his breathing slow and settle. I can't move, too filled with guilt to even speak.

"You don't have to sleep in your jeans. I won't try anything, I promise." His voice is soft and quiet. I cannot detect the anger that must surely be lying underneath. I unbutton my jeans and slide them off, letting them drop over the side of the bed. He loops an arm around my waist and pulls me against him, our bodies aligning. The desire he had for me, which was so evident before, is gone. I cannot feel it anymore.

Before long, a heavy breathing two degrees shy of a snore begins. His arm grows heavy around my stomach. I am crushed under the weight of my shame.

Chapter Fourteen

For the past few months, I've been haunted by a nightmare that won't go away. At first it happened nearly every night. I would jolt awake from a dead sleep drenched in sweat, pulse racing so fast I thought I might be suffering a heart attack. As time passed, it grew less frequent. Maybe once a week it would come back to me. And then once every two weeks. The more spaced out it was, the worse it felt when it finally returned.

In the dream, I am roaming a house that I do not recognize but I somehow know is my house, in the way that only makes sense in dreams. There are so many rooms, stairs, and colors it feels like something out of Poe's "The Masque of the Red Death." I know Mama is somewhere in the house, though I cannot hear her calling to me. It feels like I am a compass and she is true north, pulling me to her like a magnet.

What I can hear, however, is Mark's voice. I never see him. I only feel his presence behind me like a breath making the hairs on the back of my neck bristle. I am running from his voice. I want desperately not to hear it. I am trying to get to my mother, to protect her from Mark. I don't know what will happen if he finds her first. I only know that I can't let that happen.

At first I am just walking through the house, trying to get my bearings. It is only when Mark's voice fills the hall I am in that I break out into a run, my lungs splintering into shrapnel in my chest. I run through the endless labyrinth that is the house, a mere step ahead of Mark. Always miles from my mother.

This is the dream I am rescued from by a knock at the door. My eyes peel open, sore from sleeping so hard. My head pounds, though decidedly less than it would have had I not taken the ibuprofen Chase gave me before we fell asleep.

Chase.

I look around at his room, suddenly remembering where I am. I have no memory of falling asleep. Only the soft vibration of his snore and the jolting of my stomach as I tried to suppress my sobs so as not to wake him.

I look over at him, and he is still sleeping soundly, flat on his back with his arms above his head. He looks so young, like the boy in the picture with his father rather than the grown man who had just hours before been on top of me, skin to skin. The knock sounds again, and I debate whether to let it go, desperate to avoid running into someone we know. The sound of a key in the door makes my decision for me.

I jump out of bed and pull my jeans on but have no time to strap on my bra and change back into my own shirt before a woman in her sixties walks into his living room, dressed in a black dress and carrying a bouquet of flowers. She smiles at the sight of Chase sleeping before her eyes pan over and she sees me standing beside his bed. She jumps, placing a hand on her heart to steady it.

I quickly wrap my discarded blouse around my bra and clutch it tightly in my fist before walking out of his room and pulling the door to a close. I turn to face her, hoping I don't look as humiliated as I feel. While I expect to see contempt or judgment, I'm instead met with a smile on her face and a crinkle in her eyes so similar she could never deny being Chase's mother.

"You must be Eden!" she shout-whispers. She puts her arms out and embraces me before I even have time to react. A floral perfume lingers on me when she pulls away. "I'm Laura, Chase's mother."

I smile because I don't really know what to say and I am still a little discombobulated from my dream. My stomach flips. I see the moment she reads the situation, and she takes a step back to let me breathe.

"Sorry to interrupt." She gestures between me and the bedroom door. *Kill me.* "Chase always takes me to visit his dad on the anniversary of, well, you know. And then he takes me out to breakfast."

Upon further study, I realize her nose is rubbed raw and she has tried to cover this with a fresh coat of powder. Her eyes are rimmed with red, and her voice warbles when she speaks. The pieces come together in my mind, how sad Chase seemed when he arrived last night and his questions about my father. The anniversary of— *Oh shit.*

He said it had been several years since his father died, but the woman before me seems just as stricken as if it had happened last night. Her black dress is fit for a funeral. A tissue is crumpled in the fist that isn't clinging to the flower stems. Her grief hits me in waves.

Before I can say anything, the door behind me opens and Chase walks out. He's thrown gym shorts on. He brushes the hair back out of his face as he yawns. "Hey, Mom," he says when it passes.

I try to find a hint of what transpired between us last night anywhere in his expression but can't read it. He must think I led him on, or that I'm pathetic for clamming up over something as simple as being topless. Now here I am, bra in hand, in front of his mother.

"Good morning, sleepyhead," she replies, passing me to wrap her arms around her son. I see the muscles in his arms squeeze her tight, her small frame swallowed up by his embrace. He kisses the top of her head and holds her arm out to appraise the bouquet.

"These are great, Mom. Dad would've loved them."

"They're peonies, just like we had in our wedding." She looks back at me and then down at the floor, running the tissue under her nose.

"They're beautiful," I offer. She smiles at me, and over her head Chase does too, a soft one that doesn't reach his eyes.

"Well, you better get dressed so we can get going." She turns to me. "You're welcome to join us, Eden. Chase has said so many good things about—"

"I can't," I cut her off. I regret it as soon as I do because I see the excitement leave her eyes. But it's the right thing to do. She is clearly hurting and needs her son to be there for her. He doesn't need another broken woman tagging along, a burden he never asked to carry.

"I'm sorry. I hope you have a nice, erm, well, I hope your day is okay. As okay as it can be." I speed walk toward the door before I can embarrass myself even further, grabbing my purse from the kitchen counter as I go. I'm on the landing in two heartbeats.

I've made it down three steps before Chase steps out onto the landing behind me, pulling the door closed for privacy. I stop but I don't allow myself to look at him, staring at his feet instead. They are bare against the cold metal. It must be uncomfortable, but he doesn't move.

"Eden, I'm sorry, I didn't mean for you to meet her like—"

"It's fine," I interrupt. I don't want him to go down this path. To tell me how he didn't want me to meet his mom after what happened last night. We were drunk when he said he was ready for my mess. He'll regret that when he has time to think it through. He probably already does. And besides, he's been through enough with losing his dad and now helping his mom. He doesn't need another project on his hands.

"I need to go count the deposit out anyway, since we left before I finished." I finally let myself look at his face, and I can see he wants to object. He doesn't even know what is good for him. Or in my case, what is not. I guess I will have to show him.

"Last night was a mistake. We both had too much to drink. It was really..." I pause. It hurts so much to talk about difficult things. It hurts even worse to lie about them. "It shouldn't have happened."

"It didn't feel like a mistake."

I finally let myself look at him, and his mouth is set in a deep frown. "Well, it was." I don't need him to pity me. I just need this to end, so I can go cry alone in my bed.

If looks could kill, I'd be dead on this stairway. He is glowering at me with an expression that is both angry and incredibly sad. I am hurting him, but I'd hurt him worse if we drag this out. I hate living with my own trauma enough as it is; I don't want to burden anyone else with it.

"What are you saying, Eden?" he finally asks through gritted teeth.

"I'm saying it's okay." I suck in a shaky breath. I try to look confident even though I don't feel it. This is what's best for him, even if he doesn't know it yet. "We can just pretend it never happened. Go back to being friends."

"I don't want to be your *friend*," he says. His eyes are so dark

I want to crawl inside them and turn on a light. I look away in an attempt to suppress that urge.

"Fine, then we don't even have to talk," I say, though it kills me to form the words. I don't dare glance in his direction. I turn and continue down the stairs, taking all my problems with me.

Chapter Fifteen

"What would you like to talk about instead?" Stephen asks.

I was fully prepared to argue over not working on the narrative today, so his easy acceptance really takes the wind out of my sails. I slump back into my chair. He takes a sip of his tea and watches me. His eyes disappear behind a film of fog that forms on his glasses from the steam. When it clears, he is still staring, waiting for my response. Only I don't have one. I never thought I'd get this far.

"Aren't you going to ask me why?" I reply, a bit confused. The hole on the knee of my jeans opens wider as I pick at the threads holding it together.

"Do you *want* to tell me why?" His expression remains unchanged.

"Well, no," I tell him honestly. "But I thought you were going to make me."

An earnest chuckle escapes him. He pulls his glasses from his face and polishes the lenses with a small cloth before replacing them. His notebook rests on his desk at the edge of the frame, right where he placed it as soon as I told him I just wasn't in the mood. I notice there's a framed photo behind it on the wall in which he is wearing the same purple plaid button-up that he is sporting today. He's standing proudly next to someone in graduation regalia. One of his children, I assume. Every so often it occurs to me how little I actually know about Stephen, and yet he knows all the darkest secrets of my life. Maybe not knowing him is the reason this works, since I can't seem to talk to anyone I *do* know.

"Eden, this isn't a hostage situation. I'm not going to *make* you do anything."

I know he's technically telling the truth. What he's failed to mention is that his gentle nudging is nine times more effective at getting me to open up than outright prying ever has been. He's the worst type of captor: a kind one.

"I just don't really see the point in continuing." I prepared for this argument, and I want to have it, damn it. "It's not working. It's not making my life better. If anything, I feel so much worse."

He considers this, the contemplative silence settling between us as it always does. Now that I've stepped out on the ledge and made my accusation, I feel unsure of myself. I try not to waiver in my defiance, but under Stephen's shrewd observance I find myself feeling like a soldier on the battlefield who's forgotten why he enlisted in the first place.

"Well, I'd be remiss if I didn't remind you that it isn't even finished yet," he says. "But I'd like for you to tell me a little more about why you feel that way, if you don't mind?"

My mind drifts immediately to Chase. The image of him on that stairwell is burned into my brain, his eyes like hot coals as I lied through my teeth. I can still taste the bitter poison of those words on my tongue days later. That agony multiplied tenfold last night when he came to pick up dinner from the bar and he took my advice. He walked right past me without speaking a word in the same spot he'd danced with me four days prior.

I have no right to be upset. It is, after all, exactly what I asked for. It is the right thing to do to spare him from the inevitable burden I would become. So why does it feel so incredibly wrong?

I've kept Chase from Stephen, thinking if I didn't talk about it, then it couldn't be real. I thought if I didn't speak it into existence, then I couldn't lose it. But here I am, alone in my sadness, and I've lost him anyway.

I let myself look Stephen in the eyes, tears pooling in mine and threatening to spill over. He must recognize something in my expression, because a knowing look passes over his face.

"There's a man," I finally say. The words are small and high-pitched in the way they always are seconds before I begin sobbing. I take a shaky breath and desperately try to cling to my composure by looking skyward in an attempt to dam the waterfall. "He's a good man. Better than I deserve."

"What makes you say that?" Stephen grabs his notebook again and scribbles something there. *Ugly Crier,* probably. The inside joke helps me steady my footing, if only slightly.

"He's so different from me. So easygoing and optimistic. He is so patient with me, and I still manage to screw it up, Stephen," I tell him. "He's like the sun, bright and warm all the time. I feel like all I do is rain on him."

Questionable Metaphors. He sets his pen down.

"Could you give me an example, Eden? Of how you've 'screwed it up'?" He doesn't immediately disagree with me, and it makes me feel better. So many people dismiss self-criticism as a knee-jerk reaction without ever considering that you might actually be right. No matter how much I want to be told that I'm wrong, I deeply suspect that I have assessed myself accurately.

So I tell him. I tell him about the hike and Chase carrying

me for miles and the feeling in my bathroom like my skin was crawling off my body. I tell him about dancing with Chase and how he didn't make fun of me for stumbling on my sore ankle. I tell him the abridged version of what happened in the bedroom, and how even as much as I desperately wanted to be there, my body betrayed me.

Stephen waits for me to finish, for the hiccupping sobs to subside. I wonder if he ever gets sick of me crying. I wonder if I'll ever be able to talk about these things without being reduced to a pool of tears. I grab a napkin from the metal holder in the center of the dining table and blot at the puddles under my eyes.

"I think so many people wrongly assume that trauma presents itself as this blatant memory. And it may, sometimes. But a lot of times, it comes back as a reaction instead, stimuli your body reads as a threat, whether it is one or not."

I let the words rattle around in my brain for a moment, turning them over and inspecting them from all angles. They nestle like perfect puzzle pieces into a gap I didn't know needed filling.

"Eden, you've been hurt by someone society tells you should be trusted innately. Someone you loved and depended on in a very vulnerable way," Stephen continues. "Your body is designed to adapt as it takes in new information in order to keep you alive. So, when you feel yourself getting close to Chase, your body reads that trust as a threat. And it reacts in a way that it thinks will protect you from harm."

"How do I stop it from happening?" I ask. "How do I convince my body that I know what I'm doing?"

"First you have to let go of the belief that you could have known better with Mark. You've convinced yourself you're a bad judge of character because you didn't see it coming. You had no way of knowing, Eden."

His words hit me square between the eyes and cause the

tremors to return to my fingers. Mercy when you don't feel like you deserve it is a painful gift.

"Second, you talk through the story of what has happened to you. You start by telling the story to yourself with me in the safety of therapy, and then you tell it to people like Chase, who you trust, so they know how to help you. Then you slowly have new, more positive experiences over time to rewrite the narrative your brain has created for what happens when you let yourself be vulnerable with someone."

Before my brain will let me believe it, my heart recognizes what he is saying as the truth. Everything in my body says to run from it, to bury the past as far down as I can dig and to build walls so tall around myself that no one will ever get in again. Stephen's words are like a small chisel. He demonstrates how that tool can chip away at the wall of fear, and then hands it to me, telling me to get to work.

"This is definitely a hostage situation," I finally say. The seriousness melts away from Stephen's expression, and he groans at my attempt at humor.

"Well, let me give you one last piece of advice before I release you for today. The next time you feel that familiar panic coming on, try to focus on your surroundings through the lens of your five senses. What can you taste? What can you hear? What can you see?" He counts them off on his fingers. "It's called *grounding* and can be a great coping mechanism in a pinch. It keeps you in the present when your mind tries to slip into the past."

I nod and tuck this information into a file folder in my mind, hoping I never have to use it while knowing I probably will. Stephen smiles and scratches his goatee, satisfied that I'm actually listening to him.

"Great work, today, Eden." He sincerely means it, and I contemplate requesting a trophy when this is all over with that phrase inscribed on the nameplate. I have to remind myself that healing is never technically over. It is a tide that flows in and out, not a pool that can be drained.

"Thank you, Stephen." I feel like I've been passed through an emotional meat grinder, but I am grateful, nonetheless. "Am I free to go now?"

He smiles at the joke and closes his notepad with all my imaginary insults inside. "Until next time."

Chapter Sixteen

I knew taking this job I'd be working pretty much every day we are open, helping Zoey get her financial foot in the door. Today is a rare exception where Maddie and Zander are both bartending and my paperwork is caught up, resulting in an opportunity for an extra day off to relax and recharge. Unfortunately the Venn diagram of my group of friends and my coworkers is a circle, so I find myself pushing open the heavy oak door to the bar and walking inside.

I freeze when I realize the bar seating is packed, save for one stool next to Chase. He's preoccupied with shoveling a giant burrito into his mouth and hasn't seen me in his peripheral yet. I'm not about to sit in a booth on the opposite side of the room by myself, and with full plates of lunch specials in front of everyone, the next bar seat won't be open anytime soon. I swallow down the lump in my throat and force myself to move forward.

When I climb onto the seat, Chase pauses mid-chew but gives no further indication that he's noticed me. He arches his back in a stretch and settles with his shoulders squared, exchanging a fork for a beer glass that he brings to his lips. For every inch he has expanded, I shrink in on myself. I can't blame him for doing what I asked, but understanding the reason doesn't take away the sting of being ignored.

"Ed*en*! I thought you were taking the day off?" Maddie asks. She places a small square napkin in front of me and then a glass of ice water. She's dyed her hair a vibrant magenta that stands out in stark contrast to her pale skin. I force my eyes away, staring instead at the small silver snake ring she spins on her pinky around and around as she waits for my response.

"I was," I say sheepishly. "Turns out I lack hobbies in general and also wanted to spend time with Zoey before she leaves for vacation."

As if I've summoned her, Zoey walks out of the office door with the ordering binder tucked under one arm as she twists her mane into a tortoiseshell clip high on her head. The flowy halter dress she is wearing shows off newly bronzed skin courtesy of a thorough self-tanning session. The rust-colored stains from helping with her back stand out in stark contrast on my pale fingertips.

"I don't know how much of a vacation the annual Allen Family Beach Trip can be considered. They pile every cousin up at a kids' table as if we are not all pushing thirty. But I appreciate the jealousy nonetheless," she says in passing. She saunters through the double doors into the kitchen to go over the food order with Santi, I presume.

Maddie makes a face at me with her nose curled up in mock disgust. The diamond stud in her nostril glints in the light. "I can't imagine spending an entire week with my extended family in the same condo. Big yikes."

"Same," I mumble. Her phone chirps an alert for an incoming text and she pulls it from her apron, still scowling. I have to admit, Maddie's unaffected demeanor and general distaste for most people has really grown on me. Annoying when trying to manage her, but great when I need someone to complain with.

She finishes the text she's working on before tucking her phone back into her apron, rolling her eyes lazily back up to meet my gaze. "Want anything for lunch?"

"I'll take a burger," I reply. My entire right side is homed in on any movement Chase makes, which admittedly has been very little since I sat down. It makes it difficult to offer any meaningful conversation to anyone else.

"Everything on it?"

"Is there any other way?" I ask.

Maddie shrugs and walks away, typing my order into the ticketing system and then wandering to the end of the bar where her girlfriend, Camille, is sitting. They join hands across the countertop and lean in close to each other as they speak, laughing over something Maddie has said. The intimacy in that small movement causes a sharp pang of jealousy in my gut, making me even more aware of the distance between Chase and I that is more than just physical.

Zander is deep in conversation with two older men to my left who, from what I've gathered, hiked the PCT back in the eighties and want to share all their wisdom with him. With all avenues of conversation blocked off, I sit in silence next to Chase and watch the condensation sweat down my water glass onto the napkin, soaking it through. Out of the corner of my eye I can see his half-eaten plate of food remaining untouched, his hands clenching and releasing around an imaginary stress ball.

Finally he turns slightly toward me and sucks in a breath like he's preparing to speak. I feel a surge of hope in my veins when suddenly the wind is knocked out of me by a firm hand slapping against my back. I cough and sputter, turning to see Gary with a grin stretched across his face. He slides his other arm around Chase's shoulders, and we are locked together in this three-way embrace, with Chase looking anywhere but at me and myself unable to look at anything but him.

Gary's wearing a thin light blue shirt with two pockets on the chest and a flap across the back. He smells of sunscreen coupled with the sour smoke of cigars. He looks proudly back and forth at our faces, oblivious to the tension in the air.

"How are you two lovebirds doing?" he asks in a low voice, head tucked between ours. Chase chokes on his sip of beer and looks straight at me over the arch of Gary's nose. It's the only direct eye contact he's made with me in a week. His irises are dark and unreadable as they level with mine.

Gary laughs and squeezes the back of Chase's neck. "Relax. It's not often I get woken up in the middle of the night by two people chasing each other up my neighbor's staircase."

Chase's Adam's apple bobs as he swallows and turns to face forward. I wince internally but manage to maintain what I hope is a neutral expression. I should've just stayed home today.

Zoey times her return perfectly, carrying my burger and fries over at that exact moment and setting them down in front of me. The hinges on the saloon doors squeal as they swing shut behind her. Her blue eyes brighten when they land on Gary.

"What have you been up to, stranger?" she asks, looking him up and down.

"Went fishing on the lake this morning." He leans over and grumbles into my ear. "Much more fun than solitaire."

Chase lays his napkin across the remains of his half-eaten burrito and swallows the last of his beer.

"Gary, the usual?" Zoey asks, grabbing Chase's plate with one hand and depositing his empty glass into the dishwasher with the other.

"No, my stomach is still bothering me," he replies with a mild grimace. He rubs high up on his belly to show the source of his discomfort. "I'll have something light when I go back upstairs. Just wanted to see my girl before she leaves."

"I swear, Gary, if you're skinnier than me when I get back, I'll never forgive you," she warns playfully. I see the concern flash across her face, just a brief cloud that most people wouldn't even notice. The fact that he hasn't stolen a single fry from my plate fills me with a mirroring worry. Before I can ask him more about it, Chase clears his throat and finally speaks for the first time since I sat down.

"Zo, can I get the street tacos for Aaron to go. I promised I'd bring him back lunch." His voice is hoarse from lack of use, but just the sound of its familiar rumble fills my fingers and toes with a tingling sensation. From the moment I got here, I've wanted desperately to take back everything I said on his staircase. To beg him to look at me, speak to me, forgive me. The sound of his voice is the last straw, crumbling what remains of my defenses. I begin mentally rehearsing my best apology for the next time we are alone.

"Sure, which reminds me," Zoey replies, gesturing toward us and then over to Zander. "Next Sunday after I get back, the five of us are going on a hike together."

Zander nods over at us to acknowledge her plan in between his commentary on water purifiers.

"The five of us?" I ask, filled with nervous excitement. It's the perfect fresh start.

"Yeah, Aaron, Chase, Zander, me, and you," she explains.

"I don't think that's a good idea," Chase says curtly. The bubble in my chest pops, and I deflate along with it. Everyone grows silent, even Zander, as they try to understand his response. I don't have to try. I start erecting the walls back into place, higher than they were before.

"Oh, don't worry, her ankle is healed completely. She'll be fine," Zoey says with a dismissive shake of her head.

Before Chase can object further and explain that really, it's because I am an asshole with mood swings that could touch each side of the Atlantic, I push back from the bar and clutch my purse to my side. I haven't taken a single bite of my burger.

"Guys, I completely forgot I have an appointment today. Sorry about the burger. Gary, you should at least try to eat it," I say, backing away from them all. Everyone is looking at me like I've grown a third head, except Chase, who hasn't moved a muscle. "Zo, I'll be ready tomorrow morning to drop you at the airport."

Before they can respond, I duck out the door and down the sidewalk until I am out of their line of sight. I stop on the corner and inhale a sharp gust of air into my lungs in an attempt to calm my nerves. The realization that the damage I've caused with Chase is permanent rests heavy on my shoulders. It's exactly what I was afraid of, and now there's no going back.

An insistent growl rips through my stomach, undeterred by the events of the last twenty minutes. Three teenage girls leave the coffee shop at that exact moment, releasing the aroma of Rose's baked goods out onto the street. The few french fries rolling around in me are desperate for company, and so am I, so I retrace my steps and open the door just as it is closing.

Rose looks up at me through the glass of her display case, flashing a smile my way as she stacks the last scone on its stand and slides the enclosure shut. When she stands, her head barely clears the top of the case. My stomach rumbles so loudly when I'm in view of the array of goodies that I'm certain she can hear it from her side of the counter.

"What can I get you, Eden?" she asks, her voice light and cheery like a radio jingle.

I want to say everything, but I settle for a banana nut muffin and a large mocha. She throws the muffin in the warmer and sneaks an extra molasses cookie into the bag for good measure before passing it over to me. She presses the warm coffee cup into my hand, and it feels like the hug I desperately need right now.

"I saw Chase carrying you down the sidewalk last week," she says as she returns my card to me, wrapped in a receipt. "I knew you two would be a fit the minute I met you."

I know she means well, but her comment follows my sip of coffee down into my stomach and sours there. I must grimace because she stops smiling and I can see the gears turning in her mind.

"I just mean—" she pauses to measure her words like they are flour in one of her recipes. "I just mean that you seem like you could use a little light in your life, and Chase is just a big shining beam of it, you know?"

I do know. I know exactly what she means, and it hurts so much in that moment I have to give her a curt nod and turn away before I can think about it any longer. I hear her rounding the counter behind me but keep walking. The only other person in the shop is a gentleman in the corner by the window, and he stands, blocking my exit. He drops two crumpled dollar bills on the table next to his empty mug before slinging a bag over his shoulder. As I wait for him to leave, Rose catches up to me.

She touches my elbow, and I turn to her, feeling a little like a punching bag must after a training session with a boxer. Her expression is kind, her wide hazel eyes catching every thought that passes over my face. I've really got to work on not being so much of an open book. It's like all the words I refuse to say end up scrawled across my forehead.

She watches over my shoulder until the door closes behind the man, then settles her gaze back on me.

"I'm sorry if I overstepped, before at Zoey's and also two

125

seconds ago," she says sincerely. "And I'm also sorry because I'm about to do it again."

"You're fine, Rose. I'm just not good at talking about... anything really," I explain, staring at the stained toe of my white canvas shoe.

"That's okay. I'm only good because I've had lots of practice." I peer up at her and find a sad smirk twisting her lips. "Eden, my dad was an alcoholic my whole childhood. He didn't get help until I married Mitchell and my mom filed for divorce. He's better now, and so is their marriage, but there's lasting damage that I still deal with every day."

"I'm so sorry," I say, taken off guard and uncertain how to comfort her.

"I'm just telling you because I know what Zoey said, and I don't know what you've been through. But I just wanted you to know if you ever do want someone to talk to, I'm here. You're not the only one with daddy issues."

I laugh softly and she smiles, though it doesn't quite reach her eyes.

"One more thing," she says. "Chase is amazing. And I know you know that. But also know that it's okay if it still isn't easy for you. It wasn't for me with Mitchell at first. But it gets better. You just have to be willing to show them where it hurts."

She pinches my elbow again and turns to walk back behind the counter. "Okay, that's enough unsolicited advice from me for the day. Would you like me to warm the muffin up again before you go?"

"No, it's still warm." I offer a shadow of a smile since it is about as much as I can muster. "Thank you, Rose. For everything."

"Not a problem. Come by anytime."

I know she means it, and I want to be the kind of person that takes her up on it. I want to be like her, open and vulnerable about the grim details of my story. I want to pull up a chair at the table with her and tell her it hurts everywhere.

Instead I clutch my lukewarm muffin tightly to my chest and leave without another word.

Chapter Seventeen

The shrill alarm of my phone ringing catapults me out of my dream into the waking world. I'm disoriented at first, the room spinning in muted shadows around me as I try to adjust. I sit up and pat my hand across my bedside table, feeling for the familiar smooth plastic of my phone case. The light of the screen is blinding when I flip it over to see who is calling me in the middle of the night. Once my eyes are able to focus, I see that it is one in the morning and Gary's name is displayed under the time.

"Hello? What's wrong?" Panic runs like ice through my veins. There are only a handful of reasons Gary would be calling me at this hour, and none of them are good.

"Eden, thank God," Gary says. He pauses to groan in pain. "I think I need you to take me to the hospital."

I catapult out of bed and yank open the top drawer of my dresser, pulling out the first pair of pants I can find. Flipping the call to speakerphone, I set down my cell so I can clip a bra on under my shirt. His labored breathing fills the dark room. I shove my feet into a pair of slides and grab my purse as I fly out the door and down the stairs.

"Are you at home? Are you having a heart attack?" Fear grips my heart in a tight fist. I shift the car into reverse and stare at the dark windows of Zoey's house as I back out of the driveway, wishing desperately that she was here now instead of on a beach somewhere in Florida.

"I'm at home. I don't know—gah!" he exclaims in pain. "My stomach hurts. My back hurts. Everything hurts so damn bad!" The distress in his voice drives my foot down harder on the gas pedal.

"I'm almost there, Gary, just hang on. Shouldn't I call an ambulance?" I blow through a stop sign and round the corner onto Main Street, driving past the silent businesses illuminated only by moonlight. I see one window above the bar glowing yellow as I make the turn by Rose's coffee shop and park haphazardly in the lot.

"I'm not paying the bill for an ambulance. It's only fifteen minutes by highway," he grumbles. Even in his pain, he's still Gary.

I leave the car running and take the stairs two at a time, swinging open his unlocked door and rushing into an apartment identical to Chase's with a flipped floor plan. When I don't see him right away, I round the corner of the kitchen wall and walk through the doorway to the bedroom, where there is light pouring out of the bathroom.

Gary is lying on the floor beside his toilet, the acrid smell of bile in the air. There is vomit splashed into the bowl and across the porcelain seat. I fight the urge to gag and look away from it, focusing my attention on Gary. He's clutching the center of his abdomen below his breastbone, wincing with each shallow breath he inhales. The color has drained from his face, and sweat beads on his bald head.

"I'm here. Let's get you up. It's going to be okay." I scoop my arms under his and lift with everything I have. He manages to use my body as a pull bar to hoist himself off the ground with loud moans accompanying every inch of progress. I kick the toilet flusher with my foot before hobbling alongside him out of the bathroom and through his bedroom doorway. We are almost to the hallway before he doubles over in pain, and I think for a moment he's going to vomit on our shoes.

"I don't know if I can make it down the stairs," he huffs. I help him settle onto the recliner in the corner of the room when he is able to move again.

"I can't carry you!" I reply.

"Go get Chase," he manages to say. "He can help." He makes a motion to shoo me away with his hand, so I don't hesitate, I just run back down the stairs the way I came and up Chase's flight. I'm banging on his door before it occurs to me that I'm probably the last person he wants to see.

When he opens the door, he is still rubbing sleep away from his eyes. He's wearing low-slung gym shorts and nothing else, and suddenly I'm grateful for the panic because it keeps me from being distracted.

"Eden? What the hell?" The confusion on his face is replaced with worry when he sees my stricken expression.

"Gary's sick, he needs me to take him to the hospital, but he can barely walk and I need to get him down the stairs." Before I can finish my sentence, he's retreating into the dim light of his apartment and reappears moments later with a T-shirt and Vans on. I make the trip back down and up to Gary's door with him on my heels.

"Gary, what happened?" Chase asks, concern coloring his tone. He lifts Gary to his feet with minimal effort and attempts to take him forward a few steps with just an arm wrapped around his waist before running into the same issue we did when I tried it. He looks over Gary's hunched body at me with fear widening his eyes.

"This is what all those workouts are good for," Gary says. "Plus, you got practice getting her off a mountain."

"I don't know if you've noticed, but she's a little lighter than you." Chase hesitates for a few more seconds before making up his mind and kneeling in front of Gary. "Hop on, old man."

It'd be a hilarious sight if I weren't so scared. Gary releases the death grip he has on his stomach and locks it around Chase's shoulders instead. Despite the tremble in his legs as Chase shifts from his knees back to his feet and stands, he makes it look easy. I let them exit before me and grab Gary's wallet and keys from the kitchen counter, locking the door behind us to give them time to make their descent. At the base of the stairs, I rush ahead of them to hold the passenger door open, where Chase slowly lowers Gary to his feet.

Gary drops into the seat and takes a shuddering breath. I shut the door behind him and race around to the driver's side. Chase slides into the back without a word, and I don't bother to question him. I tear out onto the street and head in the opposite direction from what I normally do, following the GPS instructions I loaded on my drive to get him.

The drive is mostly silent save for Gary's intermittent moans and the engine whirring. I feel like I'm moving in slow motion down the highway. It always strikes me how time creeps by so slowly in moments of suffering. Why can't these minutes fly past just as quickly as the ones we enjoy?

After what feels like an eternity later, we are finally pulling into the emergency bay. I abandon the car and its inhabitants to run into the ER and let them know the situation. When I return with two nurses on my heels, Chase has opened Gary's door and helps the male nurse lift him out into the wheelchair they've brought along. Chase rounds the car and slips into the driver's seat.

"I'll park; you go with him," he says when I peer through the cracked window. He pulls off before I can respond, and I turn to follow Gary through the door. The sterile scent of the hospital disinfectant burns my nose.

They help him onto a stretcher in the waiting room and roll him back through double doors into triage. A plump nurse in dark blue scrubs with teased salt-and-pepper hair hands me a clipboard with paperwork attached to it.

"Where are they taking him? Can I go back?" I ask. The automated doors behind me whoosh open, and Chase marches through, joining me at the desk.

"They're going to run a few tests on him first, if you could fill out the paperwork, please." Her voice is nasal and disinterested. I know she sees worse all the time, but a little compassion wouldn't kill her. Chase rests a hand at the small of my back and gently guides me to a hard plastic seat along the wall. I am grateful for his support because as the adrenaline crashes, my body feels like it might collapse beneath me.

He settles into the chair beside me and takes Gary's wallet from my outstretched hand, thumbing through the contents. He pulls out Gary's ID and insurance cards from their slots, reading the information I need in a hushed voice. I don't know much about his medical history, but Chase mentions he complained a few months ago that his doctor wanted his cholesterol to come down. I complete all that I am able to and stand to bring it back to the nurse just as the man who wheeled him back returns through the double doors.

"Are you Eden?" he asks. His hospital badge has a tiny photo of him next to the name *Jackie*. I look at the clipboard in his hands, noticing the dark ink of a tattoo on his brown skin forming a ring around his third finger. I try to read what is scribbled on his papers, to see if Gary is okay. Chase walks up behind me, and his hand returns to its place on my back, calming the panic rising in my throat.

"Yes, she is," he answers for me.

"Mr. Barbeau says you're his daughter. You can come back now; he's in a triage room." I set the forms I've completed down in front of the nurse at the reception desk and look at Chase.

"Can he come, too?" I ask, gesturing toward him.

Jackie looks at him and considers the arm he has wrapped around me. "Is he your husband?"

Before I can open my mouth, Chase answers firmly. "No."

It shouldn't crush me the way it does. It's the truth, after all. But the quickness with which he dismissed the question adds insult to the injury of this evening's events. He could've at least lied like Gary did so we could both go back there.

"Sorry, man, family only for now." Jackie does seem genuinely apologetic. Chase steps away from me, dropping his hand from my back.

"You still have my keys. You can drive yourself home. I'll reach out once I know more," I say.

He nods but doesn't reply. His face has the same solemn expression as the night he sat down at the bar and ordered whiskey.

I follow Jackie through the double doors, and Chase stands there watching us leave.

Chapter Eighteen

"**G**od, I'm so hungry I could eat a horse!" Gary laments. I laugh and turn to look at him in the hospital bed. The crinkling plastic of the pillow under my head accompanies my movement, joining the melody of other beeps and drips from the various monitors throughout the room. The color has returned to his skin, and apparently so has his appetite.

"I doubt there are any horses around here, and Chase will be bringing food and our escape vehicle in about an hour, but let me see what I can do." I slide my feet into the soft soles of my shoes and pad out into the hallway. It's early in the morning, just after shift change for the nurses. A housekeeper pushes her green dust mop past me, a smile accompanying her quick greeting. Before I can reply, she's moved on, busy corralling dust bunnies.

Five women in periwinkle scrubs scurry around one another behind the nurses' station. They speak in low voices as they work, gathering what they need and dispersing once more to the next patient who requires their attention. I approach the petite red-headed woman seated at a computer behind the desk. She pauses typing and looks up at me with a bright smile.

"Everything okay, sweetheart?" she asks.

"I was wondering if you had any snacks I could give to my father to hold him over until we go home?" She gives me a conspiratorial look and holds up a finger to wait. She returns moments later with various flavors of Jell-O and two small tubs of vanilla ice cream, the kind that have a wooden spoon tucked inside. I take them from her and give my thanks, excited to show my bounty to Gary.

When I drop the goods on his lap, he shouts in joy. "You might not want to yell in here," I tell him, laughing. "They'll cut you back open thinking they didn't get it all."

"Believe me, there's no gallbladder left to take." He peels off the aluminum lid to a strawberry Jell-O, slurping it directly from the container. I nudge a spoon his way, and he waves me off. I dig into one of the ice creams, though it tastes more like a tongue depressor than vanilla given the utensil provided.

"I can never tell you how much I appreciate you taking care of me, Eden." He's watching me with a smile, a glob of red Jell-O stuck in his white beard. I gesture for him to wipe it and he does. "You're very good at it, you know. How'd you know they'd have snacks?"

I finish my ice cream and stack the empty container in his before tossing them into the trash can a few feet away. I return to the nest I made in the recliner where I slept no more than an hour total throughout his surgery.

"When my sister had her second son, Mama and I flew out to Texas to be with her. My brother-in-law is a big-shot oncologist at MD Anderson and couldn't take off work for her whole hospital stay. Mama kept my older nephew at their house, and I stayed in the hospital with Jarrett and Ella so there'd be someone with her if he got called in."

The memory of curling up in Ella's hospital bed next to her floods my mind. I tell Gary about staring down at Austin's sweet, chubby face and trying to decide who he favored more, with Ella's chin and Jarrett's nose. Making padsicles out of maxi pads and witch hazel for Ella to use and laughing at their matching diapers. And my favorite part, eating ice cream from the nurse's station while Austin nursed in Ella's arms.

"I learned who to ask for the hookup," I say, smiling as the mental images fade away. Gary is watching me thoughtfully as he swallows another bite of Jell-O. "What?"

He shakes his head. "Nothing, you just remind me of Wendy. So good at being there for everybody, taking care of them. Always knowing what they need."

"Sounds like a good thing to me." I'm flattered to be compared to his late wife.

The corners of his mouth pull down, the opposite direction I expected them to go. I must look confused because he tilts his head to the side and shakes it some more.

"Don't get me wrong, it's a lovely thing," he says. "I just wonder if you, like her, struggle to ever let somebody else take care of you for once."

I shrug because I don't know what else to say. We sit in silence for a moment longer, and I check my phone again for any news from Chase. Gary notices this and sets aside his second empty Jell-O cup, folding his hands over his lap.

"What's going on between you two?" he asks, pointing at the phone in my hand.

"What do you mean?" I reply, feigning ignorance.

He purses his lips at me, an expression that suggests I know exactly what he's talking about. "The other day at the bar you both were acting strange. Chase isn't the silent type, and you're not one to willingly surrender a burger."

I roll my eyes. "If you noticed how awkward it was, why'd you say all that stuff about hearing us on the stairs?"

"Because I love to meddle!" He chuckles. "If I never opened the bar, I would've started a newspaper just to dig around in other people's business."

I pull the lever to extend my recliner, looking at the ceiling instead of at Gary. I don't know if it's the sleep deprivation or the ordeal we've gone through together tonight, but I want to be open with him. I just can't make eye contact while I do it.

"I screwed things up with him," I admit. "I freaked out and I told him we didn't have to talk anymore, and he's been doing a very good job at it."

"Then apologize. Chase is an understanding guy," he says as if it's that simple.

"I wish that were all it would take. It's probably for the best, honestly," I say, more to convince myself than him. "I have a lot of work to do before I can be the kind of person Chase deserves in his life."

Gary shifts in the bed to look at me, pain meds making him oblivious to the consequences of his movements for now. I force myself to drag my eyes from the water-stained ceiling tile I've been examining down to meet his scrutinizing gaze.

"So get to work," he says firmly. "And not just for Chase. Because although he is a great guy, the person who most deserves the best version of you, is *you*."

I look down at my hands so he won't see the tears welling in my eyes. I'm still contemplating his words when my phone chimes with a text from Chase. "He's here."

The doctor comes in one last time to go over Gary's care plan before discharging him. He changes out of his hospital gown, nearly flashing all of us. Once he's back in his normal clothes, he drops heavily into a wheelchair, which is held steady by a transporter who rolls him down to the car where Chase is waiting. Aside from Gary's medically induced sleep, we're all running on fumes at this point. No one speaks on the drive home nor as Chase assists him up the stairs.

I warm his breakfast wrap in the microwave before bringing it to him where he's curled up on the couch. He takes a bite and throws his head back, moaning like it's the best food he's tasted in his whole life. I leave the two of them to talk while I clean up the bathroom using chemicals from under the sink. It's sparkling and smells as sterile as the hospital when I'm finished with it.

Chase is laughing when I return to the living room. He grabs Gary's empty plate and carries it to the kitchen. "What's so funny?" I ask.

"Nothing, Chase was just ribbing me for calling you instead of him last night." Gary shrugs. "What can I say? Women are more dependable."

"I'll remember that the next time you call me looking to borrow a cup of sugar," Chase warns. I try to smile, but a yawn takes over.

"Get going, you two. I'm fine. I'll call *Rose* if I need anything." He winks at me as Chase throws his arms up in the air in exasperation. I lean over and plant a kiss on Gary's forehead.

"I'll bring you up some dinner tonight when I'm working, and make sure you take your pain meds on time," I tell him. He thanks me and then I follow Chase out the door he is holding open, letting him close it behind me as I move lazily down the stairs.

"You know you're wearing my shirt," Chase chimes from behind me. I pause, looking down at the gray T-shirt I never changed out of when I ran out the door last night. It has the logo for a music festival I've never been to emblazoned across the chest. It's the one he gave me to cover myself with that night in his apartment. My cheeks flush with embarrassment.

I turn to apologize and find him smirking at me. It's the friendliest expression I've seen on his face since the last time we stood like this on his staircase ten feet away.

"I'll wash it and bring it back tonight," I say apologetically.

He looks me up and down, a spark in his eyes that reminds me of the first time we met. "Keep it. Looks better on you anyway."

Chapter Nineteen

W hen we arrive at the trailhead on Sunday morning, the sun is just barely beginning to stretch its arms into the air, yawning beams of light out over the meadow. The guys are meeting us here, having camped out last night nearby. Zoey pulls into the spot next to Chase's truck, her headlights panning across the three of them sitting on his tailgate sipping from a shared thermos. Once she cuts the ignition, we both retrieve our packs from her back seat and make our way to the party.

My ankle doesn't hurt anymore, and though I know I'm more prepared mentally for the type of trail we'll be hiking, I can't help but be filled with trepidation at the idea of possibly getting injured again, this time with a much larger audience. If I mess up another trip, I doubt I'll receive a third invitation.

Aaron is chattering excitedly to a silent and sleepy Zander when we round the bed of the truck. Chase finishes taking a swig from the silver thermos before capping it and extending the offering to Zoey, who reaches him first. She takes it and twists off the cap, sniffing it suspiciously before taking a sip.

"How'd you make coffee?" she asks once she swallows. She

passes it on to me, and I sample the molten liquid, savoring the warmth that fills my tired body if not the bitterness that accompanies it.

"On a campfire, boil water and add instant coffee packets. It's no 8th & Main lavender latte, but it'll do," Aaron answers with a wink. Apparently, they're at the casual name dropping of her signature order level of *just hooking up.*

She rolls her eyes and punches his shoulder with so little force he doesn't even flinch. He's wearing a floral tank top that shows off his lean muscular frame but looks ridiculous in contrast with his professionally rugged hiking boots. Zoey doesn't seem to notice.

"Everyone ready?" she asks, ever the cheerleader of the group.

"Yep," Zander replies, though his coastal accent makes it sound more like *yahp.* He and Aaron hop off the tailgate, abandoning Chase, who lingers where he is sitting, finishing the coffee before tucking the empty cup into his pack. I notice a brown box resting behind his back, though in the hazy dawn light I'm unable to read the writing on it. The others move toward the front of the truck, leaving the two of us staring at each other.

He breaks eye contact first, letting his gaze fall lazily down my body. It stops when he lands on my feet and he sees his arch nemesis: my trail runners. The crinkle I love returns to the corner of his eyes, and his teeth glow white in the shadow of his face as a smile spreads across it. In between working daily to cover Zoey's absence and checking in on Gary during his recovery, I haven't had a moment to go shopping for this hike. I shrug my shoulders to offer my apologies.

He hops off the tailgate to stand in front of me but turns and grabs the box resting in the bed of the truck. When he passes it to me, I realize it's a shoebox. "Open it," he says.

When I lift the cardboard top, I see a pair of tan women's hiking boots with orange laces woven through that match the inner lining. I look up at him, confused but honored at the gesture.

"I didn't want any more injured ankles on my watch," he says matter-of-factly. "Put them on."

I do as he says, stepping on the heels of my running shoes to slip out of them and pulling the boots on one at a time. When I finish lacing them up, I walk a few steps to test them. It's a perfect fit. "How'd you know my shoe size?"

"Lucky guess." He shrugs, that familiar smirk returning to his face. For a moment things between us feel almost like they did before, and I'm afraid to move and shatter that magic. Since that night with Gary, we've tag teamed caring for him despite his threat to outsource Chase's services to Rose. Chase has dutifully kept Gary fed while I clean his apartment, wash his laundry, and check that he's taking his pain medication. When Gary commented yesterday that we were like annoyingly overbearing parents, we shared a smile that felt like an offering of peace.

"It's not lucky; he asked me for your size, and I told him," Zoey snipes from behind me. "Let's get a move on, you two." Chase slams the tailgate shut and I toss my sneakers into Zoey's car before we fall in line behind the other three making our way down the wide dirt path beyond the marker that signifies the start of the trail.

"So if all three of you are here, who's watching the store?" I ask on a huff of breath. The thin air feels crisp in my lungs this early in the morning.

"Our boss gave everyone the day off!" Aaron calls over his shoulder. A chuckle travels through the group. There's a glint shining in Chase's dark eyes when I peek up at him.

"I put a sign on the door that we were closed for a team

meeting," he says with a snarky grin. He stretches his arms wide, adding, "I consider this market research!"

My gaze follows his gesture, sweeping across the vista. No matter how many times I see it, I don't know if the landscape of Colorado will ever get old to me. We hike in silent companionship at the pace Zander sets from his place at the front of the group. All around us, the world is waking up. The morning sun burns dew off the wildflower petals, filling the air with the scent of steam and grass.

"How did you guys meet?" I ask, projecting my voice from the back of the group. I know from Zander's accent that he isn't from here originally, but beyond that I realize I know extraordinarily little about their bond.

"Chase and I were in Boy Scouts together," Aaron calls back. When he turns his head, I catch a glimpse of glistening sweat on the dark skin of his brow.

"You mean we were kicked out of the Boy Scouts together," Chase says, grimacing.

"How do you get kicked out of the *Boy Scouts*?" I ask for two reasons. One, because I can't imagine it's an easy task. Two, because Chase doesn't strike me as someone who's been kicked out of anything. Aaron maybe, with his cocksure attitude, but not Chase.

"Let's just say it was a mixture of breaking into my dad's liquor cabinet, getting some weed from friends, and taking Chase's mom's car for a joyride," Aaron says.

That'll do it.

Zoey smacks Aaron's shoulder, the skin-to-skin contact making a solid *splat*. "What?" he says, rubbing the muscle.

Chase slows his pace, glancing at me out of the corner of his eye. Mine are wide open as I study him more thoroughly in light of this new information.

"Told you I had a wild phase," he says. His mouth curves

downward in a rare frown, cheeks sporting a pale pink. As someone whose wild phase consisted of skipping school to attend a book signing from her favorite author, I don't comment.

"I just bought gear from the Landing for a climb when I moved here," Zander says without looking back at us. "Don't lump me in with their criminal activity."

"Says the guy who does shrooms on a regular basis!" Aaron adds, earning another smack from Zoey. I'm beginning to think he likes the abuse.

This gets Zander to turn around, gaze more serious than I expected. His blond baby hairs form a frizzy crown framing his flushed face. "You haven't seen nature until you've seen it on a trip."

"I'll take your word for it," I reply. I've never tried a drug in my life, and I'm not about to start now. I like to maintain control at all times, *thank you very much.*

We pass the rotting remnants of an old mining shack, splintering boards crumbling from the frame in jagged piles. Beyond it, there's a rusting metal box half fallen over in the grass beside the path.

"What is that?" I ask, pausing to examine the bucket. It's balanced on two slate rocks, and shrubs are growing wild and unruly around it.

"It used to be a mining cable car," Chase tells me, smiling while he watches me explore it. "Left behind by the same people who abandoned that building when coal mining fell out of fashion." He nods his head toward the shack behind us, and I glance back at its hollow windows leading into darkness.

We walk farther, the burning in my lungs and my legs becoming another heartbeat, just evidence that I am alive and my body is in fact working. When the roar of rushing water reaches our ears through the maze of towering fir trees, I know that we have almost made it to our destination.

The trees thin as the terrain grows rockier, and there is less grass beneath our feet to cushion our steps. My ankles are grateful for the extra support as I sidestep cracks in the crumbling black stone. The sound of the falls is deafening when I walk up behind the rest of the group where they stand looking over what seems like a cliff edge. I follow their gaze down below as the boulder we are standing on curves into a sheer drop cut by the torrent of white water. The falls are stunning to behold, their power reverberating through my body as sprays of water mist my already sweaty face. I let out an involuntary laugh at the magnitude of it all, which the others quickly chime in on.

"Take a picture of us!" Zoey asks, grabbing Aaron around the waist before he has a chance to react and passing her phone to me. Even after hiking for several hours, she looks beautiful. Her wild curls whip around her face free from the ponytail she used to imprison them. Her color-coordinated leggings and sports bra make my black shorts and long-sleeve top look sloppy in comparison. I snap one normal photo of the pair grinning beside one another before Aaron scoops her up and pretends to throw her over the edge, resulting in a much better candid shot.

We tiptoe carefully along the edge of the falls to a calmer basin below. Zander strings up his hammock between two trees and flops back into it, hat pulled low to shield his eyes. Chase drops his pack on the ground beside me before walking over and climbing on top of Zander, straining the weight of the trees as they try to support the two grown men.

"Come on, man!" Zander cries, though his tone doesn't carry any real annoyance on it. "We cuddled all night; I need some alone time!" Chase laughs but rolls out of the hammock, landing with a solid thump on the ground before standing and dusting himself off.

"Zander, why do I get the feeling that you could live like

145

this forever, sleep in a hammock like that every night, and be perfectly content?" I ask.

"Come to think of it, I've never seen any real evidence that you have an actual house that you go home to," Zoey adds, laughing. Aaron tosses a handful of blueberries into the air above her, one of which she catches in her mouth while the others pelt her in the face.

"Because he absolutely could," Chase replies to my question. "Zander is a nomad."

"A nomad?" I ask.

"Don't listen to him, he just says that because I travel around a lot," Zander mumbles from underneath his hat. "Nomads don't have a home to come back to. I definitely do. It just so happens that my home isn't a place, it's you guys."

The sweet sentiment makes me smile, even as Aaron pipes up. "That's just a nice way of confirming you're a couch surfer." We all laugh except Zander, who appears to be dozing off.

Aaron and Zoey round the shoreline to a shallow outcrop, slipping out of their shoes and wading into the pool just out of earshot. I'm sitting at the edge of the water, dangling my bare feet in the cool current. Though the shoes have saved my ankles, blisters have formed where my no-show socks could not protect me.

Chase unzips his pack behind me, and I hear the clinking of glass and his footsteps approaching. Something cold presses against the nape of my neck, and I turn to see him holding out a familiar bottle of lemonade. I smile, take it from him, and swallow a sip. He joins me on my boulder, and we sit there, taking drags of lemonade and watching the water glisten under the bright sunlight.

"I'm grateful he called you, you know," Chase says after a while. I look up at him to find he's already watching me. I wonder how long he's been doing that, while I've been daydreaming about everything I wish I had the courage to say. "Gary, I mean."

"Why's that?"

His eyes are a warm caramel today, his lashes casting a shadow across the irises. His bronzed skin is smattered with even more freckles than when we first met, a collection he adds to every time he goes outside, it seems. He searches my face, for what I don't know. After a moment he either finds it or gives up the search, because he finally answers me.

"I couldn't have done what you did. Stayed calm. Gotten him where he needed to be and told the nurses everything they needed to know. You never showed a moment of fear."

The awe in his voice washes over me, making me feel braver than I am. "What do you mean? You were so calm the whole time!" I remember my heart in my throat the whole drive. The only thing allowing me to breathe was the knowledge that Chase was a foot behind me.

He shakes his head at me, and it occurs to me that his face has never been this much of an open book before. There is admiration and something else, a hidden layer of fear stepping out into the light. "Eden, I was scared shitless. Every time I looked at Gary, I just saw my dad. When he had his heart attack, I was the one who rode with him in the ambulance. I was there when they lost him." He clears his throat as emotion fills his voice, and he can't bring himself to continue.

The image of this bright and beautiful man watching his father die right in front of him, helpless and terrified, makes me want to pull him into my arms. But I don't know where we stand yet. I still haven't even apologized. Before I'm able to, he sucks in a breath and plasters a small smile on his face, the happy filter returning to his expression.

"Anyway, I would have absolutely lost it if it hadn't been for you. I'm such a coward. I couldn't go back with you and see him like that. Especially not knowing what would happen." He looks at his hands, picking at a cuticle with a loose piece of skin. "I'm sorry I left you alone to handle it all."

The realization sinks like a stone in my gut, weighing me down. He didn't want to leave that night because of me. In my own fear, I hadn't even considered how scared he must've been. The guilt turns my body cold, and I pull my feet in from the water to warm them on the sun-soaked boulder.

"You don't have to be sorry, Chase," I say, my voice wavering. I reach out and touch just the tip of his fingers, testing the waters. I think about Gary's words in the hospital, about doing the work now not just for Chase but for me. I realize more than anything I want to be as brave as Chase thought I was that night, brave enough to apologize. Brave enough to tell him the whole truth. "I'm the one who should be apologizing for—"

"You guys, we should probably start heading back!" Zoey calls. An intense breeze rips through the valley and tousles her hair. Her cheeks are flushed, and she bites a lip nervously as she points to the sky where a dark cloud is swirling in the west.

Chase, who hasn't looked away from me since my sentence trailed off, follows my worried gaze upward and then jumps to his feet. "Time to go, sleepyhead," he says, grabbing the side of Zander's hammock and flipping him out onto the ground. I pull my socks on and stand, lifting one leg to slip my foot into its waiting boot. Another strong wind swoops down, causing me to stumble on the boulder. Chase reaches out to catch me just as I lose my footing and slam down hard on my knee, his tight grip around my elbow the only thing standing between me and an icy swim in the swirling water below.

Our eyes meet as a crack of thunder shakes the trees.

"Uh-uh, Eden, I'm not trying to get stuck out in the rain just because you wanna get carried again!" Aaron shouts. Chase chuckles, pulling me back to my feet.

"Maybe put your shoes on over there, away from the water," he says, pointing to the rest of the group. Every nerve ending in my elbow is a live wire that sparks and misfires until he lets me go.

We pack our bags in record time and hit the trail at a hurried pace. I force myself to watch the path instead of Chase as we attempt to outrun the storm.

Chapter Twenty

Mama: I miss you so much, baby.

I re-read the words for the hundredth time since they appeared on my phone an hour ago. The perfect little boost I didn't even know I needed. For months it has felt as though I'm marooned on an island, looking at her on the mainland, with no boat to bring me across. It is so foreign to me, this distance between us. I want to shout to her that I'm coming. That I'm building a bridge back home to her.

Me: I miss you more.

For now that will have to do. My computer speaker chimes to indicate Stephen has joined the call. He's freshly shaven today, a sight I've never seen before. His chin is smaller than I imagined it would be, but the smooth skin makes him look younger. I realize he's probably closer to Ella in age than I previously realized.

"How are you today, Eden?" He reaches beyond the frame, and I hear the distinct sound of blinds opening. A pale light brightens the shadows of his office, allowing me to see him even more clearly.

"I'm doing better, thank you," I answer politely. "You have to know that I can't just let the lack of a goatee go, right?"

He chuckles and scratches where he once had hair to stroke. "What can I say? Change is afoot!"

Indeed it is, I think to myself, glancing at my phone where it rests facedown on the table.

"So, Eden." His deepening voice tells me the conversation is about to shift to a more serious topic. He doesn't have to say the words; I already know what comes next.

"I'm ready, Stephen." I hold Mama's shirt in my lap and rub the threadbare hem between my thumb and forefinger. "I can do this."

He raises an impressed eyebrow at me, although there is no surprise in his expression. A hint of a smile pulls at the corners of his newly exposed lips. "Well then, the floor is yours," he says, gesturing for me to take the stage.

I startle awake to the quiet trilling of my alarm, volume low so it alerts only me. I don't remember drifting off to sleep. I rub the grogginess from my eyes and silence the alarm, the same one I've set for as long as I can remember. It's five in the morning, Christmas Day.

The tradition started two years after Ella left for college, when I was five years old. It was the year she started dating Jarrett, and they spent Christmas together in Vermont with his family. It was the first time that my mother and I would spend the holiday alone together.

Before she left town, Ella told me the truth about Santa Claus. That Mama worked hard to get the right presents for us each year, and in turn, Ella did the same for her. And since Ella wouldn't be home for Christmas that year, it was my turn to be Mama's Santa. She left the gifts she'd bought hidden in my toy chest and showed me how to use her small black alarm clock. I felt so grown-up, sneaking out of my room and stuffing her stocking with the goodies Ella had brought and a few handmade crafts from me. Mama cried happy tears when she woke up that morning.

A little over twenty years later, here I am, slipping out of my bed and tucking my feet into a pair of fuzzy slippers. I gather the bag of gifts and stocking stuffers from my suitcase and crack open my door as quietly as I can.

The first thing that catches my eye isn't the light on in the spare bedroom, it's the pile that it allows me to see of scattered photo albums strewn across the floor. Plastic tubs have their white lids ripped off and their contents spilled. Scrapbook projects Mama has worked at for years lay wide open on the carpet.

The house is hushed, the only sound is a whirring box fan running in my parents' room. I can hear it through their door that remains ajar, which I see when I tiptoe to the end of the hallway. My newly awake brain can't quite process what I've just seen, but I'm nervous that I'll be discovered. Though Mama knows it's me that delivers her gifts each year, the magic is in the mystery of the delivery.

I peek into their cracked bedroom door and find their bed empty, the quilt Mark inherited from his mother folded back on just his side. I set down the bag of gifts and look around the living room, realizing none of the stockings have been stuffed. As my eyes scan across the presents under the tree, a flickering light catches my eye through the slatted blinds of the window. I part them with my fingers, peering out into the darkness. The glow belongs to a bonfire burning in our fire ring, and my parents stand beside it.

They are arguing, I can tell. I can't see their faces, but I can see Mama's wild gesturing and Mark's slumped shoulders. I'm still numb, trying to process what is happening. The front door pulls open with some effort, flurries of snow sucking inward onto the living room floor. Their voices reach my ears, more heated than the fire. Heart-wrenching sobs crackle between Mama's shouts, like the air is no longer compatible with her lungs. I shuffle across the yard to them, crossing my arms tightly against the cold. My thin flannel offers very little protection.

The snow obscures the sound of my approach, so I am only a foot away when Mama finally sees me. Her face is distraught; in the amber glow of the fire I can see streams of tears pouring down her cheeks. Her mouth has paused, agape, and icy dread freezes inside my chest. I have never seen that look on anyone's face. I hope I never do again.

Her outstretched arms close the gap between us, two frozen hands pressing tightly to my cheeks. Everything she says hits my ears in slow motion. "We have to leave; we have to leave. Eden, I'm so sorry. We have to go."

Terror is the only word I can use to describe the feeling that floods through me. Ella has died. That's the only thing I can imagine, the very worst thing. What could possibly be worse than death? Behind Mama, Mark watches with tears in his eyes and something else coloring his face that I don't understand.

"Mama, what's happening?" I manage to choke out. It's not my voice that I hear, not a version I recognize anyway. I can't move. My feet are cemented in place. I cover her hands with mine, silently pleading with her to tell me I'm wrong.

Mark opens his mouth to speak but Mama rips her hands from my face and turns to swing at him, and for the first time I have a name for the look in his eyes. Guilt. Like a dog caught with something it shouldn't have between its teeth. He flinches back from Mama, and she practically growls at him, "Don't you speak to her. You're lucky I haven't killed you for this."

"I wish that you would," he cries out, falling to his knees in the snow. None of this is making sense. The bones in my toes scream in pain from the cold seeping through my cloth slippers.

"What is happening?" I plead again. Mama turns back to look at me, appearing utterly devastated.

"I am so sorry, baby. I'm so, so sorry. I didn't know; how could I have known?" she chants, her eyes drifting from me to somewhere far away. "There were so many pictures of you, how did I not know?" She chokes on the last word as Mark's head falls into his palms.

Pieces of a puzzle swirl around in my brain. Slowly they fall through the haze and settle into an image I don't want to under-stand. I stumble forward, past Mama, toward the flames. She reaches for me as I pass, but so does Mark, which causes her to intervene and nearly snarl at him. It leaves me free to approach the fire pit, and there in the glare I see the confetti of photos. I kneel to get a better look at the pictures being slowly engulfed in fire. They are all of a body, a woman's body. No, not a woman. A girl. Me.

In one, I am sleeping, and a hand has lifted my shirt to reveal two barely forming breasts. The flames lick at the edge of the photograph, swallowing up the purple and white pattern of the Paris comforter I begged Mama for when I was fourteen.

I reach into the embers, burning the sensitive flesh of my wrist on the metal ring in the process. The pain of the seared skin is overshadowed by the horror that presses behind my eyes as I recognize the scene. I'm peering under a door at a more recent version of myself, my nude body on full display. I have a foot raised to step into the shower, unaware of the audience I'm enter-taining. Bile rises in my throat, and I drop the photo back into the fire as I turn and retch onto the powdery snow. The flames reclaim what is theirs, and the edges of the image curl tightly inward until the whole thing disappears into ash.

I feel Mama grabbing at me, pulling on my sleeve to urge me off the ground. She's trying to talk to me, but there is a roaring in my ears drowning out her voice. Slowly her words seep through. She is telling me to go into the house, to get my things. I struggle to stand, held up by her small but strong arms. I am a spinning top that she sets off, drifting dizzily away from the funeral pyre of my life. She orders Mark to stay where he is, his expression pathetic and sickly. He begs Mama once more to kill him.

In the shocked calm of my brain, I consider it. How easy it would be.

Before I know it, I am falling through the front door of the house. My house. My childhood home. The backdrop for every photo in that fire.

My hands are numb and blistered red from the cold as I stuff my belongings into my suitcase on the floor. Somewhere in the quiet corner of my war-torn mind, it dawns on me that I will never see this room again. I fall to the floor, a croaking sound coming out of my throat as tears I didn't notice falling blur my vision. I sense more than see a hand reaching for me, and I flinch away before Mama's words push through the fog.

"We have to go. We have to go," she urges. She is talking about packing a bag, about money in a gun safe, talking about a lot of things that I cannot hear over all. This. Noise.

Before I realize where we are, the living room door is swinging behind us, casting a long fluorescent beam out onto the lawn. Dawn is breaking, and everything glistens in the early light. I can't help but stare as I pass the house where I have lived more of my life than anywhere else. Where I learned to read, to cook. Where I hosted sleepovers and cried over the first boy who ever broke my heart while Mark held me and reassured me all men wouldn't do the same.

He was right. My heart is not breaking now. That word does not do justice to what has happened to it. It simply existed one moment and then was gone from my chest, and only a black hole remains, swallowing the essence of who I am into its ravenous throat.

A memory from Sunday school creeps into the forefront of my mind. A story about a city, burned to ash by God for the sins committed within its walls. Of a woman who wasn't supposed to look back but did. Of the pillar of salt she became.

So I look forward. I'm vaguely aware of Mark on my right, begging us not to go as we head for the car. I glance at his face and see that it is awash with what could almost be construed as regret if his eyes weren't so dead and still. There is nothing but iciness in his stare. No emotion. No remorse. I feel cold from the inside out as Mama shuts me into the passenger seat and shouts something at him that is muffled by the insulated bubble of the car. I watch as she pulls the gold band from her finger and throws it in the dirt between them. She climbs into the driver's side and changes gears, tearing down the driveway. As we turn onto the gravel road, I manage to face her.

Her stare is trained on the rearview mirror, and I wait for her to suffer the same fate as that woman, to crumble into salt before my very eyes. When she doesn't, I put thoughts of God behind me since he clearly isn't concerned with our fate.

When I finish, I look down at the fabric between my fingers. I've opened a new hole in the worn threads. I release my grip on the shirt, and it falls listlessly into my lap. Movement in my peripheral catches my eye. I zero in on a small black house spider darting toward the miniscule gap under the baseboard. My skin crawls, and I instinctively draw back my foot to stomp it. The spider pauses beside my chair, and I realize he has no clue. No clue something so terrible is about to happen to him. Something I can prevent.

I rest my foot back on the bar of my seat, watching as he scurries into the safety of the wall, blissfully unaware of the fate he's just avoided.

When I finally look back at the screen, I'm surprised to find that Stephen is watching me with a glint of pride in his eyes. "That was so powerful, Eden." I nod bashfully to acknowledge the compliment. He reaches behind his computer, returning to the frame with a white tissue dangling from his grip. He pats it under his eyes, which I now notice are glistening with tears.

I reach a hand up to gently touch my cheeks, amazed to see that for the first time since beginning this journey, my palm comes away bone-dry.

Chapter Twenty-One

Geronimo is staring down at me with a plastic-wrapped cigar stuffed between his teeth. The chalkboard sign he holds informs me that Yeti travel mugs are twenty percent off this weekend only. *What a deal,* I want to say, but I don't think the bear really cares. I sidestep around him and make my way toward the back of the store.

"There's our favorite klutz!" Aaron cheers as I approach him at the counter. Several customers turn from perusing the racks to see who it is he's referring to. Even knowing I've rightfully earned the title, I put a hand up to shield my face from them, mouthing, *You suck,* to Aaron from this side of my palm.

He lets out a hearty laugh as Chase strolls through the archway behind him. When he sees me, he stops in his tracks. "Eden, what's going on?" He lifts his baseball cap to smooth his dark waves back before resettling it on his head.

I look from Aaron's amused face back to Chase's expectant one. He watches me waver for a moment before clearing his throat. "You can come back to my office, if you'd like."

I nod sheepishly, suddenly fascinated by the display of lighters next to the register. He turns to retreat back down the dimly lit hallway, and I offer Aaron a strained smile before following Chase. We pass a bathroom and a door marked with a sign that says *Inventory*. The last door in the row is decorated with printed and clipped memes surrounding an 'Employee of the Month' sign on posterboard. In the open space below the words, they've stuck a black-and-white photo of a golden retriever with its paws propped on the checkout counter.

Chase smiles when I point at the picture with an eyebrow arched in confusion. "A customer's dog. Otter is the friendliest cashier I have."

He pushes open the door and steps aside for me to pass. It's a small, organized room with a simple oak desk supporting a laptop hooked up to a monitor. Stacks of manilla folders are tucked into a slatted organizer on the wall. Aside from the obvious lack of potted plants, it could be a replica of our office at the bar.

He gestures for me to sit in the only available chair and takes his place in the opposite corner of the room. He leans against the wall and crosses his arms over his chest, which makes the curves of hardened muscles more visible through his army-green T-shirt. His intense stare measures me carefully, and I suddenly feel more naked here than I did laid out underneath him on his bed.

I pat my hands on my knees, casually wiping the nervous sweat off onto my jeans. All the resolve I had built up when I marched out of my kitchen this morning seems to be leaking out of my pores.

"Is everything okay? Is Gary all right?" he asks, an edge cutting the hoarseness of his voice.

"Oh God, yes, he's fine," I reassure him, anxious laughter bubbling over. I press my lips tightly together to suppress it. "I'm here because I never got to finish my apology last weekend, on our hike."

Chase raises his eyebrows, shifting his weight from one foot to the other. "It's okay. You don't have to talk about it if you don't want to."

I'm overwhelmed with gratitude for this man, who even when he undeniably deserves the truth, still offers me an escape route to avoid the thing I hate doing most.

"I want to," I tell him, though my voice, thick with imminent tears, would suggest otherwise. When I finally found my words and handed them over to Stephen, I felt strong and capable. Here, standing on the precipice and looking down at where I must fall, I'm terrified. "What I said that morning on the staircase...I didn't mean that. About it being a mistake."

I watch as he absorbs the shock of my statement, a shuddering sigh of relief filling the space between us.

"It's been horrible, you know." He shakes his head softly. "I don't really understand what I did wrong."

The break in his voice is enough to shatter me. "You didn't, Chase. I did. Everything was going so perfectly that night before I ruined it, and you were so kind. You didn't even complain. But then I saw your mom, and I realized it was the day your dad—" My voice falters, unwilling to go there.

"And she needed you," I manage to continue. The tangible grief that rolled off her washes over me now in residual waves. "I couldn't be some lost and damaged woman adding her burdens to the stack of your own."

I don't know what reaction I expected, but his sharp laughter certainly wasn't on the list. I startle, meeting his eyes and expecting anger, only to be melted by their warmth. He tries to politely cover his bright smile and suppress another laugh, and I'm so endeared I can't manage to feel confused.

Suddenly we are eye to eye as he kneels in front of me, clasping my hands in his and resting them on my lap. "First of all, my mother doesn't need me. Not in the way you think."

My brow furrows, urging him to explain.

"When I said that's not how I wanted you two to meet, I meant it. Most days, my mom is a brighter force than any star in this universe. Sure, the first year was difficult as hell. But her grief is the least important thing about her," he says.

I wonder for a moment if we are talking about the same woman, dressed as if she were ready to attend a funeral and not an anniversary lunch. I ask him as much.

"Has anyone you love ever died?" he asks, his voice soft. He tucks a lock of flyaways behind my ear.

"No, not really," I explain. Lost, yes, probably permanently. But still living, which seems like a cruel joke on behalf of the universe.

He looks down at our hands and rubs a thumb steadily over mine. "Some days are harder than others, with a loss like that. Most of the time, you feel pretty okay. Even fantastic. Like the 'you' you were before you ever lost them. And then a certain day will come. Their birthday, a wedding anniversary, the day they died." He pauses on the word. It sounds so foreign on his tongue, such an ugly word from such a beautiful mouth.

"For me it's the same week every year in the fall, the same week we hiked in Zion." He looks up at me, and though his eyes are rimmed red, there's a ghost of a smile on his lips. "In those moments it's as fresh as the day he left."

I reach out and tenderly pull the hat off his head. I lace my hands through the strands of hair on the back of his head and pull him forward till I am able to press my lips into his soft waves. When I inhale his scent, I am transported. We're no longer locked in this haphazard embrace on the floor of his office. We're in that alpine lake, floating on the water, sky above and all around us. Ethereal and infinite.

He pulls away and I'm back in this room with pain running like a current between us. "What I'm trying to say is, sure there

161

are days like that one where Mom is sad and she leans on me. There are days when I lean on her even harder. That's what you do with the people you love; you lift each other up when it all gets too heavy."

He strokes the tender skin of my forearm, tracing a pale blue vein until it lands at the puckered scar curved in a half moon around my wrist. My breath halts in my chest, the memory of the smoldering metal of the fire pit twisting a sharp knife in my lungs. "When was the last time you let someone carry you without thinking of yourself as a burden?" He asks it so quietly I have to lean in to hear the words.

Just when I think he is going to lean forward and close the distance between our lips, he presses his forehead against mine and lets the gentle breeze of his breaths kiss my face instead.

"What happened to make you so scared to let me in?" he whispers.

A traitor tear blazes a trail down the curve of my cheek. I focus on its path, the way it pools at the tip of my chin before dropping onto my jeans and blooming. I watch the flower it forms evaporate in the time it takes me to decide not *what* it is I need to tell him, but *how*.

The shrill music of my phone ringing slices through the air and severs whatever thread is holding us so close. Chase shifts back onto his heels as I reach for the phone in my pocket, pulling it out and laying it on my lap in between us. I'm so surprised when I see *Mama* on the display that I almost drop it. I look up at Chase with an unspoken request, and the permission I'm seeking is there on his face.

"Hey, Mama, is everything okay?"

"Everything's great. I'm just sitting here with Zoey having coffee, waiting for my baby to come see me!" Her words slowly register in my brain, and the excitement and relief filling me in that moment are enough to leave me speechless.

"Close your jaw, Eden," Zoey's voice calls from the background. "She's really here. And we'd like you to be, too! And could you please bring some of Rose's pastries with you? We're starving."

"I'm on my way!" I say, still in a state of disbelief. I hang up the phone, looking at Chase with an apologetic smile. "My mom is here—"

"Go," he interrupts, having heard every word. "We can talk later."

I stand to leave, hesitating before wrapping my arms around him in the tightest embrace I can manage. He presses his face into the curve of my neck, breathing deeply and placing a soft kiss beneath my ear. Every inch of his body melts into mine, like the answer to a question I didn't know needed asking.

"Get the sticky buns," he suggests when I finally peel myself away. "Trust me, they're the best thing she's got."

I smile, clutching the phone tightly in my hand as I take a step toward the door. "I trust you," I say, not missing a moment of the light brightening his entire face as my words land perfectly in the expanding space between us.

Chapter Twenty-Two

The box of sticky buns warms my hand as I use the other to push open Zoey's front door. As soon as I do, the musical sound of laughter reaches my ears. The juxtaposition of the joy I feel now brimming in my body compared to the nervousness I felt an hour ago before talking to Chase is enough to give me whiplash. I bump the door closed with my hip and round the corner into the dining room.

Zoey and Mama sit across from each other at the end of the table, Zoey gesturing wildly as she tells a story I recognize as the night I got sprayed while changing a keg. Mama covers her thin lips to disguise another trill of laughter. My heart swells at the sight of her, and I feel tears welling in my eyes. Looking at the two of them, I can't even be embarrassed about the story. I'm too distracted by memories of so many moments like this before life got so complicated.

The shock of gray dominating Mama's hair now doesn't exist in the flashbacks I'm having. I can see her as she was, dark red curls in a small ponytail at the base of her neck. I've just walked out of my bedroom in a blush dressing gown we found in my grandmother's old trunk. A teenage Zoey is wearing the black pleated swing skirt discovered alongside the gown, and Mama is sporting a lime-green jumpsuit from the disco era.

Elvis Presley's "Hound Dog" is blasting out of the surround-sound. Mama twirls Zoey under her arm before embracing her and rocking in circles. When she sees me, she breaks one hand from Zoey's and reaches for me, pulling me into their lively embrace. We hold on to each other as we do a little jig, shimmying our hips to the beat of the music and collapsing into a fit of giggles when Mama yells, "Elvis with the pelvis!"

Zoey brings me back to the present with an excited squeal, taking the warm box of buns from my hand and running it to the kitchen to divvy them up onto plates. Mama stands to greet me, and I'm struck by just how different she looks.

The woman in my memories is petite but muscular, an immovable force with a vibrant personality. She's so small now as she stands before me, so frail. She's easily lost fifteen pounds since December, weight she didn't really have to lose. When she wraps her arms around me, I can feel her ribs. There are even more wrinkles forming around her eyes and mouth, like the stress of the past few months has aged her ten years. The sudden realization of her growing older causes a pang in my heart.

"I've missed you so much, baby," she says as she squeezes me into a tight embrace. I tuck my head down against hers, inhaling the familiar scent of her sweet-pea shampoo that costs ninety-nine scents at the only store in my hometown. Her voice warbles like she's going to cry, so I push down the wave of emotion brought on by her aging appearance and plaster a smile on my face as I pull away.

"I've missed you, too, Mama. I'm so glad you're here!" And I mean it. The magnitude of how much I've longed for her presence over the past months is like a tsunami crashing down on me now. It's amazing to me that no matter how old I get, I still need my mother so desperately.

Zoey comes back into the dining room with three syrupy sticky buns stacked on plates that her waitressing career allows her to carry precariously in a way that would make me nervous with anyone else. The two of them return to their seats, and I take the one next to my mother. Groans of satisfaction fill the air as everyone digs into the pastries.

"Where were you this morning?" Zoey asks around a mouthful of dough and caramel.

"Out for a run?" Mama follows up, patting her mouth delicately with a napkin. Zoey looks at her and then over at me, her expression unreadable.

"Um, I actually haven't been running since everything happened." I say it quietly with my eyes trained on my plate. A heaviness settles in the air around us, and I'm filled with regret for always being the one to ruin the party.

Mama mulls this over, chewing on the inside of her cheek. When she finally speaks, her words come out sharper than I imagine she intends. "You know, it's been almost six months. Maybe it's time to get back out there."

Given that she's not the member of our family known for her tough-love approach, her out-of-character suggestion feels like a slap in the face. Mark has always been the one rushing us women along when he feels we are being too sensitive about something. Six months feels like no time at all for a wound to heal that isn't even closed yet. I would think Mama of all people would understand that.

To end the awkward silence that ensues, Zoey repeats her question.

"I was talking with Chase at his store," I explain, trying to cover up the wounded tone in my voice. Before Zoey can respond, Mama excitedly jumps in on her favorite subject: romance.

"Oh yeah? And who might this boy be?" she asks playfully, her cutting comment from a moment before forgotten. She nudges me with her elbow, and I roll my eyes at Zoey. She hides her smirking mouth behind a coffee mug as she takes a sip.

"Well, he's almost thirty, so hardly a *boy*," I clarify.

"Eden, when you get to be as old as I am, they're all *boys*," she says with a snort. Her delicate hand pats my arm, the metal of her gold watch clinking with the movement. "How did you two meet?"

"He owns a store next door to the bar." I don't mean for my words to come out sounding so sickly sweet, and I'm grateful when neither of them acknowledges how pathetic I am.

"And keeps me in business," Zoey adds, gathering our empty plates and walking them over to her sink, where she rinses them of caramel residue before loading them into her dishwasher.

Mama looks from her over to me with a stern expression magnifying the wrinkles between her thin eyebrows. "He's a drinker?" The warning in her voice is apparent. From what little she and Ella have told me, I know my biological father liked to drink, though in terms of his poor qualities it was never the most significant one on the list.

"Only socially, and only a few beers with his dinner," I explain.

"He never even gets drunk," Zoey adds. *Except that one time*. Not that she needs to know about that.

The incredulous expression on Mama's face causes a spark of unfamiliar anger to burn low in my gut. It strikes me as odd for her to judge my taste in men, given how horrible both of her husbands have turned out to be.

That's not fair, I correct myself. *It wasn't her fault.*

The anger is gone as quickly as it came, replaced by the shame of having felt it in the first place. How can I blame her for something no one could have predicted? It blindsided all of us, the devastation unanimous, and she's handling it the best way she can. She's found the strength to leave not once, but twice. My admiration for her bravery overshadows any hurt from her snide comments.

"Well, just be careful," she warns. "That's how your father seemed at first."

I bristle at her comparison of Chase to my father, then quickly push aside the unwelcome sensation. I don't know why I'm so on edge with her. It's uncharted territory in our relationship, one that has always been rooted in a closeness my friends envied growing up. I focus on the knowledge that she only shares her fears in the hope that I won't repeat her mistakes.

"Don't worry," Zoey says, stepping in. "He's a good man, and if they could ever move past this flirtationship, we'd all be better for it."

I wince but keep my expression neutral, suddenly aware of how many details I've kept from her. In all my indecisiveness and embarrassment over how I've handled things, I've accidentally kept Zoey more in the dark than usual.

"Well, Mama, I'm sorry but I actually have to get ready for work. I didn't know you were coming, and one bartender won't cut it for a Saturday night," I say, trying to change the subject.

"Don't worry about it; I can cover for you. I still owe you for working my entire vacation," Zoey says. Mama smiles at me expectantly, and I shrug at both of them.

"Thank you, Zo. I really appreciate it." I stand and walk through the archway into her living room, grabbing Zoey into a quick embrace.

I throw finger guns at Mama. "In that case, I can give you a tour of my humble studio apartment and then we can explore my new town a little?" She returns the gesture with a click of her tongue and a smile.

"Whatever you want to do. I'm just here to spend time with my favorite girl," she says.

"I'm telling Ella you said that," I reply. She laughs and threatens my inheritance before standing to follow me out the door. We toss a "See you later!" to Zoey in unison before stepping out into the dry heat of the morning.

"*Ghost* or *Pretty Woman*?" Mama holds up the two DVDs she's pulled from her decades-old suitcase. Every night is a movie night where she's involved. My gaze switches back and forth between the two before I point a decisive finger at Richard Gere. She examines my selection with a smile. "I knew I raised you right."

"I'll go pick up dinner so we can eat while we watch. What would you like?" I ask her as I tie the laces on my shoes. She takes a sip from the bottle of lemonade I forced her to buy when we stopped by the Raven for lunch. Turns out everything on the menu is as good as their signature beverage. I finally understand Chase's obsession. Afterward we drove to the nearby lake Gary mentioned he frequents for fishing, and we walked the nature trail that overlooks the scenic waterfront.

It's something we loved to do together anytime she'd visit me in Nashville. We'd drive to Radnor Lake and meander along the wide paved path that surrounds the water, reminiscing on the past and making plans for the future. Today, that same conversation felt forced and unfamiliar. The past too tender to touch. The future too unknown to predict.

"That burger you mentioned sounds perfect!" she replies. I nod and promise I'll be back soon before stepping out onto the staircase and shutting the door. The relief that floods my body is unexpected and confusing. Why do I feel so on edge around my own mother? Sure, the conversation hasn't flowed as easily, but it's been months since we last saw each other, the longest we've ever been apart. She's still the person who knows me best, the only one who can truly understand what I've been going through.

I shake my head to derail the train of thought as my keys find purchase in the ignition. It's a quick drive to the bar, and when I get there, it's slow enough that I can absolve myself of the guilt I felt from letting Zoey cover my shift. Maddie smiles when I approach the bar, a new silver hoop pulling tight against her purple-painted lips. I toss my small purse onto the counter in front of her.

I catch a glimpse of myself in the mercury-glass mirror mounted on the wall behind her, reflecting back a warped view of the stacked liquor bottles and the small gaggle of customers moving about the room. My auburn bangs are pinned back from my face, giving a clear view of the wrinkles forming at the edge of my eyes, as if one day reliving the past has jolted me forward ten years into the future.

"I heard your mom is in town," Maddie says in lieu of a proper greeting. Zoey rounds the corner to toss a crumpled receipt in the trash can under the counter. The apron tied around her waist is dusted with evidence that she's been helping Santi in the kitchen, powdered seasonings and puffs of flour standing out against the black fabric. She brushes a curl away from her face before training her tired blue gaze on me.

"Yeah, I just came to order something to go for our movie night. I've been bragging about Santi's cooking all day, so she wanted to try it," I explain. Maddie nods and takes my order, running my card before returning it with my receipt. I sign it and add her tip, leaving it on the counter for her to retrieve when she finishes delivering a round of rocket pops to some college girls at the end of the bar. The girls each take photos of the festive cocktails, evidence of the free advertisement I'd hoped to garner.

Zoey leans against the counter and places her forehead against its cool surface. So much for being relieved of the guilt of making her work.

"I think it's time we start interviewing some line cooks," I say. Her head rolls to the side, a hard stare peeking up at me from the corner of her eye. Her eyeliner has smudged from sweating over the hot cooktop.

"I think you're right," she groans. "Yours is the last to-go order we're taking tonight. It's too much."

"Best food in town. It was bound to happen," I say. This earns a modest smile.

The business has really thrived under her directive, though it's taken her this long to fully appreciate that. Zander helped ease the stress on the bar, but she always dismisses me when I suggest the kitchen—her true baby—needs the same. The fact that she's accepting it now means she finally realizes how successful she's been, even if she's too humble to say the words.

"Zo, I can't thank you enough for bringing Mama here. Even though it's hard, I really needed to see her," I tell her, genuine emotion flooding my voice. Her eyebrows pull together, and she purses her lips, sitting up to face me.

"I had nothing to do with it. It was just as much of a surprise to me when she knocked on my door this morning."

"What do you mean?" I ask, gears turning in my head. "How in the hell did she get here from the airport if you didn't help her?"

"Maybe she took an Uber?" Zoey suggests, shrugging her shoulders. A polite smile passes over her face when a customer behind me calls over a farewell. Something nags at the edge of my brain like a loose thread in a pair of tights, and it takes everything inside me to ignore it.

"All the way from Denver? I don't think so," I say.

Her mouth opens to respond and then shuts when no good explanation comes to mind. She's rescued from having to formulate any answer when Santi delivers two foam to-go containers out of the kitchen and onto the counter between us.

"Tell your mamá I said, '*Provecho.*'" He doesn't even wait for the thank-you to finish falling off my lips before returning to the sanctuary of his kitchen.

My gaze drifts back to Zoey, and I find a storm brewing in her normally vibrant eyes. That dangling thread tempts me, begging to be pulled. I grab the to-go containers and clear my throat, giving her a strained smile before thanking her again.

When my feet hit the pavement out front, I realize my bumper is sticking out of my parking spot into the street. I mentally kick myself before climbing in. All along the street, strangers wander up and down the sidewalk, enjoying the reprieve from the oppressive heat of the day. I wait for an opportunity to open up and pull out into the flow of traffic.

The whole drive home, it is just me and the echo of my thoughts. I dance around that thread, unwilling to acknowledge its presence for fear of unraveling it and leaving a hole that can't be repaired.

Chapter Twenty-Three

Any tension built up inside me dissipates like cotton candy at the suggestion of rain as I'm swallowed up by the darkness of my apartment. Mama has pulled the blankets from my bed onto the floor in front of the love seat, creating a pallet like what I'd make as a child at sleepovers. Every light aside from the one atop my oven is off, and her face is illuminated solely by the soft glow of the television. Everything hard inside of me softens when I recognize the gray, threadbare shirt she has piled in her lap.

"I found this when I was looking for a sweater to cozy up in. I can't believe you still have it," she says tenderly. She holds it close to her heart while her eyes remain far away. "I spent a lot of nights like this, piled up on the couch watching movies when you just couldn't fall asleep."

The upturned corners of her lips wipe my mind of any questions. I want nothing more than to curl up next to her, safe from the world and all its evils in the arms of my mother. Whatever method she used to get here, I'm just grateful that she did. You don't question why you got a miracle; you just hold tight to it with both hands so it doesn't slip away.

I set her meal on the coffee table in front of her and then join her on the floor. She hits play on the remote to kick off the movie. As the opening credits roll, the mouthwatering scent of Santi's cooking fills the air. We both dig into our burgers. As soon as the flavors hit her tongue, she turns to me with wide eyes and a dribble of green chili running down her chin.

"I'll get some napkins," I say, giggling. She laughs in earnest while cupping a free hand under her mouth to catch the drippings. When I hand her the paper towels, she dabs them against her skin, and they come away soaked. "I told you it was to die for!"

"You weren't kidding. My compliments to the chef," she says, nodding her head vigorously. Before we know it, our to-go boxes are empty and Richard Gere is climbing up a fire escape with roses between his teeth.

"So romantic," Mama says, wiping a tear from the corner of her eye. I smirk at her and roll mine.

"You hate heights. You would *not* find that romantic *at all*."

She shoves me playfully but can't deny what I'm saying is the truth. I gather our trash and bring it to the kitchen, throwing it away before washing our silverware in the sink, the metal glinting in the soft light. Mama pads over to my side, leaning one arm on the counter and watching me work.

"That man could bring me roses on Mount Everest, and I'd still find it romantic," she clarifies. "And immediately after I'd faint."

We laugh in unison at the mental image of her anywhere near the top of a mountain. Not her scene, at all. I look over at her, exploring the face I know almost better than my own. Her pink lips come to a soft close, capturing the last of her laughter. Eyes that have always reminded me of the grassy fields of pasture sprawled on the outskirts of our hometown watch my hands scrub my coffee cup from this morning.

"So, I've been meaning to ask you. Before you left," she begins, her voice tightening like a rope pulled taut, "did you get a letter? From Mark?"

The hairs on the back of my neck stand up, and a cramp forms low in my stomach. I clear my throat to try and swallow back the bile as quickly as it rises.

"Yeah, it was ridiculous, just page after page of him talking about how much *his* life has been ruined by this whole thing. As if *he* was the victim," I scoff, my words coming out sharp as knives. "Can you believe that?"

She doesn't respond immediately, and that cramp intensifies, like the worst period I've ever endured. My eyebrows pull together as I try to make sense of her question. "How did you know about the letter?"

She examines her fingernails, decorated with chipped, espresso-colored polish. "Brother Richard gave it to him as a project in our couples counseling."

The pain is instantaneous and all-encompassing. The blood in my veins turns into a river of razor blades coursing through my body. For a moment I don't know if my legs will continue to hold me up. I brace my hands, still slick with soap, against the laminate counter to steady myself.

That thread dangles right at the forefront of my mind. Her words pull at it even as I recoil from its presence. *Couples counseling.* Surely I've misunderstood. She takes a step closer to me, covering my white-knuckled grip with her petite hand. When I look down at where we are joined together, what's left of my world falls away from me.

There, on her left hand, third finger, is a familiar gold wedding band.

"Mama?" I ask, my voice having to claw its way out of my throat. It is the last tug that the thread can withstand. As she draws an anxious breath in, everything unravels, and the truth is laid bare before me.

"Eden, you can't possibly fathom how sorry he is," she whispers. I am frozen in place, my brain unable to keep up. The words she's speaking are in a language I don't understand. They must be because they are incomprehensible.

She removes her hand from mine and rests it on my lower back, trying to pull me toward her into an embrace. I am immovable, drowning in the quicksand of this new reality. My eyes lock onto the photo I hung above the sink, a stretched canvas of a photo I took all those years ago in London. I pretend I'm running down that cobbled street toward the Piccadilly Circus, Zoey hot on my heels, this moment an unknown destination far down the timeline of my life instead of the one I'm currently living through.

"When did this happen?" The words take more focus than anything has in my life. It feels like I'm in the final push of a cross-country race, every muscle in my body screaming for me to stop. To end this pain before it gets any worse.

I finally force myself to meet her eyes, once the familiar trait that anchored me to her. Now they don't look anything like mine. They are emeralds in desperate need of a polish, an echo of their former glory.

"When we told Brother Richard, he thought counseling could do us some good," she explains. She's looking at me, but I get the sense she isn't really seeing what's in front of her. We're stuck in this half embrace, neither of us sure where to go from here. "You'll understand one day when you get married. Men have needs, you know? I wasn't giving him what he deserved, and you are so beautiful, Eden."

I'm definitely going to throw up.

Every cell in my body recoils. I can't believe the sickening words coming out of her mouth. How, in this moment, is she still able to find a way to shoulder the blame? Why does she even want to?

"He's a pedophile," I say it firmly, leaving no room for interpretation. "You understand that, right? He can't *pray* that away."

She shakes her head softly, dismissing the truth before it even has a chance to reach her. "He never touched you."

I draw back from her as if she's slapped me. She startles and her face crumples, the dam of her tears breaking and letting them fall freely down the canyons her wrinkles create. I don't know how to make her understand that he didn't have to touch me. That the wounds he left behind are just as deep as they would be if he'd used his hands to create them.

For a second it's like I see her clearly for the very first time. Not as my mother but as another person. Whole and separate from myself, with her own failures and mistakes and dreams she never got to make a reality. It takes everything from me in that moment to keep from hating this stranger, and even then I can only scrape together some pity.

"Why are you saying these things?" I plead with her, sounding the same way I did when I was five years old and she explained to me that one day she would die. I didn't understand back then that she had no choice. It's so much worse now, knowing that she does and still, she chooses the wrong one.

"Honey, it's what God would want us to do. To forgive Mark like God's forgiven us," she says. She crosses her arms and rubs them like she's cold. She's never looked more fragile than she does right now, like one light gust of wind could blow her away. "We just want you to be part of the family again."

Something inside of me snaps, and suddenly my voice comes out in a roar rather than a whisper.

"Mama, you and Ella and me? We're the family. Not him." I'm trembling with rage and indignation and disbelief that this is somehow my life. *This can't be my life.* "I'm not the one who did anything wrong."

A wall comes up behind her eyes and I'm shut out. She straightens her back and purses her lips, looking like she used to right before she spanked me for talking back, long before I gave up on telling my truth at all.

"Why do you insist on being so bitter?" she asks.

My anger is a white-hot lightning strike coursing through me. "You need to leave. Right now."

Shock ripples through her, my command skipping like a rock across the surface of her body. "Eden, I am your mother."

"I don't know who you are right now." I shake my head vigorously, willing the memory of these last fifteen minutes to erase like drawings on the Etch-a-Sketch I played with as a child. The question I've avoided asking rises to the surface.

"How did you get here?" I ask her through gritted teeth.

"Mark drove us. He's staying in town at that motel." She says it the way a child admits to doing something they know they'll get in trouble for. I rip my hands away from where they've remained locked on the edge of the counter.

"Go. *Now.*" I march across the room and nearly rip the door off its hinges, holding it open for her to exit. She watches me fearfully, desperately pleading with her eyes and her folded hands.

When I don't waver, she slowly gathers her things into the suitcase she packed and walks through the doorway past my rigid body. Even as the rage rolls through me, a current of sorrow flows under the surface. I want to cut off my own arm as it points toward the direction she needs to go, down the stairs and away from me.

"Call him to come get you. I can't be near you right now," I tell her, the words opening wounds in my body I don't think will ever heal. She dials the phone, watching me the whole time she is speaking. The call is quick, and we remained locked in this standoff as the minutes tick by. When the familiar rumble of his truck meets my ears, I fight to keep a shiver from running through my body.

Mark parks at the end of the driveway, and I am grateful when he doesn't get out of the truck. My gaze flickers back to my mother, and I don't recognize the person in front of me. She sobs so violently that her shoulders tremble and snot pools underneath her nose. She reaches out for me, and I'm frozen in place, desperately wanting to be as far from her as possible while needing my mother's comfort more than anything else.

"You have to understand, baby," she whispers in my ear. "I didn't want to die alone."

When she pulls away, her cheek brushes against mine, leaving a wet spot on my skin. No tears of my own form to wash it away. I'm suspended in disbelief, my eyes dry as the scene plays out before me like a bad dream I'll awaken from any moment. She walks down the driveway, opening the back seat to toss her suitcase in before climbing into the front. I look away so I don't see him in the shadows.

I stay there, on the last step of my staircase, listening to the sound of his vehicle grow quieter. Her absence is a rock through the glass case around my heart. In the silence of the night, under the cover of darkness, the first sob shakes me to my core. It is the raindrop that precedes the torrential downpour, and soon I am crying so hard I can't breathe between the surges.

You hear people toss around the word *agony* from time to time. You think you know what it means, can imagine how it would feel. Until this moment, I would've told you I did, too. But the echoing in the chasm of my chest where my life-giving organs once were, the tremors of absolute anguish wrecking my body—*this* is true agony.

I don't know how long I've been here when Zoey's headlights wash over me. Her car lurches to a stop, and through the haze of tears I watch her feet hit the pavement, her door still hanging open as she closes the distance between us. Aaron steps out of her passenger seat at the same time her arms wrap around me. A wail rips through the night. It takes me a beat too long to realize the unfamiliar sound is coming from the depth of my lungs.

"Eden, what's happened? Where's Julie?" she asks, her voice distressed. Aaron blocks the light blinding both of us when he comes to a stop at the foot of the stairs. He searches my face and Zoey's, unsure what to do that could possibly help.

"She's staying with him," I tell her finally on a series of choppy breaths. "She's staying with Mark."

Chapter Twenty-Four

It takes both of them to lift me from my place on the staircase, and once I'm standing, Aaron scoops me into his arms while Zoey runs ahead. In the depths of my mind, there is a small piece of me embarrassed for him to see me like this, but so much of me is focused on surviving the pain overwhelming my body that that piece is unable to take hold. I inhale his expensive cologne, willing the fumes to put me under.

When he steps over the threshold, I catch a glimpse of Zoey quickly shoving a lump of gray fabric into the bottom drawer of my dresser. I'm lowered onto the love seat with a tenderness I'd never have guessed Aaron was capable of, his scent lingering on my shirt. He steps away from me to make room for Zoey, who kneels in front of me and peels the strings of tear-dampened hair away from my face.

"He drove her here," I cry. The sobs have subsided, and it's just a steady stream of tears flowing from my exhausted body. "She let him put that letter in my mailbox. She told me it happened because they weren't *fucking* enough and I was too pretty to resist!"

Her skin takes on a tinge of green that echoes the rolling in my gut, and Aaron reads enough of the context clues to curl a lip in disgust.

"How can she stay with him? After what he did to me?" I don't know if I'm asking Zoey or the supposed God who let this happen to me or the whole damn universe. I don't believe any of them actually have an answer.

As I suspected, Zoey shakes her head and presses her lips tightly together. Tears are brimming in her eyes, and she brushes them away with the hand that isn't holding on to me. "I don't know, Eden. I really don't."

Aaron watches over us with concern etched in the chiseled angles of his face. Zoey notices me looking at him and turns to follow my gaze.

"Aaron, I'm sorry, but I've got to stay here tonight," she tells him, her voice thick with unshed tears. He nods in understanding, then leans down to kiss her forehead. If that display of affection wasn't enough to surprise me, the matching one he presses into my hair definitely is. It's a side of him I never imagined existed, and I see him differently when he pulls away.

"That didn't seem very casual," I murmur. They exchange a look, Zoey shaking her head while scowling. Aaron winks at her, unbothered, before looking back at me.

"Feel better, Eden. I'm sorry for whatever you're going through." His words are unsure but comforting, nonetheless. "I'll have Chase come get me and bring me back to my car."

"Aaron—" I start to say. I must look as panicked as I feel, because he shakes his head softly.

"Your secret is safe with me," he replies to my unspoken request.

He closes the door behind himself, the breeze it creates ruffling the sheer curtain I added to cover the window beside it. Zoey climbs over me, into the minuscule space left behind me on the couch. She wraps her arm around my stomach and tucks her head into the curve of my neck, and we cry in unison, our weeping the saddest song I've ever heard.

Sleep comes in spurts, brief moments of agonizing consciousness broken up by a dreamless haze. Sometimes Zoey is there, insisting I eat or drink something she's brought me. Sometimes I am alone, and I'm not sure which is worse. Ella calls me several times, but I let them all go to voice mail. I wonder who told her, Zoey or my mother. She'd get very different versions from each.

Only now has the answer to Stephen's question come to me. I never called Mark *Dad* because I didn't truly see him that way. I couldn't possibly have, because the pain I feel now from my mother's betrayal is tenfold that which followed his. Probably because I could allow myself to hate him for it, and that loathing distracted me from my suffering. Even now, as my mind begs to be set free from this agony by hatred, I remain imprisoned by the love I still feel for her.

The sun has fallen low in the sky at the end of the longest day of my life, and Zoey is in front of me again with a sandwich and a bottle of water. She struggles to find an empty place to stack it amid her other untouched offerings on the coffee table. I watch a fly buzz excitedly from plate to plate, and I'm grateful someone is benefitting from all of this.

"I know you're upset, but you have to at least drink some water," she says. I reach out and grab the most recent addition, unscrewing the plastic cap and pressing the bottle to my chapped lips. She smiles at me, and I mirror her expression, though with decidedly less enthusiasm.

"Thank you for taking care of me," I tell her. My voice

croaks after hours spent bawling. "I know this is hard for you. You love her, too."

Growing up, when we weren't at her house, we were at mine. Her mother, though I love her dearly, is waspy and uptight. Nothing like the woman who raised me, willing to climb trees with us and throw dance parties and gossip about boys while our faces hardened under green clay masks. I know this is as much her loss as it is mine.

The corners of her lips turn down, a tremble shaking them ever so slightly. "I just don't understand how she could do this. To you. To herself."

"I don't either," I say. It's the one thing I keep coming back to. *Why am I not enough for her?* plays on repeat in my mind, like someone put all their nickels on that one track in the juke-box. "Could I have some Advil? My head is killing me."

She nods and leaves her spot beside me on the love seat to go rummage through my kitchen drawers. A knock at the door startles both of us. Our eyes lock and the same thought passes between us.

"I don't want to see her," I finally manage to force out.

The knock comes again, softer this time, and Zoey drops the pills into the palm of my hand before opening the door just wide enough to peek through. Her body blocks my view of who is on the other side, but a familiar deep voice releases the tension I'm holding in my spine.

"Now isn't really a great time," I hear Zoey whisper.

"It's okay, Zo," I tell her. Despite every protest in my head, my heart whispers that seeing him will make it all better. I have to at least give it a shot.

She looks back at me and then steps aside and pushes open the door. Chase is there, the setting sun casting him in a glow that is almost angelic. He's carrying two glass bottles in his hands, and the amusement I feel spreads a warmth throughout my chest that I never thought I'd experience again. That's how a pain like this feels: all-encompassing, like everything good is gone from the world.

A smile blooms across his face like the dawning of a new day, and I'm reassured that there is definitely still good in my life. That some of it is standing right in front of me.

"I brought lemonade," he offers with a shrug. "It's kind of my thing."

He holds a bottle out to Zoey, and she takes it with a smile. He looks over the plethora of uneaten food on the table and passes right by it, extending the other bottle directly to me.

"You're too kind," I mumble, the hint of a smile pulling at the edges of my lips.

"So, I've been told," he replies, searching my face for I don't know what. Reassurance, maybe? An explanation? I know how terrible I must look, and yet the blatant affection I can see in his eyes suggests he doesn't seem to care.

"God, what am I, chopped liver?" Zoey says, throwing an arm in the air in exasperation. "I've been trying to cheer her up all day, and you manage to do it in two seconds."

"What can I say?" he says over his shoulder with a smug look on his face. "I've got the magic touch."

"I don't want to know anything about your magic touch," she says in mock disgust.

Weak laughter bubbles up in my chest, and it's the lightest I've felt all day. Chase turns back to me, resting a strong hand on my thigh. Despite everything currently going on in my brain, heat spreads through me, sparked by the place where our bodies meet. We both look down at his tan hand pressed against the bare skin of my leg, and he pulls away while sucking in a quick breath.

"I know now is not a good time to finish our discussion," he begins. He looks from Zoey back to me as she suddenly becomes fascinated with the label on her lemonade bottle. "But Aaron just mentioned you were upset last night, and I wanted to at least try to make it better."

I nod my head almost imperceptibly, those damn tears I thought I'd run out of pressing behind my eyes again. He doesn't wait for an explanation, thankfully recognizing that I'm not in the best position to give one. Instead he leans toward me, slowly, to give me a chance to object. When I don't, he presses his lips tenderly against mine, his stubble abrading the sensitive skin of my face. He lingers for a moment before pulling away, locking his eyes with mine and making a silent promise to finish where he's leaving off.

"Thank you," I whisper. His eyes crinkle at the edges.

"Anytime," he replies. He stands and ducks his head to Zoey as he passes her, pulling the door shut behind him when he leaves.

Zoey turns to face me with her mouth so wide open I'm afraid she'll catch the fly that's hanging around.

"I'm sorry, *what?*" She jabs a thumb over her shoulder in the direction he left. "When did *that* happen? I mean, I knew you guys were into each other, but that didn't look like a first kiss to me!"

Heat crawls up my neck and incinerates my cheeks. She storms across the room and takes the seat Chase just vacated.

"Spill."

The look on her face is priceless as I tell her everything I've been neglecting to share. From the kiss we shared at the lake, to the night we danced in the bar, to our attempted rendezvous afterward and how I ruined it—and continued ruining it—until we finally started talking again after we both apologized. The whole time I am talking, I don't think Zoey's jaw ever leaves the floor.

"You mean you went on that hike with us knowing you were in the middle of giving each other the silent treatment?"

I nod, too embarrassed to say the words out loud. She tilts her head back in a fit of laughter, the light finally returning to her eyes.

"Girl, that is so awkward. And explains so much," she says between giggles. She finally sucks in a calming breath while I take a sip of lemonade. An unexpected bitterness hits the back of my tongue and I almost choke before forcing myself to swallow.

"That is not good," I manage to say, smacking my tongue against the roof of my mouth. Zoey takes a sip of mine and puckers her face.

"That's on whoever made it," she says decisively. "They didn't add enough sugar."

I wash the bitter flavor from my mouth with a gulp of water, mad at whoever's fault that was.

"Why didn't you tell me all of this sooner?" Zoey asks, handing me the bottle of lemonade Chase gave her. It's sweet and refreshing, the way it should be. "I tell you about all my hookups."

I don't know why the implication that it was just some hookup feels like she's cheapening what has happened between us, but my immediate reaction is a flash of irritation. A harsh laugh claws its way up my throat, and the words are spoken before I've cleared them with my filter.

"That's because your hookups are a dime a dozen." I regret the words as soon as they're out of my mouth, but they aren't on a fishing line that I can reel back in. The damage is done; I can see it on Zoey's face.

She stands and grabs the sweet lemonade back from where I sat it on the table, leaving the undrinkable one next to all her other untouched offerings. "Just because you're hurting doesn't mean you can be cruel."

She shuts the door behind her, and I'm alone once more. I take a sip of the tart beverage, knowing it's probably exactly what I deserve.

Chapter Twenty-Five

"What the actual *fuck* is wrong with her?"

It's the seventeenth F-bomb Ella has dropped in the thirty minutes we've been on this phone call. I have to focus on counting them to prevent myself from thinking too much about the conversation at hand. Plus I can't say I don't love hearing my innermost thoughts spoken aloud, with all the anger I won't allow myself to express.

"Is it some kind of fucked-up Stockholm syndrome thing?" she continues, ranting to no one in particular. I just happen to be on the other end of the call; it could be anyone at this point. "And what the fuck is wrong with that pastor to even suggest this is okay?"

Nineteen now. And she's got a very good point.

As it turns out, Ella got neither side of the story until I finally gathered up the energy to reach out this morning. Zoey just sent a text suggesting she needed to check on me, and when I didn't answer any of her calls, she tried our mother, whose phone is apparently turned off. The first five minutes of our phone call was just me painfully dragging word after word out of my brain, like trying to form a path by laying stone pavers. But the path leads somewhere you don't want to go. And every paver makes you cry.

"I'm so sorry, but I just pulled into work. I have to go," I tell her, regretting it even as I say the words. With my whole family imploding, everything in me screams to cling tightly to her so she can't slip away. Even the sound of her breathing on the other end of the call is a comfort. "I wish you were here."

The last words are a whisper, a quiet prayer.

"I do, too." I can hear it in her voice, how badly she wants to take this pain away from me. I rest my hands on the handle of my door, watching them tremble. This was just one of a few hard conversations I need to have today. Zoey's inside, waiting for an apology she is owed.

"I'll talk to you soon, El," I say, swallowing back the lump rising in my throat.

"You better," she replies with a quick huff of laughter. She clears her throat before adding, "I just want you to know that I'm here. I'm in your corner, and I'm not leaving. Okay?"

I nod even though she can't see me. Her words illuminate the darkest part of my fear, a lantern in a room I thought no light would ever reach again. "Okay."

The line severs with a soft *click*, and I'm left to put on my big-girl panties and go to work.

Zoey wipes a hand on her olive overalls, leaving freckles of dirt on the material. She tips her watering can over the unbridled ivy plant currently commandeering the wooden beam above the bar. I cough into a closed fist to get her attention. She looks over her shoulder at me, and I can tell by the curl of her lip when she sees me that I better get straight to the point.

"Hey, Zo," I start. My hands are folded together, hanging listlessly in front of me. "I need to tell you how sorry I am."

She harrumphs as if to say, *Obviously,* but leaves the floor open for me to continue. I walk over and brace the bottom of the ladder as she slowly climbs down.

"I had no right to say that about your, erm, relationships." I'm talking to her through the slats of the ladder steps, and she regards me thoughtfully, chewing on my words to decide if they taste genuine. "There's no excuse. It was just an asshole thing to say. And I'm sorry."

"You said that already," she points out, but the edges of her red-painted lips are curling up, and I know I'm forgiven.

She steps around the ladder, and I meet her halfway, throwing my arms around her narrow shoulders and squeezing her tight. I don't know how I can feel so lucky in the midst of all that has happened, but I know that I am, to have a friend like her.

She pulls back and plants a firm grip on both of my arms, demanding eye contact with her steady gaze. "Remember, just because the family you were born into has been shitty doesn't mean I will be. Blood might be thicker than water, but a choice is more powerful than both. And we chose each other. So you're stuck with me."

"That might be the most profound thing you've ever said," I tell her, laughing so I'm not tempted to cry.

"Every now and then, there's a nugget of gold in this river of rocks," she says with a wink, rapping her fist against her head.

"And that might be the most *Alabama* thing you've ever said," I reply. She covers up her nose in an attempt to hide her snort. I let out a relieved sigh and collapse my upper body across the counter.

"Okay, two out of three painful talks down. One more and I'm home-free."

Zoey steps up beside me and straddles a barstool, propping her head on her hand. "What were the other two?"

"I called Ella this morning and told her about Mom." My cheek is squished against the wooden countertop, making my voice sound like I'm chewing on something. Zoey's eyes grow wide, and she blows out a shrill whistle.

"How'd that go?"

"She said 'fuck' nineteen times," I say matter-of-factly. Zoey purses her lips like she's impressed.

"Honestly," she says. "Even that is probably not enough to do this situation justice. The man was getting off to child porn. Of his *daughter*. And now Julie's just going to brush that under the rug and stay married to him like none of it ever happened? And she expects you to just forget it, too? That's supremely *fucked. Up.*"

I stare at her, letting the words batter my ears. They sound so absolutely ridiculous that I almost can't believe it's my life she's describing.

"What are you going to do?" It's a gentle prodding, but a prodding nonetheless. My fingers drum an unsteady rhythm while I consider my answer.

"I honestly have no idea," I reply. I look away from her pitying expression, planting my forehead firmly against my forearm.

"Have you told Chase?"

She scratches her pointed nails up and down my back, soothing me like you would a baby. All I can do is groan. "That's the third conversation."

"Oh, come on, that's the easy one," she says, pinching my vulnerable side. I scoot away from her without ever looking up. "Chase is even easier to talk to than Aaron. You know he'll be understanding."

"I *do* know that, deep down," I admit. The sound of the door opening behind her is muffled by the next words that come out of my mouth. "I just feel like Stephen is the only man I've ever been able to truly talk to."

Feet shuffle on the floor, and I lift my head to follow the sound at the same time Zoey turns to look. Chase stands on the black-and-white tile of the entryway, seemingly unsure if he should move any closer. There's a look on his face that's so familiar to me, I'd be knocked off my feet if I weren't already sitting.

It's a potent mixture of anger and disappointment and just plain hurt, twisting his features into a heartbreaking expression. My mind spins in circles to find a possible source for that look of betrayal, a replica of the one from that morning on his front steps when I told him we'd be better off as friends.

"Stephen?" It's one word, but it's the final clue I need. My words echo back to me the way he would have heard them, and I jump to my feet with my hands outstretched, ready to explain. He looks from me to Zoey before pivoting on his heel and marching through the door, his long legs crossing the distance faster than I can close what existed between us.

"I really need to put a bell on that door," Zoey mutters as I race past her.

By the time I step out onto the street, he's nearly rounded the corner by Rose's shop. I curse under my breath and break out into an awkward jog, my legs wobbly from lack of practice. I finally catch up to him, grabbing his arm so he'll turn to face me at the foot of Gary's stairs.

"Is that what you've been so afraid to tell me? All this time?" The words are angrier than any I've heard from him before, causing me to recoil. He grabs a metal rung to brace himself, his jaw clenched so tightly the muscle twitches. His eyes go skyward like he can't even stand to look at me as he says the next part. "That there's someone else?"

Every inch of him is a taut wire, waiting to snap. Which is why I cover my lips in an effort to disguise my laughter. I don't know if it's nerves from the intensity of his presence or the mental image of Stephen popping into my head, but I'm hoping the shaking of my shoulders passes for crying.

"Are you laughing right now?" He sounds disgusted. "Eden, I really care about you; this isn't funny to me. All you had to do was tell me from the beginning so we didn't waste all this time. Instead you've been stringing me along like there's some big thing going on when it was just some other guy."

I bite a lip to ground myself before responding. He finally looks at me, his burning gaze falling to my lips. "Do you love him?"

The words knock the laughter right out of me along with my breath. Not for the reason that he's probably thinking, but because the emotion in his voice is so strong it leaves me wondering if *he* loves *me*.

I shake my head to dismiss the thought. He can't possibly love me; he doesn't even know me.

And whose fault is that?

He's still looking at me, waiting for some kind of explanation. The vein in his forehead looks close to bursting.

"Stephen's my therapist." It's the quickest way I know to diffuse the situation, and it works like a charm. He deflates like a popped balloon, and the anger and hurt are replaced by relief and confusion.

"*Oh*. What?" He crosses his arms over his chest but gestures for me to continue. I don't know what comes over me, but suddenly I want so desperately for him to know the truth that I don't have time to find the right way to articulate it. It tumbles out of me with about as much grace as a confetti cannon.

"Last December, my mom discovered a stash of nude photos my stepfather had taken of me over the years without our knowledge. It's why I moved out here. It's why I'm in therapy. With Stephen, who is very much not my type, by the way."

It's so unlike me to be this vulnerable, and I've been doing it so much today, that I immediately start shaking as the adrenaline drains from my body. I feel like an exposed nerve, and it's all too much too quickly. His eyes remain locked on mine, his lips pressed tightly together. I wish more than anything in this moment that I could read his mind—or crawl under a rock. Or both.

Instead I get the next best thing. He steps forward and encircles me in an embrace so tight that I'm unable to draw in a drop of air. One of his hands laces through the hair at the base of my neck, and the other holds me securely around the waist. I'm aware of the hard ridges of his chest against the rolling hills of my body, and I hear his breath hitch in his throat. For a moment it feels like he might be able to push all the shattered pieces of me back together. Like I could step away from this embrace whole once more.

Neither of us moves for a small eternity, and then finally he leans back enough to settle his warm hands on either side of my face. When I look into his eyes, they are dark as night and red around the edges, and so filled with sorrow that I have to force myself not to cry.

"God, Eden, I'm so sorry," he says, the rasp in his voice slicing through each word. "That never should've happened to you."

They are words I didn't know I needed to hear until they fell from the beautiful precipice of his lips. I'm trembling from head to toe, awash with a merciful sense of gratitude. And validation. My legs have no strength left in them, but I am held steady in the safety of his arms.

He presses his forehead to mine, and the heat of his body all around me combined with the calming scent of fresh pine trees stills the shaking within me. I lick my lips self-consciously, suddenly aware that we are two degrees shy of a kiss.

"Thank you for trusting me enough to tell me."

I imagined a lot of reactions when I thought about telling him what happened to me. Nervous avoidance of my perceived fragility. Righteous anger like you see in men on television. At times I even craved the latter, desperate for someone to want to go to war on my behalf. Ella and Zoey's shared fury flashes through my mind, and a phantom of a smile passes over my lips.

Chase takes that smile captive, drawing my lips tenderly to his. His hands cradle my face with reverence, holding me close as he presses deeper into me, the kind of kiss meant to take away my pain. He ignites a fire in the pit of my stomach, warming me from the inside out. That last fragment of fear, the one I barely would admit existed even to myself, is uncovered by the light. The one that told me he'd be disgusted if he knew the truth. The tip of his tongue gently explores the curve of my bottom lip, and I'm no longer afraid.

"Glad you two have made up, but I have a hot date with an Americano and kind of need to get past." Gary's voice bursts the bubble of magic we are trapped in, and I startle in embarrassment. He smirks, looking from Chase's face to mine. We step away from the foot of his stairs, stumbling over each other's feet. "Took you long enough."

The tone of his voice tells me he's talking about more than just us getting out of his way.

He slaps Chase on the back in congratulations before shuffling down the sidewalk and disappearing around the corner of the building. Chase throws his arms around me once more, scooping me up and swinging me around to the tune of me squealing, "Put me down!"

He finally sets me firmly back on the ground, poking my nose with his finger. The edges of his eyes crinkle, and a blinding smile spreads across his face.

"For the record, I think we are right on time."

Chapter Twenty-Six

I swing open my door to find Chase on the stoop, his flirtatious smile deepening the cleft in his chin. He's leaning against the railing nonchalantly, but he's dressed more formally than I've ever seen. That is to say, he's wearing jeans and a lightweight teal button-down with the sleeves rolled up. "Are you ready for the most romantic, first official date ever?"

"Am I underdressed?" I ask nervously, looking down at my cotton romper and sandals. "I could change."

"No need," he says, still grinning. I smirk at him but take his outstretched hand, allowing myself to be pulled out of my house. His truck is still running where he parked it in Zoey's usual spot.

"I do have to be at work later to run the evening shift. Zoey's taking the night off," I remind him. I clip my seat belt over my lap, smoothing out the tan fabric of my romper where it bunches. He shifts into reverse, watching the side mirrors as he replies.

"I haven't forgotten, you turn into a pumpkin at one o'clock."

He travels the opposite way than I'm used to, toward the outskirts of Loveless. We pass a behemoth of a brick building with black painted letters on the side reading *Loveless Tobacco Factory*.

"I bet that place would smell interesting if it burned down," I muse. Chase gives me a pointed stare filled with mock alarm.

"Is this how I find out you're secretly a pyro?" he asks warily.

My laughter stalls in my lungs when he rests his hand casually on top of mine where I've propped it on the center console. He strokes his thumb gently over each knuckle, then trails a fingertip down to my wrist until it finds purchase in the edge of my scar.

"How'd you get this?" His tone is still playful; he doesn't know he's striking a nerve. I study the planes of his face and swirls of dark hair defying whatever gel he tried to use to tame them. There's a freckle behind his ear I never noticed before. I get so lost exploring his features, I forget about the question for a moment. He clears his throat to remind me to answer, smirking when he catches me staring.

My gaze falls to that crescent moon of pale white scar tissue. I'm mesmerized by the rhythmic movement of his fingers tracing it back and forth.

"My mom put all the pictures she found in our fire pit. I burnt myself trying to grab one." The dark mood that arrives in the cab on the coattails of my words is exactly what I wanted to avoid. I try to pull my hand into my lap, but he captures it and holds me there.

I look back up at him as we pull to a stop at a red light. We're in a part of town I haven't been through before, mostly residential. Bungalow-style homes line the side streets that we pass, where small children draw hopscotch squares on the sidewalks, oblivious to the summer heat. He meets my gaze with a sympathetic smile, lifting our joined hands and pressing his lips against the tender skin on my wrist.

When our arms fall back to their resting place on the console, he continues driving forward like nothing has happened. But everything has.

"All my scars got covered up by tattoos," he jokes, dispersing the dark clouds with his sunlight smile. "Remember I told you I shattered my arm?"

He fills the rest of the drive with the story of how he managed to flip an ATV while off-roading in the mountains as a teenager. The Alpine Rescue Team had to get involved, and he got grounded for a month for being so reckless. Which didn't really matter, since he had several surgeries during that time to make sure he'd regain full functionality of his arm.

Looking at the sculpted muscle under the patchwork quilt of shadowed ink, I send the surgeons a silent *Thanks* for doing such a good job.

His voice trails off as we pull onto what looks like more of a grassy path than an official road of any kind. He shifts into park when the path dead ends at a wrought-iron gate joining together two faded brick walls. He smiles over at me tentatively, unbuckling his seat belt. "We're here."

I'm not certain exactly where *here* is until I catch a glimpse of headstones through the slats of the ornately welded gate. "You brought me to a cemetery?"

He takes my hand once I lower myself down from the truck and shuts my door for me before guiding me forward. As he deftly unravels the chain holding the gate closed, that shy smile returns, pulling at the corners of his lips. "Yeah, I wanted you to meet my dad."

A flutter begins low in my abdomen, spreading with every step we take. I don't know how to tell him how honored I am that he would show me such an intimate part of his life, so I just remain silent as we slowly pass row after row of monuments. A peaceful quiet has settled over the hallowed ground, reminding me of days spent with my mother visiting her parents' graves.

We slow to a stop in front of a rough-cut stone with a vase embedded in the grass before it. I recognize the disintegrating stems tucked inside as the bouquet of peonies his mother held in her hands that morning in his apartment. Their wedding flowers, she'd said. I can't imagine her pain, to bury the man she promised her future to and then to have to go on living that future without him. For a moment the depth of a love like that overwhelms me, leaving me unsteady on my feet.

Chase leans over and pulls the rotten flowers from the vase, dusting away the grass clippings sprayed over the top of the stone by the mowers. Through the warped lens of my unshed tears, I see *Hollis Taylor* inscribed on the face of the monument, but what catches my eye is the epitaph at the bottom.

"'*Live the best life you can while you're here,*'" I read aloud.

I look up at Chase, his white teeth standing out in stark contrast to his tanned skin as he smiles broadly down at me. I remember the words the way I heard them first, in his deep voice while he was sprawled out beside me on a rock warmed by the sun.

"It was his motto; now it's mine," he explains. I melt into his side, my head resting against his chest. His steady heartbeat thrums against my temple, so strong I have to remind myself that it was ever broken. "Trust me, he'd be honored that I plagiarized him."

"What was he like?" I ask.

Chase rests his chin in my hair, his breath ruffling the strands and sending chills down my spine.

"Imagine the Kool-Aid man, but in better shape." Chase

chuckles. "He had a booming voice that could fill the room. He told the dumbest jokes, but they always made you laugh because they were so unexpected. He was always up for an adventure. He thought the whole world revolved around my mom and me. He held me to a higher standard than I held myself, and it made me a better person."

Listening to him, I'm ashamed to find that above all other emotions, the one I'm overcome with is jealousy. I envy Chase that he gets to grieve his father, knowing what a wonderful man he was and having fond memories to run to when he's missing him terribly. It would've been so much easier to mourn Mark than to carry this knowledge around with me, each good memory turned sour by the revelation of his sins.

I know how horrible it is to wish that he'd died instead. But the wish is still there, no matter how bad I feel for having it.

"Well, that's enough sadness for today, don't you think?" Chase says, rescuing me from my pity party. He places a firm kiss on the top of my head, inhaling deeply before pulling back to look down at me. "Ready to re-meet my mom?"

We're only in the car for ten minutes or so when we pull into a café on the edge of the residential neighborhood. It's a house, too—or at least it used to be. It's painted robin's-egg blue with a bright yellow door and the name *Yellow Submarine* hanging on a banner above the porch. There's a wooden swing hanging by four chains at the edge of the porch, and on it sits a woman wearing a sundress just as vibrant as the restaurant. It's almost like she's part of the decor.

Her brunette hair is streaked with gray and swooped into a chiffon bun. It isn't until she pulls her sunglasses away from her face and I see those amber eyes with familiar crinkles at the edges that I realize it's Chase's mom sitting there.

She jumps up from her place on the swing, and it falls away from her in surprise. Her sundress flutters behind her as she closes the gap between us, squealing and throwing her arms around Chase beside me. If it weren't for those eyes, I might not even recognize this as the same woman who stood in his living room, clothed in black and sadness.

When she's done squeezing him, she sets her sights on me. I feel bad for the hesitation I see pass over her face, knowing I'm responsible for it. Her only impression of me was the skittish woman in pajamas that ran out the door in a panic. I inhale a deep breath to settle the nerves in my chest, then reach for her first to show I'm capable of being friendly. Relief washes over her just as our arms close around one another, and she gives me three solid squeezes the same way she did Chase.

"So good to see you again, Eden," she says, her voice warm and rich like a fresh baked brownie.

"Nice to see you, too, Laura," I reply, but my words are drowned out by Chase's correction.

"No, Mom, remember, this is the first time you're meeting her," Chase says theatrically, winking at her while playfully nudging me. She slaps his chest and *pffts* at him, looking at me like we're both in on the joke.

"Nonsense, Eden and I are already the best of friends. After all, look how happy she's made my son," she says while throwing a conspiratorial smirk my way.

I blush under the spotlight of her praise, and I know immediately what Chase meant about his mom. This woman is no burden, and I'm embarrassed I ever likened her to one. Standing here in her dramatic floral dress and perfectly coiffed hair, his mother isn't just radiant, she's Technicolor.

For a moment she reminds me so strongly of my own mom

203

that I feel the pull of my despair. Before all the tragedy, Mama was like this. Bright and nonsensical and always happy. My heart twinges when I think of how much they would've liked each other, the thought like a dark vignette around this otherwise perfect picture.

"Forgive me if I'm too much. Chase would never let me meet his girlfriends before. You must be something special," she says.

I raise my eyebrows at Chase, mouthing, *Girlfriend?*

He rolls his eyes at both of us. "What can I say? I grew up in the shadow of the *Hollis and Laura Love Story*. Didn't want to bring anyone home till I had one to rival it."

He hooks an arm around his mother's neck and kisses the top of her head while I remain utterly speechless.

"Well, enough of that. Who's starving? I know I am!" she says, turning and gliding up the porch steps to the café. The smell of fresh baked bread wafts out on the breeze, and suddenly the pun of the name makes sense to me.

I look up at the banner and then over at Chase, who's grinning at me again. He's doing that a lot lately. "It's a yellow *sub*marine, get it?" I say, jabbing him in the ribs.

He takes a moment to process what I've said, and then his eyes roll back in his head, "*Oh God*, what a terrible pun. My dad would've loved that joke. I always just assumed they were big Beatles fans."

"Have you not eaten here before?" I ask in surprise as we follow his mom inside. He holds the door open for me, letting me approach the glass display case first. My mouth waters as I scan the selection of homemade hoagie buns, the source of that delectable aroma.

"Eden, please," he replies, pinching my shoulders from behind to release the tension. He touches me so easily, like we've belonged to one another for a lifetime. "I only ever eat at the bar."

I catch his mother admiring the two of us together out of the corner of my eye, a glint of appreciation and something like a memory passing over her watchful gaze.

Chapter Twenty-Seven

Maddie's voice is the background music to the staring contest Chase and I are competing in. His dark eyebrows pull together to admonish me for not paying attention to her, or to question why I can't tear my eyes away from him, but either way it does nothing to sway me. I'm too busy admiring the thick layer of stubble sharpening his already firm jawline. Even after several days of enjoying my newfound freedom to check him out whenever I feel so inclined, it's still all I want to do.

"Eden? Are you even listening to me?" Her annoyed tone and admittedly effective way of whining my name finally breaks me out of my trance. I turn to look at her and she rolls her eyes, dropping the black lock of hair she's twirling. It's the third phase her hair has been through since I've met her, and a marked improvement over the magenta she sported for the past month. It works in conjunction with the sticker-style tattoo sleeve and multiple piercings to complete her edgy vibe.

"I'm sorry, what was the last thing you said?" I ask innocently, trying to play it off like I spaced for a moment. She groans and slams the dishwasher door shut with a little more force than is necessary.

There's a swoosh as water begins filling the bottom of the appliance. Satisfied, she wipes her hands on a nearby rag. "First of all, I'm happy you two have finally worked things out because the sexual tension was honestly a little distracting for those of us trying to work around here."

I choke on the sip of water I just swallowed, color filling my cheeks as I try to recover. Amusement turns Chase's eyes the color of a Werther's Original.

"Second, that's no excuse to be rude. Active listening is an important skill; they taught it in my speech course," she says.

"Maddie, what are you majoring in?" Chase asks. He shovels a handful of fries into his mouth as he waits for her answer.

"Finance, I thought you knew that?" she asks incredulously. Chase looks pointedly at me. The flames spread across my entire face, knowing he's calling out my tendency to write Maddie off as an airhead.

His eyes quickly flick back to her with a satisfied smile as he says, "Oh, I did."

"Anyway, I was saying Camille and I are going to a music festival next weekend, so I need someone to cover my shifts." The smug expression drops from Chase's face as we're both reminded where my preconceived notions about her derive from.

"That's kind of last minute," I say suggestively, hoping she'll get the hint.

"Yeah, she gave me the tickets for my birthday a few weeks ago, and I kept meaning to mention it. Sorry about that!" Her voice is flippant, my words flying right over her head. I hope she's not going for a career in financial planning. "Oh! Eden, isn't your birthday in, like, a week or two?"

207

Chase's eyebrows shoot up, nearly touching the brim of his black baseball cap. I shake my head at him, warning that it's not a big deal while I reply to her. "It's the fourth."

"Of July?" he asks with an excited grin at the same time it dawns on Maddie, and she says, "That's next weekend!"

"Of July," I reply flatly, ignoring her revelation. "Don't get any ideas."

"Yeah, Zoey already has all the ideas, and she's not sharing," Santi adds from behind Maddie and me, the shock of fear from being startled leaving my fingertips buzzing. "Shawn's here with the delivery."

He passes the invoice to me and then hangs his apron on the bar, taking his daily thirty-minute trip to the bathroom between the lunch and dinner rush. Maddie presses her finger against her nose. "Not it."

Chase sits up straighter, his spine now rigid. "Relax, macho man, I'll be fine," I warn him, holding my hand out to show I've got it. "Be right back."

Nervous energy is still crackling off him as I pass Maddie and head back into the kitchen. Shawn waddles out of the cooler, drenched in sweat while rolling an empty barrel toward the delivery door on his dolly. I scoot a box of bananas over until the edge holds the heavy insulated door open so I can step inside. I'm nearly finished verifying the number of replacements matches the invoice when Shawn rolls the dolly back over the cold steel floors.

I retreat farther into the cooler to give him clearance to grab the last empty keg. Even with a foot of space between us, the smell of sour beer pours off him and stings my nose. I involuntarily grimace, and he catches the movement with his glazed-over eyes. He lets go of the barrel, leaning against it instead. His stocky frame fills the space between me and the exit, leaving me stuck in this uncomfortable position. Goose bumps pucker on the skin of my forearms like apprehensive hackles raised on a cornered animal.

"What's that look for?" he slurs, all the words blurring into one. It suddenly occurs to me that the smell is not an occupational hazard, but a direct result of something he's been drinking. I'm not exactly a fan of Shawn's, but until now I've never been more than just a little wary of him. My senses immediately go on high alert. If I've learned anything from working in bars, it's that drunk people are unpredictable. And an unpredictable man is a dangerous one.

I've taken too long to answer, and he stumbles toward me, pressing me deeper into the cooler. I'm backed up against the wall, and I flinch away from him. Fear spreads through me like ice, and I'm frozen in place. He grabs hold of a lock of hair that's fallen from my loose ponytail. Nerves tighten their vise grip on my lungs, preventing any breath from entering. I press my shaking hands against the metal wall to hold myself steady.

"I've always wondered," he mumbles around the wad of chewing tobacco protruding from his lip, "if the carpet matches the drapes."

My scream is stuck behind the concrete barrier of panic blockading my throat, disgust curdling the contents of my stomach. I try to discreetly peek around him into the kitchen, desperate for Santi to hurry it up. He follows my gaze and squares his shoulders to block my view.

"Why're you so uptight?" Shawn whispers hatefully, his rancid breath dampening my face with condensation. He's so close I can count the pockmarks that long-ago acne carved out of his cheeks. A meaty hand grabs my arm too tightly, causing a yelp to break free from my mouth. "I could loosen you up."

"What the fuck do you think you're doing?"

Shawn's lazy eyes sharpen into focus, and he drops my arm quickly, whipping around to confront a seething Chase. Every vein in Chase's body throbs to the surface, and he flashes a quick look at me to assess the damage before training his withering glare back on Shawn. I half expect the smell of urine to join the stale stench of beer with the way the portly man is shaking in his boots.

"Hey, man, we were just playing around. No need to get all upset." His tone is trying to sound casual, but there's a tightness beneath his loose-flowing words that betrays his nerves.

"Hey, *man*," Chase mocks, towering over Shawn as he takes another step closer. "I suggest you get as far away from here as fast as you can, before you need an ambulance to drive you."

He steps aside to let Shawn escape with his tail between his legs just as Santi traipses back into the kitchen, humming a tune under his breath. The melody falls silent as he assesses what he's walked into, meeting Chase's eyes and seeing something there that makes him quickly pull the delivery door shut and arm the alarm.

I inhale my first full breath in what feels like an eternity when Chase pulls me against him and hauls me out of the cooler. I'm shivering, either from fear or the cold, and he rubs my back to warm me as his eyes travel over my body with concern. "Did he hurt you?" he asks, anger broiling beneath his worried question. He's staring at the bruise that's already blooming on my bicep.

I shake my head, trying to put on a brave face and failing. My mind is both racing and paralyzed, and I'm wondering how that can be. I ping-pong across the table between *Why does this shit always have to happen to me?* and *It really wasn't that bad, Eden.*

"Do you want to get out of here?" Chase asks.

I swallow over the thick tears coating my throat. I'm seconds away from descending into a breakdown, and all I can manage is a quiet, "Yeah," while staring at the wall behind him in an attempt to steady myself. He exchanges a quick look with Santi, who nods in return, his lips set in a grim line; then he presses his hand gently against my lower back to guide me forward. He shields me as best he can from the prying eyes of the few patrons at the bar, and he doesn't let me go until we've made it to our destination.

His apartment looks exactly as I remember it, different T-shirts in the same position scattered across the floor. I tell him I just need a moment to myself. I step into his bedroom while he sits down on the leather couch. Far enough to give me space, close enough to keep me safe.

I go to the bathroom and purposefully avoid looking at my reflection until I have no choice as I wash my hands. The girl in front of me is pale and rattled, my ponytail barely hanging on to a few remaining strands of hair. There's a deep purple bruise in the shape of a hand gripping me just above my elbow.

A sickening feeling overwhelms me slowly, creeping from my hands and feet inward. That familiar panic climbs hot and steady up the ladder of my spine, and I look away from the mirror to try and tamp it down. I focus on the cool granite countertop underneath my clammy hands. I listen to the steady dripping of the faucet. I taste the metallic blood spilling into my mouth from biting down too hard on my bottom lip.

A bottle of pine-scented body wash on the shelf behind the porcelain claw-foot tub catches my eye. I take three unsteady steps across the room and grab for the soap, hoping the smell will bring me back from the brink. I pour it out onto my hand and drop the bottle in the tub, scrubbing the soap desperately against my bruised arm to wash away Shawn's filthy touch.

"Eden? Are you all right?" Chase's words follow two soft raps against the bathroom door. A sob rips its way out of my throat as waves of fear wash over me. For the first time I notice the gap under the door, with no towel stuffed against it.

How could I be so careless? *He can see me.*

I grab a striped towel from where it's tossed over the drying rack and kneel on the ground to block myself in. Rivulets of soap run down my arm. I'm crying in earnest now, little hiccups rattling my chest.

Those quiet knocks happen again. This time I'm right on the other side of the door. Fear and reason are at war within me, and reason is getting ready to wave a white flag.

"Eden, you're safe here. Just let me in. Let me take care of you," he says, his voice muffled by all my barriers. I press a slick hand against the wooden door, willing myself to be brave. *I want to let you in,* I want to tell him. *I just don't know how.*

"Eden," he says again, his voice like a metronome to my uneven whimpering. "Do you trust me?"

His words land like a lifesaving ring into the ocean I'm drowning in. I don't have a clue how the hell to swim, but I grab on. I open the door.

Chase steps over the piled-up towel and joins me on the floor, gathering me against him. He rocks me steadily like a mother would a fussy child. When he feels the slick residue of soap all over my arms, he pulls back to look at me, and all I can manage to say is, "I want him off me."

His eyes are as dark as night as he captures my gaze and holds it, a strong hand cradling my tear-soaked chin. "Do you trust me?" he repeats.

I nod my head because I realize I do. I trust him intrinsically, here on the other side of my walls. It feels in a way like my heart has always known it, and my brain is finally catching up.

He leans over and turns on the faucet to the tub, steam billowing out from the water as it fills. He turns to face me, pulling his shirt over his head and then unbuttoning his pants. Between each movement he pauses, giving me space to object.

When I don't, he strips down to his underwear, then reaches behind me and turns off the lights.

I expect to be lost in darkness, but a swath of blue light filters in through a small stained-glass window I didn't notice perched high above the tub. It blurs the edges of the details, but I can still see the outline of his body in front of me. He reaches out a hand to lift me off the floor, and when I stand before him, he runs his fingertips gently under the hem of my shirt, a question in the subtle shine of his eyes.

I close my hands around his and pull them up, letting go when he tugs the fabric over my head. Steam is filling the room around us, and coupled with the warmth spreading through my body, my trembling finally subsides. He unbuttons my shorts and slides them over my hips. They fall to a puddle at my feet, just as he leans forward to press a kiss against my forehead.

I reach between my shoulder blades and unclip my bra, letting it join my shorts on the floor. I've never felt more present, more grounded, than I do the moment his rough hands slide under the waistband of my underwear and push them slowly down my legs. They are joined on the floor by his boxers in a quick swish of fabric.

When we are both bare to one another, he takes my hand in the twilight of the room and pulls me with him into the water. He settles his back against the porcelain tub and cradles me in front of him, every inch of our bodies pressed against one another with no shame left to separate us. I wait for some type of apprehension to come for me, but it never does. He grabs his soap and fills a dampened loofah with it, reverently exploring the topography of my skin.

"Do you want to talk about it?" he asks. His words are punctuated by the slow drip of water as he lifts the loofah to brush softly over the sensitive bruise on my arm. I shudder against him, and his other arm around my waist tightens. "I know it's hard, but you keep so much inside. Maybe it would help to let some of it out."

My head is resting against his chest, eyes trained on the dust particles swirling in the spotlight of the window. I'm suddenly so tired, exhausted from the effort of holding it all in. My trembling hand clenches around his thigh, as if the secrets are my only anchor, and without them I'll float away.

"Shawn is insignificant," I say, and I mean it. In the grand scheme of what has happened to me, this is a blip. An outtake. A minor plot line to my greater tragedy. "I just wonder when the universe will run out of blows to deal me."

He drags the loofah across my collarbones, a thoughtful hum sounding in the back of his throat.

"He took so much from me." I choke on the lump in my throat. Shawn is gone from my thoughts. The real monster has reared his ugly head. "He took my family, my home, my body. I have nothing left to give."

"You have everything to give, Eden." He says it firmly, the words whispered right into my ear. "You have rebuilt your life from scratch, and it's all yours. He can't take that. He'll never see you again. He can't hurt you anymore; I won't let him. I won't let anyone."

He growls the last part, and I know it's true. I can still see his pulsing anger as he stared Shawn down. The only hesitation he showed was refraining from killing the man, which I could see in his eyes that he desperately wanted to do. On the other side of that coin is the gentle man who holds me now. He never takes more than I'm willing to give. Even with me naked in his arms, he awaits permission before each touch. My body feels like it belongs to me for the first time in months.

"Why the bath?" I ask, watching a particularly large piece of dust flutter and dance in the light. I feel the swell of his cheeks as he smiles.

"My mom used to babysit the neighbor's kids when I still lived at home. She always said when a baby is upset, you take them outside or put them in water. It worked every time."

"Are you saying I'm a baby?" I ask incredulously, turning to look up at him. His eyelashes are so dark and long, fanning out beyond his cheekbones.

"No," he says, holding the loofah over my head so water dribbles in my face. I sputter as it flows onto my lips. "But anytime I'm having a bad day, I go for a hike or I take a shower, and the concept still stands. I figured it would for you, too."

He returns to his rhythmic washing, swirling the pine-scented suds over my knees. "Thank you for trusting me, Eden."

The light turns from blue to the gray of evening as the bath grows lukewarm around us. Still, he holds me against him. He sets aside the loofah, replacing it with the gentle kisses he trails along my shoulders as he breathes quiet words of admiration into my sensitive skin. "You are the most incredible woman I've ever met," he whispers. *Kiss.*

"So unbelievably brave." *Kiss.*

"I'm falling in love with you, Eden."

I tip my head back and steal his next kiss for myself, covering the perfect cupid's bow of his lips. I let my head fall into the curve of his neck, his rough stubble scraping against my skin. Three words, I tell myself. It's just three words. I can do it. With him holding me like this, I can do anything.

"I love you," I say, my lips brushing over his pulse point. His heartbeat grows erratic, a guttural groan of relief sounding at the back of his throat.

"You have no idea how good it feels to hear you say that," he says.

Oh, but I do.

"Thank you for what you did today," I say.

The words carry more weight than either of us probably

realize, but I pray that he understands what I mean. Because I'm not just referring to him standing up for me with Shawn and preventing something horrible from happening. I'm not even thanking him for telling me he loves me, but for showing me. For stepping into the mess of my panic with me and staying to wash us both clean.

Chapter Twenty-Eight

The next day I spend so long trying to catch Stephen up on the events of the last two weeks that there's no time to even think about finishing my narrative. My vocal cords are raw from the circles I've been talking in by the time he pipes up with his first question since, "How are you today?"

"Did this man suffer any repercussions?" he asks with about as much frustration as he's ever exhibited in front of me. While I usually appreciate his levelheaded approach to all things, I have to admit there's a small part of me that revels in the fact that he's even remotely upset on my behalf.

"Zoey called his company, and they told us he'd be fired and we'd get a new delivery driver," I explain. He shakes his head in mild disbelief before the therapist hat goes back on.

"Eden, did it ever occur to you to call the police?" There's no judgment in his voice, just a clinical curiosity that usually indicates there's a lesson to be learned there, somewhere.

I rack my brain for a moment, replaying the events and trying to filter through my panicked thought process. There's a tug at the edge of my mind like a child pulling on a teacher's shirt, insisting it knows the right answer. I shoo it away.

"I guess I just didn't realize it was an option," I say finally. "I didn't think the crime was severe enough, or even know if it was in fact a crime."

He watches me carefully, calculating his response. This is usually the part where we arrive at the water he's trying to get me, the proverbial horse, to drink. "Can we circle back to your mother for a second?"

I shift uncomfortably in my dining chair, waiting to see where this is going. I managed to give him a quick synopsis of her visit without shedding a single tear, and I was really hoping to hit a two-game winning streak on not crying in my therapy sessions.

"Have the two of you spoken since she left?" he asks, a gel pen poised above his notebook.

I study my cuticles while I deliver my response. "No, she hasn't reached out."

Truth be told, I'm not sure whether to be hurt by or grateful for her radio silence. On one hand, I secretly hope for her to send a message saying it was all some cruel joke, that of course she's not staying with him. On the other, the reality that this is a moment that we can't come back from, not the same as we were before, sits like a stone in my gut. For as long as we don't talk about it, no further decisions have to be made.

In those first hazy days after Christmas, I remember looking at my life in two parts. There was the *before* and the *after*. The moment life as I knew it had ended lay like a line drawn in the sand, with everything good before it, and nothing but a bleak unknown to follow. I didn't know how to navigate this new reality, so for months I just didn't even try. Moving to Colorado was the first big step I took to regain control of my future.

My mother's decision to stay married to Mark feels like another line, an impassible one. I can't imagine another day on this earth without the woman who brought me into it. I also can't fathom spending another second in her presence knowing who she goes home to at the end of the day. Knowing the same eyes that violated the sacred trust of a child in their parent, the same hands that held the shirt up above my sleeping body and snapped a photo, will be the eyes she gazes into over every dinner, the hands she holds as they curl close on the couch each night.

I think of the way Chase didn't hesitate for a second as he stared Shawn down, barely contained rage boiling underneath his skin. In the same flash of memory, I see my mother's eyes trained on our rearview mirror, even as she drove us away to what I thought would be safety. I didn't understand it then, the regret filling her expression. I'd assumed it was a response to having trusted the man behind us in the first place, not for leaving him behind.

When Chase walked me away from the bar, and for the rest of the night onward, all he could look at was me.

The question I've neglected for so long, scared to know the answer it would garner, bubbles to the surface of my lips. "I just don't get it," I manage to say through the vise grip my pitiful excuse for anger has on my throat. "I can't wrap my head around it. She raised me, she's supposed to love me more than anything —or anyone—else in the world. Why would she choose him over me? Why couldn't she stand up for me? I *want* to understand, I do."

He chews on the inside of his cheek for a moment, the regrowth of his facial hair sparkling in the light of his office. I watch his eyes flicker to that photo of him standing proudly next to his graduating child. A traitor tear trails down my cheek, too far gone to be contained.

"Eden, the short answer is, I truly don't know how she came to this decision." Something like sorrow colors his otherwise neutral tone. "What I *do* know is that people can't stand up for others when they are unwilling, or unable, to even stand up for themselves."

The simple truth of his statement settles over me. I imagine the million and one times in my life that I've watched my mother shoulder someone else's blame, stay quiet in the face of a false accusation, accept the offered truth without question that her first husband had to be shitty so God could give her a second husband that was the kind of man she deserved. Every remembered moment reinforces the validity of this fact: my mother cannot see that she's disrespecting my worth when she lets her own be ignored every day.

"So where do I go from here?" I ask, desperately hoping that for once he can give me a clear direction instead of a compass and a map to figure it out. "How do I move forward from this?"

"No one can decide that but you," he says. I sigh. Another damn atlas to add to my collection. "You have to decide what you're willing to tolerate and create a firm boundary to protect that decision. *You* have to be willing to stand up for *yourself*, or else the cycle will only continue."

My head bobs up and down, a buoy on the ocean of my thoughts. Growing up, I always thought I'd become a mother someday. I love my nephews and I'm fairly good with children after years spent aiding in the nursery at my mother's church. I figured when I finally found the right person, it would just happen naturally if it was meant to. But from the moment this all came to light, the fear that I could choose someone as the father of my children thinking they were wonderful, only to be surprised with an awful truth the way my mother had been, caused my decision to waver.

It never occurred to me in that recalculation that I, too, could be the one to damage my kids, simply by not valuing myself enough.

"You don't have to make your decision today, or on any timeline in general. Take the time to choose what feels right for you. I'll be here when you're ready to help you decide what healthy boundaries look like for whatever path forward you take."

His kindness beyond a clinical obligation threads through every word. I let myself wonder for a moment how so many people—Stephen, Zoey, Chase, even Gary—can care for me so well without sharing any familial ties when my own parents couldn't manage to do it. It's like Zoey said, a choice is more powerful than any blood. I thank my lucky stars that these people have chosen me.

"I'll be sure to let you know," I tell him with a faint smile. He scribbles something on the notepad resting in his lap, and for once I let my curiosity get the better of me. "Can I ask what it is that you write in there?"

He looks up at me over the wire rim of his glasses, pushing them up from where they've fallen down the bridge of his nose. The corners of his mouth twitch upward as he lays his pen to rest.

"It's a list of every bit of progress you make, any break-throughs you have. I keep it for all my clients. Everything from the first time you mentioned what had happened to you outside of me reading it on your intake form, to you seeking help to find a way to be vulnerable with Chase. All of it is a step forward." His voice trails off, letting his words take hold in my brain.

"Baby steps," I say. It's the only luggage that my stunned train of thought can deliver to my tongue. All the subtle insults I threw at myself over the months with the mental game I played suddenly go flying out the window.

"Baby steps," he agrees, closing the notebook to let me know my work is done for the day.

Chapter Twenty-Nine

My eyelids are stiff with resistance, begging me to let them close. Despite the fact that I'm definitely sleeping better lately, I'll never be a morning person. I've spent too many years working late-night events and tucking drunk people into cabs after last call to see being awake with the sunrise as anything but a nuisance.

I tie my long-neglected running shoes onto my feet, imagining how Stephen will write about this breakthrough in his notebook. *Began running again, something she's loved all her life.* The thought makes a sleepy grin stretch across my lips. My internal monologue is much kinder today. For that, I am grateful.

My feet hit the pavement just as tendrils of sunlight begin spilling over the mountain range onto the town. Aside from the low thrum of early morning commuters and the slap of my shoes, not much else disturbs the quiet that has settled around me. I chose to forego my headphones this time, wanting my first run in half a year to contain little in the way of distractions.

I focus on the steady pattern of my breathing, the strain of underutilized muscles in my legs. Weaving throughout the neighborhood and beyond, I pass dog walkers and a few other joggers. I try not to let my gaze linger on the ease with which they move at a much faster pace than me. It's like my high school coach told me after I finally returned to cross-country from a monthlong bout of mono: *Today, don't focus on being better than anyone but yourself.*

Sweat is pooling in every nook and cranny it can find when I finally give in to the screaming coming from my lungs and calves. I slow to a stop just shy of 8th & Main Roasters, leaning forward to grab my toes and curl them upward. Every muscle running the length of the backs of my legs breathes a sigh of relief when I finish stretching. I stand with my hands on my hips, red-faced and proud of myself.

A major benefit to forcing my sleep-drunk body out of bed this early presents itself: there is no line for one of Rose's coffees. *Or pastries*, my growling stomach would like to add. My birthday isn't for two more days, but I tell myself an early treat never hurt anybody. Besides, I've earned it.

I step into the tranquil shop, warm from the ovens and filled with the heady scent of cinnamon and espresso. The top of her assistant manager Jessie's head is just visible through the window into their kitchen, but otherwise there's no sign of life. I take a moment to scan the walls, looking over the intricate mosaic tile that borders the top of the batten board, which is painted the same color as my coffee after I add three teaspoons of creamer. My eyes are drawn higher until I'm looking skyward at the giant white chandelier hanging from the middle of the ceiling, each LED light a floral chute coming off the center.

"You're up early!" Rose says, interrupting my mental tour of the place. I'm often in such a rush as I pass through here that I've never taken the time to appreciate how beautifully deco-rated it is. I let my gaze fall to meet hers and notice a second pair of eyes staring back at me.

"Yeah, I decided to go for a run," I say casually, though for me it feels like I'm sharing that I climbed Mount Everest. The simple act of reclaiming something so important to me fills me with crackling energy, like I've got a mouthful of self-improvement Pop Rocks.

"Good for you," she says without even a hint of sarcasm. Cleo, however, pouts at me, big hazel eyes unimpressed by my accomplishment. "Can I get you anything?"

She bounces the baby on her hip absentmindedly while she waits for my response. She must notice my eyes flickering between the two of them because she adds, "Little Bit is just hanging out with me until Mitchell can come pick her up. Don't worry, no spit up has made it into the muffins."

I smile at her and shake my head, "Oh, I wasn't worried about... I'm sorry." I reach across the counter to pinch the thick roll of Cleo's thigh. "I just love seeing the two of you together, that's all."

My words coax out that dimple in Rose's cheek. She smooths the growing fuzz of hair back from Cleo's face, which is as close to happy as I've ever seen it be when aimed my way.

"I was just going to get a mocha if you don't mind." I hate to bother her when she's got the baby, but my mouth is watering with all the smells swirling around me. Not to mention my spine is pulling my belly button inward following that run on an empty stomach. "And what the hell, I'll get the chocolate muffin, too. It's almost my birthday anyway."

I say the last part mostly as an excuse to myself, but Rose perks up as she pops the muffin into the warming oven. "Oh, I know. I can't wait! Jessie's manning the store for me tomorrow so I can help Zoey with everything."

One of my eyebrows nearly hits the roof, and Rose begins backtracking to save herself. "Just pretend I didn't say any of that."

"I will feign absolute surprise," I promise, wondering what Zoey could possibly have planned. She knows birthday parties are not my thing.

Cleo tugs at the strand of her mother's hair she has snagged with her tiny fist, causing a wince to pass over Rose's face in conjunction with the grateful smile she sends my way. She slides my coffee across the counter, steam rising from its travel lid. Just as I've tapped my watch against the payment terminal, Jessie calls out for Rose's help from the back.

She looks over her shoulder through the kitchen window and then back at Cleo, unsure how to proceed. Her eyes level on me just as I'm popping a piece of my gooey muffin into my mouth. "Do you mind?" she asks, grabbing Cleo and holding her out to me.

Jessie hollers again in the time it takes me to process her request. I give a panicked nod and dust the muffin crumbs off on my leggings before reaching across the counter. Cleo watches me warily as I grab her and pull her to my hip. She turns to watch just as her mom disappears into the kitchen.

I half expect her to burst into tears. After all, she doesn't seem to be my biggest fan. To my surprise, she bobs her little head over and leans back, looking up at me with more curiosity than annoyance. I'm suddenly self-conscious that I probably stink, and then remind myself that she's a baby and I don't need to impress her.

She chatters mindlessly with such determination I'm certain she actually thinks she's telling me something important. Probably to wear more deodorant next time. "Why don't you tell me all about it?" I ask her playfully.

It's the same phrase my mom always used to start conversations with my nephews when they were infants. I'm reminded that just like Cleo's big hazel eyes are an echo of Rose's, Mama is woven into the very fabric of who I am.

I grab one of Cleo's chubby hands and pretend to eat each finger, a go-to move to get the kids laughing. She just stares at me, eyebrows furrowed, as if this childish game is beneath her. "Wow, tough crowd," I tell her.

"Don't worry, she's just picky," Rose tells me, returning to her place behind the counter with an additional dusting of flour across her right cheek. I gesture to wipe it off, and she grabs a paper towel while nodding her thanks.

I bounce Cleo against me, pinching a cheek more delicious than the muffin in an attempt to win her over to me. "How old is she?" I ask, not looking away from her stone-cold stare.

"She'll be seven months here soon. She was born on Christmas."

My rocking stills, and I watch her thoughtfully. The thought occurs to me that I can measure the time that has passed since my world unraveled in the life of this little girl.

"I was born on Independence Day," I offer her. "We're both holiday babies."

A miracle of a smile turns her scrumptious cheeks into rosy rolls of fat, and an amused giggle fills the air between us like music. Pride swells in my chest, and Rose exchanges a surprised look with me over this accomplishment.

"Well, I'll be damned. She likes you," Rose says happily. "Jokes on you, now you're on the list of people to call when I need a babysitter. It's a *very* short list."

I pass Cleo back to her mother, watching as she folds easily into the curve of Rose's side. Her head falls against Rose's shoulder, and she brings a thumb up to her mouth to suckle, exhausted from her little adventure. Watching the two of them in their familiar embrace causes my heart to test the boundaries of my rib cage.

"How did you know you'd be a good mom?" The words come out before I've had time to properly vet them. To my relief, Rose doesn't seem put off by the question. In fact, the gleam in her eye suggests she's pleased that I'd feel comfortable enough to ask. Like I'm the skittish stray dog she's been feeding that finally came close enough to be petted.

"Well, of course, *good* is subjective. But I assume you're asking how I knew I'd be a *healthy* parent, given the example I had growing up," she says. The way she's read right through my facade makes me feel simultaneously seen and examined.

"I guess so," I tell her, sipping my coffee as a distraction. When I set it down, I see that Cleo's eyes have drifted shut, cradled in her mother's arms. I decide to go with the brave side of me that brought this up in the first place rather than cowering behind my fear of her answer.

"Actually I guess it's a few things. How did you know you'd pick a man you could trust to be different from your dad? And how did you know *you* wouldn't screw your kids up?"

That gleam turns into a full-on twinkle. "Oh, I'll definitely screw them up, no doubt about it. That's parenting, baby."

She must see the horror I feel reflected clearly on my face because she quickly adds, "It's human nature to mess up, Eden. What matters is that the moment you know better, you have to do better."

"I don't think my mom has figured that last part out yet," I say, my voice stiff with bottled-up frustration. A sympathetic frown pulls on the corners of her mouth.

"The day I found out I was pregnant with Cleo, I had a really firm talk with myself. I love my mother desperately, but she projected a lot of her fears from her life with my father onto me. I told myself I would not let Cleo grow up with a mom who was afraid of the world and the what-ifs. I'd just teach her how to be strong enough to handle any possible outcome."

Cleo's thumb pops out of her mouth now that she's sound

asleep. Her thick eyelashes flutter, reacting to whatever dream she is having.

"And as far as Mitchell, part of me just knew. I don't know how to explain it," Rose adds, looking at me pointedly. "But I'd venture to guess you know exactly what I mean. I felt safe with him, safer than I felt just by myself. And he loved Cleo from the moment she was a faint line on a plastic stick. I could see it even then, that he'd leave me just as quickly as I'd leave him if one of us ever posed a threat to that baby."

A hairline fracture opens up along my heart. I tear another piece of muffin off, not even tasting the bite as I struggle to come up with a reply. Her words have weighed me down just as much as they've set me free.

"Not to be overly presumptuous, but Chase is that kind of guy, too." It's her final piece of advice, her checkmate to drive her point home.

"Yeah, he is," I say, because I know it's true. It was never a question in my mind. The real concern is whether or not I am that kind of woman, and if my mother still can be.

A broad smile takes over Rose's delicate features. She rests a hand absentmindedly on the back of Cleo's head, the diamonds in her wedding band sparkling in the morning light filtering through the windows.

"You're going to be fine, Eden. I've just got this feeling."

"Thank you," I tell her, humbled and also hopeful that she's right. "I want to be like you when I grow up."

Twinkling laughter spills out of her in response. "I've got bad news. I'm younger than you."

I groan as a reply, and she laughs even harder. Just then the door opens behind me and a tall, gangly man with a tangle of curls on top of his head comes striding in. He's dressed in jeans and a button-down over work boots, a neon yellow safety vest topping off the look. He waltzes confidently around the counter and scoops Cleo right out of her mother's arms, planting a kiss on Rose's head in the process. Cleo doesn't stir in the slightest from the disturbance.

"Hey, I'm Mitch," he offers, extending a hand to shake mine.

"Eden," I reply. "It's good to meet you."

A goofy grin takes over his face in response before giving Rose another kiss, this time on the lips, and then grabbing a muffin right out of the case. Rose swats at him as he makes his retreat. "I've got to go; see you guys later!" he calls as he disappears out into the morning, baby in tow.

Rose transfers her withering stare back to me from his retreating form, though there's an obvious undercurrent of amusement. "Well, you can't demand perfection, but maybe also request that your man not be a thief."

Chapter Thirty

"**O**uch! Damn it." My toe throbs in response to the rude assault. I can't see what I've tripped over because Zoey's hands remain tightly clasped over my eyes. She doesn't slow down to let me recover, either. Next thing I know, I feel my sandal catch on the base of her front porch steps.

"Take a step up *carefully*," she warns. Her words are laced with anticipation. I gingerly hover my feet over where I think each step will be, not shifting my weight until I'm confident I'm right. I focus on putting one foot in front of the other so dread at the idea of an impending surprise party can't spread any further through me.

"Zo, not to sound ungrateful, but if a bunch of people jump out at me and yell, I will probably have a heart attack."

I hear a sharp *pffft* and the opening of her front door. "Please, you think I don't know that?"

As soon as I've cleared the threshold without error, her hands fall away from my face. A theatrically whispered, "Surprise!" is my cue to open my eyes.

I'm temporarily blinded after having them squeezed shut

for so long. As the room comes into focus, I see a cluster of pastel balloons hanging from the ceiling over her kitchen island. On the counter, an arrangement of champagne flutes and chilled bottles in ice baths borders a selection of fruit juices. An elaborate charcuterie board tops off the display sporting both a savory and a sweet side, overflowing with cheeses and chocolates alike.

Excitement flutters in my stomach. "It's *perfect*," I sigh.

My gaze pans over to the living room where face masks and nail polishes are laid out with all the necessary tools for a manicure. The television is paused on the opening credits of *Practical Magic,* and there are piles of plush blankets folded on the corner of her green velvet sectional.

But that's not why pricks of tears are forming in my eyes. Despite the fact that it is quite possibly the most stunning display I've ever seen, and truly the nicest thing anyone has ever done for me, the thing I can't tear my eyes away from is Ella, practically vibrating with anticipation on the couch.

Our joint screams are so loud that Rose, who is seated next to Ella, covers her ears at the same time as Zoey. I close the distance between us in a flash, tackling her petite body into the cushions. I'm squeezing her so tightly it's quite possible I'll smother her, but she doesn't protest. She just squeezes me right back.

"How are you here?" I'm cradling her face in my palms, and my half-yell at such close proximity causes her to wince, but her green eyes, which are darker than mine, shine with excitement. I drink in the familiar sight of her button nose and heart-shaped face, her strawberry-blonde waves and freckled skin, as though I am a person wandering through the desert who has stumbled across an oasis.

"I'm your birthday gift!" Ella says happily.

"Rose did me a solid and picked her up from the airport this morning while I got everything ready here," Zoey replies from behind me.

That's nearly four hours round trip. The fact that she would do something like that for me makes those tears sting even worse, like a thousand bees are swarming behind my eyes. I lean over from where I'm straddling Ella and pull Rose into a hug.

"Thank you so much," I say.

"Happy to do it! Besides, your sister and I are best friends already," she replies, my tight embrace straining her normally singsong voice.

Considering how talkative the both of them are, I don't doubt what she's telling me for a minute. A loud *pop* coming from the kitchen startles me out of our three-way bear hug. When I turn around, the champagne bottle in Zoey's hand is just settling down from its exciting debut.

"Mimosas, anyone?" She wiggles her eyebrows at us to complement her come-hither tone.

She fills a flute for each of us before sliding it down to where the juice selection sits. Grapefruit juice turns mine a pale pink, the sour-sweet combination fizzing all the way down my throat.

"Drink up!" Zoey says, holding her glass of champagne with a drop of orange juice up in a toast. "This is how twenty-eight-year-olds get shwasted!"

"I'm still twenty-seven until tomorrow," I remind them all, clinking my glass against hers.

Zoey rolls her eyes at me. "I know, but Chase called dibs on your actual birthday so let's just pretend. And anyway, it worked out because it allowed this special surprise"—she squeezes Ella around the shoulders—"to be here."

Just the mention of Chase's name sends a little thrill through my body. The fact that he cared enough to hog my birthday makes me feel like a teenager again, finding out my crush is planning on asking me to the homecoming dance. The anticipation mixes with the alcohol in my stomach, making me woozy.

Ella groans before taking a long drag of her mimosa. "Please, I don't want to be reminded that you're twenty-eight because that means I'm almost in my midforties."

"Before you know it, you'll be the big 5-0," I tease her, tugging on a lock of hair that just barely brushes her shoulder.

She glares at me with only a hint of genuine disdain. "You take that back."

We make our way to the couch with plates loaded full of rosemary crackers and slices of gourmet cheeses along with a selection of shortbread cookies and chocolate truffles that are calling my name. We arrange our feast on the round surface of Zoey's marble coffee table. Ella examines the selection of nail polishes while I peel open the foil packet of a mask that I'm hoping will fight off any sugar-induced acne caused by the truffle I pop into my mouth.

I've just been swallowed by the velvety warmth of the cushions when I shoot up, the slimy sheet mask slipping down my face.

"Wait, who's watching the bar? I can't leave Zander alone on a Saturday," I say, the paper vibrating against my lips. Maddie is off at a music festival, and with it being a holiday weekend, I know vacationers will fill the town in search of a base camp for their outdoor activities. Luckily Santi hired two new line cooks just in time, which is probably the only reason Zoey's so relaxed right now.

"Relax, Gary's got it," Zoey reassures me, her firm arm stretching across my chest and shoving me back into the couch. I right the mask on my slick face so I can see out of the eyeholes again. "And he asked me to let you know you owe him one since this is the second time he's covered for you."

My snort of laughter nearly sucks the flap of my mask up

my nose. "I'll be sure to remind him that sleeping on a hospital chair and scrubbing his toilet should more than cover my debt."

Zoey shrugs her agreement and takes a sip from her glass. Rose lifts the remote but settles it back into her lap when Zoey raises a finger to interject.

"Speaking of Zander though, do you remember us talking about him living in a hammock?" Zoey asks.

The telltale dimple appears in Rose's cheek, this time from a confused frown. I comb through the files of my brain and come up with a dusty transcript. "On the hike? Vaguely, I guess."

In my defense, a lot has happened since then. She huffs but doesn't let my inability to follow her down the rabbit hole deter her from the path.

"Yes, on the hike," she says, her face comes alight the way it always does when she has an idea to share. "Anyway, I was thinking about what Chase said—when he called Zander a nomad? I think it could be a cool name for the bar, with all the people who pass through town coming to the mountains. Loveless Nomads. What do you think?"

"Your bar doesn't have a name?" Ella asks, then takes a sip of her mimosa to hide the concerned-mom tone she's famous for using. Zoey shrugs like, *What can you do?*

"Maybe just Nomads," Rose suggests. We all turn to look at her, and she takes it as a prompt to elaborate. "Look, I love my town as much as the next person, but adding *Loveless* in front just makes it sound a little sad."

I normally refrain from throwing my hat into the ring when it comes to naming the bar due to my decided lack of creativity. The last time I was allowed to name anything, I was eight and it was a stray kitten that wandered onto our property. I called it Rachael because that was my favorite babysitter's name, and all I could think of at the time. I was apparently a rather progressive child because the cat was a male.

That being said, even *I* know Rose makes a good point. Ella and I nod to give our endorsement as Zoey nails Rose with an aptly named throw pillow. Rose tucks the faux fur pillow under her head, tossing a wink toward the three of us.

"You guys are *so* helpful," Zoey replies, voice thick with sarcasm, though I can tell she's mentally noting the advice.

"All right, any more objections, or can I start the movie?" Rose asks, finger poised over the play button. Our muffled giggles blend into the opening score.

I lay my head against Ella's shoulder, savoring her closeness. It's so rare that I get to see her, and even more rare that she doesn't have my two nephews in tow. When they couldn't come to town for our usual family Christmas due to Jarrett's work schedule, I was devastated. Her absence was felt even deeper in the days that followed.

As if sensing my thoughts, she reaches a hand up and strokes my hair, comforting me the same way our mother did when I was little. I let myself be pacified, trying to focus on the story unfolding on the screen.

Zoey and I first fell in love with this movie when we were preteens, just beginning to navigate the world of crushes and middle school bullies. Like most girls that age, we searched a million books and movies trying to understand the people we were becoming. We likened ourselves to the Owens sisters, me the reserved and practical Sally, Zoey the wild and enigmatic Gillian.

For Zoey, I think she liked the magic and the mystery of it all, but I found myself fixated on the way they looked out for one another. While I imagined myself getting married one day and having a family of my own, those were just dreams. The only concrete truth in my life was Zoey, and it struck a chord somewhere deep inside me to hear Gillian tell Sally they'd grow old together, regardless of any man.

I reach for Zoey's hand on the couch, thankful that I have a best friend who loves me more than anyone in the world. More than my parents, which I thought half-heartedly back then but now fully believe. She squeezes my hand tightly, and I can see it just like Gillian says: the two of us, growing old in a big ole house, much like the one we already live in. Dying when we're covered in wrinkles and full of memories, on the very same day.

When I look over at her, she senses my gaze and turns to face me, the light from the television reflected in her glistening eyes. We've been through a lot of life together and, in a way, are so close that even Ella and my relationship can't compare. I don't know if it's the overwhelming gratitude I feel for her going so above and beyond to celebrate my birthday, or if it's the memory of so many days spent exactly like this, but for a moment my heart feels so swollen it might burst.

The final straw comes a moment later when, in perfect sync with Gillian on the screen, Zoey whispers, "I love you."

I tighten my hold on her hand as the words open up my heart, painting my rib cage with its contents. I know what my response is meant to be, exactly what Sally says next. I've been rehearsing the line for half my life.

"I love you, too, Gilly-Bean."

Chapter Thirty-One

Skyscrapers stretch their arms up high on the horizon as the mountain range retreats in my rearview mirror. Ella pops the cap back onto her travel bottle of motion sickness medication, a necessary companion on every trip she takes. Her eyes roll over to me, the tinge of green fading from her normally creamy skin. She offers a forced smile, relieved to be clear of the winding mountain roads.

"I'm sorry you couldn't stay for longer," I say, reaching out to pat her knee. We're approaching Denver quicker than I'd like, with the airport just beyond it. I subconsciously pull my foot off the gas, slowing our speed to delay the inevitable.

"I know, but Jarrett leaves for that big medical conference tomorrow," she replies, a grimace emphasizing the new laugh lines forming like parentheses around her mouth. "My mama heart won't let me leave the boys home alone just yet."

I refrain from reminding her that my oldest nephew, Wesley, will be a senior this fall.

"You know there are great hospitals here in Colorado," I offer.

A soft chuckle is all she can manage. "Yeah, I'd definitely

lose these extra few pounds I've been carrying around just from all the puking. No mountain ranges in my future, I'm sorry to say."

I let a sorrowful groan climb out of my throat, so she knows just how I feel about that.

"I'm glad I came, though, even if just for the night," she says with a sigh, turning away from the window to look at me. "I needed to see you in person to make sure you were okay."

I keep my gaze trained on the highway, silence settling uncomfortably into the space between us. The sensation of her watchful gaze examining my facade for cracks makes my skin crawl. I want so badly not to come up lacking—if nothing more than to keep her worry at bay.

"How are you holding up, Eden?" she asks when I don't immediately take the bait. She shifts in her seat to face me fully, one leg tucked underneath the other. "I'm sorry I kind of lost it when you called. It wasn't my finest moment."

My responding laugh comes out harsher than I intend it to. I clamp my jaw shut, trying to cut off the sound. Realistically I know we're trapped in the cab of my car and I can't avoid answering her for the remainder of our drive, but there's a part of me that wishes we could skirt past the subject, ignoring the glaring mark of my mother's choices on this otherwise perfect birthday.

When her stare doesn't let up, I release the breath I've held captive in my lungs. "Honestly I'm not doing the greatest. I'm still trying to process everything."

My teeth grind against one another, chewing on the frustration I can no longer keep at bay.

"You know what really irks me?" I say too sharply, causing Ella to startle, her pitying stare giving way to nervous anticipation. "That she could leave Dad for being an abusive drunk, but Mark being a pedophile is A-OK!"

I don't intend for the double meaning to be laid so bare, but it is. My real question lies just beneath the surface of my words: *How could she leave that man for you, but not this one for me?*

Ella is quiet in the aftermath of my admission. I wish desperately that I could take it back, roll it up like an out-of-fashion rug and tuck it back into storage where it belongs. But there are no take backs in life, I'm learning. There's only what comes next.

I chance a glance her way, surprised to find a look of confusion rather than indignance.

"What?" I ask her.

"Eden," she says, ringing her hands together the same way Mama does. "She didn't leave Dad."

If I weren't flying down a crowded highway, I would slam my foot down on the brakes. My mind is spinning, desperately trying to make sense of her statement. I wait for her to continue, mostly because I'm unable to form any coherent thoughts.

"He didn't want any more children. Hell, he didn't even want the one he had." She gestures gruffly at herself. "When Mama found out she was pregnant with you, he split. We never heard from him after that."

I find my head shaking of its own volition, denial my knee-jerk reaction. "No, Mama told me she left him when I was a few months old. That he was abusing you, and she decided enough was enough."

My hands tremble on the steering wheel, struggling to grip it as I turn it to take our exit. Ella's snort of laughter is laced with hatred, though I can sense it isn't aimed at me.

"He *was* abusive. He was absolutely awful," she replies, her voice distant. She's somewhere in the past, a time before I even existed apparently. "But Mama never had the courage to leave him. Every new bruise that appeared on my body, she swore

239

would be the last. She insisted that he loved us, and he was *really going to change this time*, every time."

I picture Ella as she must've been, young and fragile at the hands of a man I've only seen in a handful of faded photographs. An angry purple bruise blossoming around an emerald eye, our mother holding a bag of frozen peas to it, making promises she couldn't, *wouldn't* keep.

"How do you stand her?" I ask, desperate for a guidebook on where to go from here. It's like the magnetic poles of my world are switching, and as a result my entire sense of reality is in an upheaval.

"I didn't for a while. I resented her a lot growing up, and we didn't get along because of it." The veil is torn, and I see my past clearly for the first time, all the short-tempered exchanges between her and Mama that were written off as teen angst rather than the righteous anger it actually was. It suddenly makes sense why she always brought me to her dorm for visits instead of sticking around at home—she was avoiding extended time with Mama at all costs.

"Then I was an adult, and I was getting married and having my own children. It was a season of life that I desperately wanted my mother to be a part of, so I made that decision to let her in. It's always been strained, but I love her as much as I'm able to without sacrificing any love for myself."

Her eyebrows draw together as she looks at me. "Though I'll be honest, lately that amount is less and less."

I'm still shaken from the revelation, my thoughts rendering me speechless. The pedestal I've placed my mother on for my entire life gives way to the cracks that have been forming for the past six months. It crumbles into a heap of granite and false truths at my feet, while I remain locked in place, helpless to do anything but watch it happen.

The soft skin of her hand meets my cheek, wiping away a

hot tear that sneaks out of the corner of my eye. I sniffle, trying to keep it together for our impending goodbye. I do another loop around the airport, purposefully missing the turn for departures.

"I'm sorry I never told you. I really thought you knew," she says.

"It's okay," I reassure her, though I'm probably the last person in the position to do so. My voice sounds like I'm talking through a mouthful of broken glass. "It just changes so much."

Watching the clock on my dashboard, I know I can't delay any longer or she'll miss her flight. I take the necessary turn, approaching a long line of cars pulled up against the curb. Hordes of travelers in various stages of goodbyes crowd the sidewalks.

"I know," Ella says, drawing my attention to her as I put the car in park. "But you know what hasn't changed? You and me. I'm your big sister, Eden. I am always going to be here for you, no matter what relationship you choose to have with Mama, or if you have one at all."

The security guard directing traffic whistles for us to get a move on. We scramble out of the car, Ella grabbing her overnight bag from the back seat and slinging it over her shoulder. I round the hood to meet her, gathering her into my arms and holding on for dear life.

She's wrong, though I don't tell her so. Our relationship *has* changed. I feel closer to her now than I ever have before, sharing this bond neither of us asked for but got, nonetheless. She's the only person with as much at risk to lose, yet she's still here, telling me it's okay to choose what's best for me.

"I love you, El," I whisper into her ear.

"Love you, too," she replies, squeezing me one last time for good measure. "Happy Birthday, old lady."

I climb back into the car, ignoring the shrill whistle urging me to move until the back of her head disappears into the crowd on the other side of the automatic doors.

I wave at the agitated guard before pulling away from the curb, beginning the long drive back to Loveless and whatever surprise Chase has prepared for me. My phone dings just as I'm merging onto the highway, fear that Ella forgot something driving me to glance at the message after I check for surrounding traffic.

My heart stills in my chest when I read the text, and I drop my phone back into the passenger seat so I can grab the steering wheel with both hands, the road suddenly blurrier than it was a few seconds ago. With every blink, the text scrolls across my eyelids, impossible to ignore.

Mama: Happy 28th birthday, baby. Your mother loves you.

Chapter Thirty-Two

I power down my phone to avoid any more unpleasant distractions. It's been hours since the text came through, and still it sits there in my inbox with no reply. I decide it will have to stay that way because I'm done crying on my birthday. Besides, why do today what you can put off until tomorrow?

At least I'm pretending that's how the phrase goes.

Chase pulls off onto a dirt road, so poorly graded that I'm practically rattling in my seat. I look over at him, my curiosity piqued, but I find no hint of what's to come. All I get is a cocky smile and a crinkle at the edge of his eyes.

We drive past a wooden sign with yellow painted letters announcing we've arrived at a group of campsites. "Are you taking me camping?" I ask.

His wry grin only grows wider, but he doesn't respond, saving the surprise for some planned grand reveal. As the normally quiet one in this relationship, I can imagine how much this pains him.

We pass several tents surrounded by families and solo

campers alike, the occasional dog barking to alert their owners of our presence. The woods grow thick around us, all signs of civilization left behind as we climb the meandering road higher. Just when I'm at the stressful end of calculating how long of a walk it will be back to the bathhouse at the main site, the trees open up to reveal a final unoccupied clearing overlooking sweeping views of the valley below us.

"Oh my God, Chase, it's stunning," I say, slapping a hand over my heart to calm its giddy thudding. "I never would've been able to keep this a secret. Kudos to you."

His smoky laugh tickles my ears. "It was easy. I wouldn't have missed this reveal for the world."

I'm still fumbling for the right words to respond when he jumps out of the truck, reaching into the bed to pull out a tent and a backpack.

"Could you grab that basket from the back seat?" he calls to me, jolting me out of my stunned silence. My eyes widen when I open the door and see a wicker basket on the seat behind mine. *He made me a picnic.* The romantic in me swoons.

What can I say? I am my mother's daughter.

Quicker than I thought possible, he has a simple two-person tent pitched with two sleeping bags rolled out inside of it, which he zips together to create one giant cocoon. Despite the fact that I've slept next to him before, this feels different. More intentional. The butterflies in my stomach feel more like birds that have been set free from their cage.

"Can I help with anything?" I ask, watching him gather kindling from the tree line and deposit it into the fire pit. With the flick of a lighter, the dry twigs and leaves are ablaze, and a cozy warmth fills the air around us.

"You can open up that basket," he says, taking a seat next to me on the blanket I've spread out. In the setting sun, his eyes are two amber pots of honey, tempting me with their sweetness. I have to force myself to pull my eyes away so I can look at the wicker lid I'm fumbling with.

I survey the assortment of homemade sandwiches and small bags of chips next to a gift box of Rose's homemade cookies tied with pink ribbon. My mouth waters when I realize they're oatmeal chocolate chip, and I have to firmly remind myself that I can't eat dessert first. When I move aside the box to see what lies beneath, a gasp falls from my lips.

I pull the bottle of red wine from where it is nestled and hold it on display for Chase, who is smiling as he watches me. "This is my absolute favorite! I haven't had it since—"

"Since your summer in England with Zoey," he finishes for me. I draw my lower lip into my teeth, biting back the grin that wants to form. "She told me all about it. The day trip you two took to that French vineyard, the sommelier who hit on you the whole time..."

My eyes roll so far back, I swear I catch sight of my brain. "He did *not*."

The man was just gay and friendly, as I'd repeatedly explained to Zoey.

Chase snickers as he reaches over me to grab the wine-glasses clipped to the basket lid, retrieves the opened bottle of wine, and pours us two servings—each. "It's okay, no need to defend yourself. My girl is a catch, and I'm proud of it."

The way he casually calls me his girl sends a zing of pleasure from the crown of my head all the way to my toes. He scoots closer to me until I'm leaning into the curve of his side, my shoulder tucked under his arm. We gingerly clink our full wineglasses together before I bring the heady bouquet up to my nose. The scent takes me to a faraway corner of the world, one I didn't even realize how much I missed until now.

"Cheers to the well-traveled birthday girl," he says, taking a sip.

"Speak for yourself," I reply, picturing the map above his bed and the multitude of parks he's already crossed off. I laugh when he winces at the dry wine, knowing he's only drinking it for me. If it were up to him, there'd be a chilled Coors Light in his hand, and that knowledge makes the gesture even sweeter.

"Oh please, I still have the whole world on my bucket list," he says, gesturing broadly to the valley below us. Twilight has swallowed much of the view in its shadows, but there's still the exhilarating sense that we are up high above it all. Far in the distance, the crackle of fireworks echoes. "Which is why we better make sure your passport is up-to-date."

I tuck my head playfully against him, each sip of wine loosening my limbs and my inhibitions. I let myself imagine it for a moment, traveling the world with him. I picture us rambling down the streets of Amsterdam or sunbathing on a beach in Mykonos. All the places I've ever dreamed of seeing, I tuck him right into those plans. I'm surprised to find he fits perfectly.

"So, did you have a good time with your sister?" he asks, interrupting my fantasies. It's a hard landing, falling from the height of those hopes to the reality of my day. I take a moment to orient myself before responding.

"Yeah, I did," I offer, but my melancholic tone alerts him that something's up. I swear, almost as if he were a dog, his ears perk up at my words. He watches me carefully, searching my face for what I'm not saying. Knowing how easily he can read me, I decide to beat him to the punch.

"My mom isn't going to leave Mark."

It's the one piece of the puzzle I haven't shared yet, but he doesn't react with the surprise I expect. He settles his barely touched glass of wine on the flat surface of a nearby slab of rock and turns to give me his full attention. "I know."

My eyes widen, and I watch as he measures my reaction.

"Well, I inferred. Once you told me about your stepdad, her abrupt exit and how upset you were made a lot more sense," he clarifies.

I settle back onto my elbows, my now-empty glass cast aside.

"So, what are you going to do?" he asks, mimicking my movement.

"I don't know," I confess. I suddenly realize how badly I want his guidance. The desire to show him this dark corner of my thoughts is overwhelming, hoping beyond hope that he'll help me find the light switch. "I love her so much, and the idea of never speaking to her again terrifies me, but the reality of having her in my life knowing she continues to have a marriage with a man who hurt me like that is almost too much to bear."

He presses his lips together, the corners of his eyes wrinkled with concern rather than joy. "Do you think she'll change her mind?"

"I want to believe there's a chance. Sometimes I think we're all just suffering whiplash from him becoming someone we didn't recognize overnight, and that given enough time we'll be sane again," I say, shaking my head at no one in particular. I picture her at the foot of my stairs, how lost she looked as she told me she couldn't die alone. "But probably not."

The last words are a whisper, but he hears them. I know because that muscle in his jaw ticks, the same way it did any time Shawn came into the bar. There's an anger simmering just below the surface, fueled by a desire to protect me, and that twitch is a leak in the dam holding it at bay.

"Can I tell you something terrible?" I ask, picking at a jagged fingernail.

"I love terrible things," he says, letting out a strangled breath.

"Every time I think I've made up my mind to never talk to

her again, I picture you standing in front of your father's grave, and I feel like the most selfish human ever because at least my parent is still alive."

"Ed*en*," he says, rolling onto his stomach to face me head-on. I bite my tongue so I can't point out that he said my name the same annoying way Maddie does. "If Hollis Taylor were here right now, do you know what he would say?"

I shake my head.

"He would tell you that being a parent isn't a get-out-of-jail-free card for shitty behavior. She only deserves a place in your life if she earns it." He reaches up and tucks a strand of hair back behind my ear, taking my already raggedy breath away. "My dead dad and I both support you in whatever you decide."

He winks to soften the edge of his dark humor, but I still let my head fall back with a frustrated groan.

"Everyone keeps saying that!" I lament to the heavens above. "I don't want to decide. I want it to be someone else's job."

He's watching me with an amused expression when I finally lift my head to face him again, done with my whining.

"Just think, someone else's terrible decisions are what got you here in the first place," he says. "Being the one in control is definitely the better option."

I glare at him even as this blatant truth shatters my resolve. "How did you get so wise?"

"Don't worry," he says with a husky laugh. "You will be too when you reach the ripe old age of thirty."

I attempt to swat him, but he catches my wrist before I can make contact, that familiar intensity flaring in his stare. My breath stalls in my lungs, and I feel warmth creep up my neck and set fire to my cheeks.

He lifts himself up and crawls forward, placing a hand on

either side of my hips. I'm trapped and I don't even care. I can't look away as he drops his head and presses his hot mouth against my collarbone where the blush began. He blazes a trail up the sensitive skin of my neck, drawing my earlobe in between his teeth and eliciting a sharp gasp, the sudden breeze ruffling his dark waves. His stubble grazes my cheek as he pulls back just enough to scan my face. Whatever he's looking for, he finds, because he closes what little distance remains and covers my mouth with his.

I let myself fall back onto the blanket. He shifts his weight to rest on top of me, settling into the cradle of my thighs. My legs wrap around his hips in an attempt to draw him closer. His tongue explores mine, our lips tangled together in one endless kiss. When he pulls away, breathless, he drags his T-shirt over his head, the firelight illuminating every contour of his body.

I tuck my fingertips under the hem of my shirt, eyes locked on his as I lift the fabric higher, higher, until it's over my head and discarded on the ground. The familiar joy passes over his face at being handed a piece of me without having to ask for it, and it's coupled with a desire so intense I feel it radiating off him. I reach back between my shoulder blades and release the clasp of my bra. His fingertips tickle my skin as he tantalizingly drags the straps down my arms.

This time, when I lay bare beneath him, I stare bravely back as he admires my body.

He inhales sharply, the twitching muscle in his jaw revealing a fight for control that he is at risk of losing. "I'm trying so hard to be a gentleman right now."

I decide the fight is over—for both of us. I'm done resisting the best thing to ever walk into my life. My finger hooks around the edge of his waistband, pulling him down to me.

"Don't."

I could be arrested for arson with the way his features become engulfed in flame. He works the button of my shorts as he leans into me, his lips closing around my nipple. Teeth pull at sensitive skin, and I think I might explode from the electricity traveling through me. It is so good. So much better than I ever thought it could be.

"God, I want you so badly, Eden." The words are a breath, a whisper, a dream.

"I'm yours," I tell him, running a hand through his hair while he makes quick work of the rest of our clothes. His gaze washes over me like it's a miracle I'm even here. "So come and take me."

His responding moan is lost when he crashes back into my lips. Every inch of my skin burns so hot I'm afraid I might combust. He slips his fingers into me, staving off the hunger that is rising fast. His tongue explores my ribs, my breasts, the hollow of my throat. My hips push against his hand of their own volition, desperate to draw him closer.

"Chase, I need you."

His heavy-lidded eyes lift to meet mine. A tease of a smile flashes pearlescent teeth my way.

"*Now*," I beg.

It's the final straw that ruins his resolve. I whimper as his fingers leave me aching and empty, eyes widening when he draws them into his mouth and moans.

Where everything else about him is soft and gentle, the way he thrusts into me then is anything but. He holds me tightly against him, each aggressive drive of his hips sending him so deep that I cry out. The sound is cut off by his lips hard against mine, swallowing up the air in my lungs until I'm convinced it isn't oxygen I need to breathe, but him.

He is inside me and all around me and I'm not sure how I ever thought I was living before this, but I come alive from his touch. I rake my nails along the broad expanse of his back, drawing him nearer to me, but he is never near enough. He drags a rough thumb over the most sensitive place on my body, building me up so he can let me fall. When I don't think I'll survive another second, I shatter into a million fragments of light beneath him.

"Holy *fuck*, Eden." His muscles grow taut beneath my grip as he holds me close through his own undoing.

When we've both drifted back down to earth, we lay curled into one another, covered only by the blanket of stars above and a sheen of perspiration. He twirls my hair absentmindedly, smiling down at me as we talk about everything and nothing in particular. I trace the outline of each clock on his bicep, admiring the artwork as much as the canvas. My fingertips explore the pattern of numbers on the digital face, and he shivers from the sensation.

"What's the significance of 12:14?" I ask. The crinkles around his eyes soften in response.

"It's the minute my dad's heart stopped beating."

I lean forward and replace my fingertips with my lips, pressing them against the inked memory. As if in direct defiance of this talk of death, his heart thrums loud and steady in my ear. His hand slides down my arm, securing my wrist and holding it up between us. The white scar tissue curved around the bone reflects back the flickering glow of the flames.

"You could turn this into a tattoo if you wanted," he says, thumb tracing the shape like always. "It's badass as is, but it lends itself to a moon."

A soft smile tugs at my mouth. He presses his gently into mine, the flutter of his tongue on my lower lip enough to rekindle that heat low in my stomach. His gaze lifts to meet mine so I feel the full weight of his next words.

"I know you don't think you can handle it, but trust me,

Eden." My name feels like velvet when framed with his raspy voice. From the intensity in his eyes, I get the acute sense that we aren't talking about tattoos anymore. "You can do anything. And I'll be there, no matter what, to hold your hand."

Chapter Thirty-Three

The first thing I hear when Mama picks up the phone isn't a greeting like I'd expect. Instead I hear the chatter of a crowd in the background, and I almost drop my cell. The plan wasn't to bombard her in public. Though if I'm honest with myself, there is no *plan*. Just the culmination of a week's worth of agonizing over the decision.

The only thing that keeps my grip steady on the phone is the resolve I've worked so hard to build up, the very reason I have to do this now, before I lose it.

She sounds muted, like she's covering the speaker with her hand, when I hear her tell some unknown person she'll be right back. The noise falls away with the shutting of a door, followed by shuffling before her voice comes clearly through the phone.

"Sorry about that. I'm working vacation bible study tonight," she says. Memories long tucked away come flooding back, of crafts and games and songs about Jesus sung in the auditorium of the church. It was the height of my summers as a child.

Whatever small part of me that has managed to be angry at her instead of heartbroken revels in the fact that she's getting this call at church. How fitting, after all. Mark's probably the one she left behind with the children since they usually teach the classes together. I feel a sharp pang of pity for every parent who trusted him with their child, dangerously unaware of who he truly is.

"Are you there?" she asks. I realize in my contemplation that I've missed something she said. I mumble a reply, letting her know I'm still here, if only for a moment longer.

"How's it going, baby? Did you have a good birthday?" Her voice is upbeat, no trace of emotion from our last interaction. For some reason, this sets my anger to a boil. How could she act like everything is normal when nothing is? When nothing has been for so long?

The first hints of panic creep in when my hands begin to tremble. I inhale the scent of vanilla wafting off the candle burning on my coffee table. My eyes zero in on the flickering flame. I run my hands across the woven blanket draped over my legs, shivers racking my body from the cold within me.

"It was great," I bite out. "Ella came to town."

She either misses the tightness in my voice or chooses to ignore it completely. "Oh, that's good! I'm glad you two got to see each other."

It's harder than I thought it would be to force the words out of my mouth. I wish I could be a coward like Mark, that I could just write all the words I need to say down on a scrap of paper and leave the letter like a ticking bomb in her mailbox. But I'm not him. And I'm not her, either. So I swallow the rising lump in my throat, putting on courage like a too-big sweater and hoping I'll grow into it.

"She told me something interesting." There is no wading into a conversation like this. I have to dive and trust that I will remember how to swim. "About Dad."

"About Mark?" she asks, confused. Even the sound of his

name is like an electric shock to my system. I shake my head even though there's no one around to see me. The serene quiet of my empty apartment holds its breath, waiting.

"No, my real father."

She doesn't immediately respond, and I try to picture what she looks like, tucked into a closet or maybe a bathroom connected to one of the old Sunday school classrooms. Wood paneling along the wall, paintings of flowers adorned with scripture meant to inspire hope where none exists. I envision her lowering herself to sit on the closed lid of the toilet, hesitant to follow the trail of breadcrumbs I've laid before her.

"What about him?" she asks. Her voice warbles over the speed bumps of her nerves. I imagine faded echoes of my own eyes, trained on a painting of a field of lavender hung on the wall across from her. Underneath the painting, an inscription of Proverbs 3:5.

Lean not on your own understanding. Even when your understanding tells you to run.

"She said he left when you found out you were pregnant with me," I say, surprised to find my voice is laced not with spite but with desperation. I want her to tell me I'm wrong. That this is all wrong. But she doesn't; she just remains solemnly speechless.

"Mama?" My voice is so shrill, so childlike that for a moment I have to look down to verify I am in fact grown. Still the only answer on the line is her breath, clipped and sputtering. "Mama, is that true? You wouldn't leave a man that treated you like that? That hurt *Ella?*"

"Eden, it's not that simple." I recognize the tone immediately, the same one she used when she called me bitter before. It implies that I don't know what I'm talking about. Her voice is a warning, a sign to turn back. But I'm tired of turning back. I'm tired of begging my mother to love me as much as I need her to, tired of trying to understand why she can't.

Tired of trying to accept the measly parts of her that she is willing to give.

Suddenly all the words I've held inside for months come rushing forward. I don't have the strength to hold them back anymore, so I stop trying. I just let go.

"*It is that simple*," I growl. There's no other word to describe the animalistic emotion in my voice. "You brought us into this world. You're supposed to protect us! And while I understand that it is impossible to prevent every tragedy, you had a chance to make this right. TWICE. And still you'd choose a man over the daughters who suffered the consequences of your poor choices."

"Eden, I—"

"No, I'm done. I'm done listening to your excuses." Hot tears are forming rivers down my cheeks, but I keep talking through the downpour, even as my voice shakes. "Mama, I love you with everything that I am, but I can't do this anymore. I can't let someone be a part of my life when all they do is hurt me."

"You don't have to see him," she says desperately, grasping at pieces of the world shattering around us both. "He can stay at home or in a hotel. You'll never have to see him, I promise."

"It's not enough," I cry, the thick sludge of snot and tears making it difficult to breathe. A small part of me cowers in the corner of my mind, and I have to strain to hear her whispered correction: *I'm not enough.*

"What are you saying?" she asks. She's defiant, backed against the wall with nowhere to go. That *bitter* part of me savors the fact, grateful for her to see how it feels. "This is my life; he's my husband. What do you expect me to do?"

It's the million-dollar question, after all. Faced with the

most impossible of circumstances, what is she supposed to do? I don't know if anyone has all the answers, but I give her the best one I can come up with. The only one.

"You leave him. You love yourself and your daughters enough to demand better. You walk out that door, and you never look back."

I clutch a fistful of the blanket to my chest, holding on for dear life. Suddenly I'm a child again, straddling the seat of a bike that's just been stripped of its training wheels. Mama is impossibly far away, telling me to trust her. *Just put your feet on the pedals and push*, she urges, like it's that simple. *All you have to do is make it to me.*

Now I'm at the end of the road, begging her to try. Begging her to pedal hard, fast, to give it everything she has to give.

"I can't do that," she says. Her voice quivers with the thickness of tears.

"Yes, you can." I wipe the blanket across my face because it's all I have, and it comes away drenched. "You come live with me. Or Ella. You let us take care of you until you can take care of yourself. We'll help you."

I let the words land between us like the ultimatum they are, a bridge from her to me.

"He's a predator, Mama. He will always be a predator. We all, yourself included, deserve better than that. You have to leave him."

It's the truth, and all I have left to give. The seconds stretch into minutes, and I think for a moment I've lost her. But then her voice, quiet and so very sorry, comes through the phone.

"*I won't do that.*"

With one simple sentence, she sets the bridge on fire, and it burns down to the ground.

The world goes black around me, everything falling away until there is only me and the phone and a voice that sounds like the person I used to love more than life itself. But it can't be, I reason. The mother I thought I knew couldn't possibly choose a man over her child.

In that impossibly heavy silence, I imagine her eyes scanning to the other side of the room, lip quivering as it always does when she's upset. There, on the wall, is a painting of a storm cloud blanketing a field in darkness. Below the picture, my favorite Bible verse is written in elaborate script. *Jesus wept.*

I am weeping, holding my heart in my own hands and crushing it as I say the words I know must be said but will kill me to speak.

"Then I love you. And I wish you the best. But I can never speak to you again."

Her shock reverberates through the phone in waves that nearly batter me into submission. But I can't let myself be swayed. I dig my heels in and I hold on tight.

"Eden don't do this. I'm your mother, for God's sake."

"I know." That simple truth is the very reason I *have* to do this, and the fact that she can't see that makes it all the more necessary. "And I'm your daughter."

I hang up the phone.

Chapter Thirty-Four

Her eyes finally tear away from the rearview mirror as the road transitions from gravel to pavement. We sit in shocked silence together, with no radio or conversation to distract us from our thoughts. My head feels at once empty and overwhelmingly full, like so much is running through my brain that I can't process any of it.

Main Street is decorated for the holiday, twinkling bells and boughs of holly strung from the power poles lining downtown Ardmore. The roads haven't been cleared of snow, and I can see Mama's hands clinging to the steering wheel to maintain control, both of the car and herself.

We pass rows of historic brick buildings hugged up against one another before they slowly give way to the newer part of town. Here, the fast-food restaurants are dark, the workers at home with their families. The world is waking up, and soon everyone will be opening presents.

The cream-colored building with the green tin roof that I assume is our destination approaches too quickly on the left. Mama's foot never leaves the gas as we zoom past it, so fast we dust the cruisers parked out front with filthy snow from the road.

"Aren't we going to the police station?" I ask her. My voice croaks around the stale tears clogging my throat. Mama's eyes flicker to the rearview mirror briefly before settling on the road once more. Her face is gaunt and void of any emotion.

"What are they going to do?" she scoffs, more to herself than to me. "A slap on the wrist for being a peeping Tom? Besides, all the pictures are gone now anyway."

The truth is a hard knot in my stomach. All the evidence burned up in the fire, alongside my view of the world as a safe place. That knowledge threatens to open the floodgates for the pain. I become a shell of myself, holding my own mind at arm's length so I'm not forced to feel the suffering.

"We don't need anybody else, baby," she says, flashing a glance my way. She merges onto the interstate, headed north toward Nashville. The roads here have been plowed, allowing her to pick up speed. "Just you and me."

I don't acknowledge her statement. Instead I stare out the window at the glistening trees, desperate to lose myself to sleep. When my puffy eyes finally fall to a close, I find myself in a house my mind tries to tell me is home even though it looks unfamiliar. Mazelike hallways leading to endless empty rooms shoot off in each direction. I run from room to room, searching for my mother, Mark's voice hot in my ear. Two tight fists squeeze the air from my lungs. I can't run for very much longer. Just as his calloused hand clamps down on my arm, whipping me around to face him, I jolt awake.

"We're here, Eden," Mama says softly, stroking the mess of bangs back from my forehead like she did when I was a feverish child. I look around and recognize my apartment complex. She's parked in my designated spot, and it occurs to me that we've left my car behind. I shudder at the thought of returning to retrieve it, residual fear from my dream creeping up the base of my neck.

With trembling hands, I pull on the door handle and grab my

small suitcase from where it rests at my feet. Mama climbs out of the car, gathering an overnight bag from the back seat that I didn't notice in our hasty exit. We take to the stairs in silence, both of us moving as if through water. When we step into my apartment, the familiar surroundings don't fill me with their usual comfort. Instead I feel like a trespasser, an unwanted transient walking through my own life.

"I'm going to take a shower," Mama says. She doesn't look at me when she speaks, just pads softly down the hallway to the spare bedroom at the end. I watch as she tosses her bag on the bed before the shutting door cuts me off from her world.

I'm suddenly acutely aware of how disgusting I feel, both inside and out. I follow her lead, trudging into my bedroom and locking the door behind me. I drop my suitcase onto the floor just before the threshold of my bathroom. I turn the faucet as far into the red as it will go, until steam billows out of the shower. Living alone, it never occurred to me to shut the door when I shower, but I find myself pushing it to a close. The hair on the back of my neck stands up, and a shiver runs through me. I stare at the too-wide gap running the length of the base of the door, and the image of Mark sprawled out on the other side with his camera pressed into the opening causes my hands to shake.

I grab a towel from where it hangs on the back of my door and shove it into the crack. The breath I've been holding filters out through my teeth. Satisfied, I remove my clothes and step into the shower, where I scrub my skin until it's raw.

"You don't have anything to eat in here." Mama's voice echoes inside my refrigerator; that's how far she's stuck her head into the empty cavern. I finish braiding my damp hair and secure it with the scrunchie around my wrist, letting my cramping hands rest on the kitchen counter.

"In my defense, I planned to be gone a few days and didn't want anything to spoil."

My words remind us both why we're here. I see it in the stiff set of her shoulders when she stands upright, letting the refrigerator door fall shut. I feel absolutely spent, like I've just run an emotional marathon. My stomach growls, but I could just as easily ignore it and go to sleep, though fear of slipping back into that dream makes me wary.

Mama purses her lips, staring into my pantry. There's tomato soup and a few slices of stale bread, a box of pancake mix but no syrup. I work so much I hardly have time to cook, existing on leftovers from whatever meal I'm catering at the hotel though I don't have it in me to defend myself right now, so I just let her continue her fruitless search.

"No restaurants will be open on Christmas," she says. I sink deeper into the palm of my hand, my elbow barely holding me up. I want to give in to depression, which hovers at the edge of my mind like a group of sharks circling their intended prey. I want to cry and scream at the world for all its injustices. I don't give a damn about dinner right now.

Her eyebrows perk up like a lightbulb has just gone off. "I'll bet that Chinese place up the street is open, right?"

I shrug half-heartedly. Her eyes soften at the edges when she finally looks at me. She comes over to where I'm seated on the barstool and wraps her arms around my waist, squeezing me against her. The dam I built up as we drove away nearly breaks, spilling all my tears with it. But she pulls away, leaving me cold and lonely, before too much damage can be done.

"Honey, do you think you could go get us some food? I just don't think I can face anyone right now." Her voice is pitiful, and the image of her stricken face highlighted by fire pops into my brain. Despite everything in me screaming in protest, I nod my head.

"Thank you, Eden. Just get me whatever you usually order," she says.

She pulls me down to her so she can plant a kiss on my forehead, and it's the quiver in her bottom lip that gives me the strength to stand, grab the keys, and go back downstairs to her car.

The door of China One chimes when I open it, and the lady behind the counter startles from where she sits slumped on a barstool behind the register. There's music playing in the kitchen behind her, and I see two men chatting while they cook. There's a father with two small children seated in a booth that hasn't been reupholstered since the eighties. He barely spares me a glance as I pass, too preoccupied with his talkative daughters.

The cashier has thick hair the color of ink, falling in a straight line down past her elbows. She smiles politely at me while I recite my order.

"Two servings of orange chicken with fried rice!" she yells over her shoulder. A grunt from one of the cooks is the only response she gets. I pay and sign the receipt, crumpling my copy in my fist before taking a seat in an unoccupied booth.

The cashier goes back to reading the folded paperback in her lap. Across the room, the father stares at his phone, trying to ignore his older daughter's inquisition about the logistics of Santa Claus. The world keeps spinning normally around me, but I feel like I've fallen off. It is so surreal, to walk right past these people with my life crumbling around me, and none of them even see the neon sign glowing on my forehead that begs for help.

When I return to the apartment, Mama is curled up against the arm of my couch, talking on the phone while quiet tears stream down her face. She glances up at me as I set the brown paper bag on the table, divvying up its contents between two place settings.

"I've gotta go, Ella. Eden just got back with the food. She's fine. We're both fine. I'll call you later," she says.

She hangs up the phone, offering a pinched smile as she

wipes at her eyes. I duck my head, pretending not to notice, pretending I'm as fine as she says I am.

Later, she falls asleep before the sun has even slipped beneath the horizon. Zoey, who flew into town on Christmas Eve to visit her parents, tells them we aren't able to have our annual joint dinner due to a family emergency. After she eats with them, she drives all the way to Nashville, pulling into my apartment complex just past nine. I'm sitting at the top of the stairs when she parks.

As soon as she sees me, she breaks out into a run, taking the steps two at a time. She sits down beside me and pulls me close as I dissolve into a puddle of tears, finally letting the pain rock through me like an earthquake. She rides out the storm, listening when I want to speak and speaking when I run out of words. The walls will come later, the inability to talk. For now I'm bleeding like an open wound. She does everything in her power to keep me alive.

Time passes in a haze. I tell my boss I have the flu, which buys some time. Zoey flies back to Colorado, but not before begging me to come with her. I tell her I can't leave Mama. She and I wander around the apartment aimlessly, passing like ships in the night. Ella orders groceries to be delivered to us so I don't have to leave again. Neither of us knows where to go from here, so we remain stuck in place.

Two days after Christmas, one of Mama's friends from church stops by my apartment. The two of them sit cross-legged on the couch, holding cups of coffee neither of them touch. I watch from the kitchen, washing the dishes leftover from break-fast. They discuss divorce lawyers and who will get the house in hushed tones they don't think I can hear.

A sob cracks in Mama's chest, and she brings a crumpled tissue up to her nose. Cheryl—at least, I think that's her name—reaches out to pat her knee. It's the most I've ever seen my mother cry, and my nerves are raw from the aching it causes. Since Zoey left, I've forced myself to hold it together. I can't be another source of her pain, no matter how badly I'm hurting.

"I just don't understand how he could do this," Mama cries.

"I don't either," Cheryl replies. The woman's Southern accent is thick, making every word she says twice as long. Her blonde hair is box-dyed and teased so high it'd make a decent helmet in a fall. "I'll never understand why men turn into such sickos around pretty young girls."

Her pointed look in my direction causes me to wince involuntarily. I know she's just trying to comfort my mother, but the words feel too similar to blame for my liking. Shame takes up residence in the chambers of my heart, slowly pumping out into every vein of my body until the poison becomes a part of me.

A week passes, and my boss demands a doctor's note that I don't have. I tell Mama I have to go back to work, and the next morning when I walk out dressed in my slacks and blouse, she's standing by the door holding her bag.

"Where are you going?" I ask, looking back and forth from the suitcase to her in an attempt to understand.

"I'll drop you off at work, and then I'll go back to the house. Zoey's mom is going to come with me to return your car this afternoon, so I have a ride back home."

My head shakes of its own volition. "What do you mean? You can't go back there."

What she intends to be a smile turns into more of a smirk. Her facade is flimsy at best, and I see right through to the fear on the other side.

"I have to. I've got to get things in order, meet with a lawyer, decide where to go from here," she says. "I've got my job at the church to get back to."

I take a step toward her, grabbing her hand. It's clammy against my own.

"Don't go. We can figure that out from here. The pastor will understand."

She bites her lip, worrying the skin until a pinprick of blood appears. Her tongue darts out to wipe it away. I feel so fragile all of a sudden, like every bit of emotion I've suppressed from the past few days is hitting me at once. "Don't leave me, Mama."

"You'll be all right." She wraps her arms around me and squeezes tight, and suddenly I'm a child desperate for my mother's comfort. "I'll just be a phone call away."

I feel her begin to pull away from me long before the embrace is over.

"The end, I guess."

Stephen presses his lips together, letting the dust settle while I wipe my tears away. I'm done trying to resist them, done seeing them as a weakness. I just let them fall and clean them up when it's over.

"And then? What happened next?" he asks when I finish. I sniffle, confused about the question.

"Um, I went back to work. My doctor referred me to you a few weeks later," I reply. He can tell that I am puzzled but remains stoic while I grasp at straws. "I don't really know what else you want me to say. That was the end of my narrative."

I hold up the pages of notes I've scribbled over the past few months, drawing a firm line under the end to prove my point.

"The end of your narrative, yes," he agrees. I know he's trying to guide me somewhere but I'm too tired to follow, so I dig in my heels and wait for him to spit it out. The corners of his lips curve, disappearing behind the beginnings of a beard he's attempting to grow. "But it wasn't the end of your story. Of your life."

"What do you mean?" It certainly felt like it at the time.

"Eden, the most important parts of our stories are not the worst things that have happened to us, but what comes after. There is a beautiful grit that only humans seem to exhibit, by picking themselves up after a tragedy and making life wonderful in spite of its shortcomings."

I think of all the beautiful moments that have happened since that day, moments I would've missed if not for the catalyst that sent me spinning in their direction. I let myself believe Stephen is right. I don't think I'll ever be grateful Mark did what he did, but I'm proud of myself for how I've handled the aftermath. Proud that I've found so many wonderful people to surround myself with, that love me as if I were their own family. Or something even greater than that.

"So what comes next?" he asks again.

I laugh a little before responding. "Well, there's a party at the bar tonight to celebrate it finally having a name."

The sign arrived this morning; Zoey texted me before my session to tell me so. In the picture she sent, bright geometric designs were painted sporadically over the stark black lettering, the word *Nomads* appearing both edgy and welcoming, exactly the way she intended. *A place for weirdos and wanderers*, she said.

"The bar hasn't had a name all this time?" Stephen asks in disbelief. He shakes his head and waves a hand through the air, putting aside the question. "Never mind, that's not the point. I meant what comes next for your future. What wonderful life will you create?"

I smile at him, finally giving in to his request. For a moment I let the past fall away and just focus on all the good that is still to come. I close my eyes, and I can't help it. I immediately picture Chase.

Chapter Thirty-Five

ONE YEAR LATER

My heartbeat pounds against my eardrums. I focus on drawing in deep, raggedy breaths to try and calm my rapid pulse, watching my breath rise like smoke in the cool air. I put one foot in front of the other, despite every muscle protesting against it. My eyes train on the back of Chase's head, his sure step moving forward with the energy I've run out of. I already know what his answer will be, but I decide it's worth a shot to try. "Chase, do you think we could take just one more short break? Penny is really worn out."

Penny perks up at the sound of her name. I look down into her soulful brown gaze, the same one as her father's. She doesn't even try to play along with me to win my case, her happy prancing not the least bit hindered.

When Otter, employee of the month for twelve months running, sired a litter of puppies in the spring, Chase couldn't resist taking Penny home. I run a hand through her downy copper fur, darker than most golden retrievers I've seen before. What can I say? Chase is a sucker for a redhead.

An amused grin thrown over his shoulder tells me exactly

what I suspected: he's not falling for it. "We're almost there, Eden. No giving up now."

I groan, throwing my head back in mock despair. With all hope of giving up shot, I dig deep to tap into my reservoir of determination. We've been at this since just before dawn, when we took off from the trailhead with headlamps to guide our steps. After our fifth break less than an hour ago, Chase began to crackle with anxious energy, urgent to get to the summit. Penny trots eagerly ahead of me, nuzzling against his palm. He strokes the wavy fur behind her ears, causing her tongue to loll to the side.

Just when my chest feels as though it will explode with the effort, we crest the hill we've been climbing and the end is in sight, a stark gray ridge cutting into the bright blue sky. I carefully navigate the crumbled boulders underfoot with decidedly less grace than my two companions. I look down at my worn-in boots, the orange lining now coated in a thick layer of dust. I force myself to trudge forward, eyes on the prize.

In the distance I see two hikers have already made it to our destination. Which, from what Chase has told me, isn't bad considering this is one of the more popular hikes in Colorado due to its entry-level terrain. I don't let myself give in to the temptation to be insulted by that. It's not about what's easy for everyone else; this is my challenge to conquer.

With the very fibers of my legs screaming to let up, I push through the last hundred feet. Chase rushes ahead of me, Penny following suit. I'm confused at first until he pulls a camera from his pack, turning to snap a photo of me as I reach the summit. His triumphant smile stretches from ear to ear, and I know there's a matching one on my face.

I let out a whoop and thrust my fists into the air, relief washing through my exhausted limbs. "I did it!" My gaze falls to meet his. "I can't believe I did it!"

"I always knew you could," he says.

Penny jumps up, planting two paws on my hips, jazzed from the aura of excitement swirling around us. I cradle her head against me, burying my fingers in the thick fur of her neck. I suck in a gust of thin, crisp air as I take in the sweeping views below us. Though it's late summer down below, up here the air is so cold I shiver in my jacket. Pinpricks of tears sting my tired eyes. It's breathtaking, being so high up.

For my whole life, with my mother's fear of heights, anywhere we went that required confronting it, she'd stay behind. From solid ground she'd watch me scale the high ropes course at a church outing or zipline through the trees on a family vacation. It became our thing that I would carry a camera with me and snap a photo of the view from up high, so she could still enjoy what her fear kept her from experiencing firsthand.

Standing here, I take the camera from Chase's hand while he fumbles in his pack for something. I take a photo of the winding mountain ranges in the distance, the evergreen valleys below. I even zoom in on a discarded cardboard sign stuck in the rocks a few yards to my right. The shutter clicks on another photo I won't be able to share with her.

I gingerly navigate the uneven path, crouching to grab the weather-beaten sign. In thick black marker, the words *Quandary Peak* are scrawled above the elevation: 14,271 feet. My first 14er.

When I turn to show Chase, he's unexpectedly right behind me, though I didn't hear him approach. I'm surprised to find him kneeling, and at first I think he's redoing the laces on one of his boots until he looks up at me and cracks a maroon-colored velvet box open in his hand. My heart stills when the midday sun sets the dazzling diamond ring alight.

"Chase, what—"

"Eden," he says, stopping my words in their tracks. He

reaches for my trembling hand, pulling it into the space between us. Penny has stopped pacing and stares at us, as if even she senses the weight of this moment. I'm vaguely aware that one of the other hikers pulls a camera out and snaps a photo. When I peek over, I'm surprised to recognize Zoey and Aaron. She smiles at me and waves, but Aaron hooks an arm around her neck and turns her away to give us some privacy. Chase follows my gaze, chuckling when he sees the struggle. "Figured you'd want your best friend here for this."

The fact that Chase convinced Zoey to hike this mountain is almost as shocking as the ring in his hand. Looking at the two of them pulls my already taut lips into a wider smile. I honestly thought Aaron would've popped the question long before Chase, as in love with Zoey as he obviously is, but she's clearly holding her ground. Having her here to support me on the best day of my life just like she has on so many of the worst is like icing on the cake. I listen to her laugh as she strains against Aaron's choke hold, letting my gaze fall back to Chase. Aaron will wear her down soon enough if he's been taking any lessons from his friend.

Chase looks back up at me, the brightest joy I've ever witnessed unleashed across his face. Like I always do in his presence, I feel warmed from the inside out, as if he is the sun shining all his light down on me. I count the freckles across his cheeks, which are red from the whipping wind. I draw my bottom lip between my teeth, trying to bite back the tears threatening to fall.

"From the moment I met you, I knew I wanted—no, *needed* — to get to know you. You were this sassy, brooding, breathtaking woman that I couldn't bear to stay away from."

A nervous giggle rattles out of me as I picture myself the first time we met, sleep-deprived and uncertain of both the world and my place in it. How confident he seemed, that first day. How I learned something new and wonderful about him each time I saw him after.

"And then I knew you, and you were even more than I could've imagined. You are fiercely loyal, almost to a fault. You see the beauty in all of this"—he juts his chin, which I notice is wobbling, toward the expanse below us—"and in me, too. You love with everything you have, and I'm so lucky that you've chosen to love me."

I can't help the tears that spill over, tears of joy and relief and hope for a future I'd nearly given up on when I pulled up in front of *Nomads* last May. Chase is so good, probably too good for me, and still, he is choosing me. He is choosing the ugly past and the beautiful present and asking to join me on my endless journey of not only healing but thriving, too.

"So, Eden Ross, I was wondering if you'd do me the honor of making this the best life it could possibly be, by becoming my wife?"

There are no words that could do my feelings justice, so I just nod my head as my heart swells beyond the borders of my rib cage, expanding outward and upward until I can hold this moment, this entire mountain and everyone on it, within me forever.

He slides the gold band slowly over my knuckle until it fits snuggly at the base of my finger. I don't even give him a chance to stand up—I fall to my knees, and he pulls me tight against him. His lips find mine, and the taste of saltwater tears mixes with the outdoors and something inexplicably him to overwhelm my senses. I'm suspended in time, in this moment. I suspect part of me always will be.

Aaron and Zoey are cheering in the background. Penny rushes over to us, unwilling to be left out any longer. We pull her into our embrace, completing the circle. Chase cradles my hands in his, admiring his work. The ring feels too beautiful for someone like me to wear, but I decide it's an occasion to rise to rather than something to shy away from. On instinct, his thumb travels to my wrist on the other hand, stroking the curve of puckered skin as he always does. I let myself study the thick black ink covering what used to be a delicate white scar. He traces the sketch of a lemon wedge. When he presses his lips to the tattoo, it no longer feels like he's touching evidence of the pain I've suffered. Instead it feels like a reminder of all the work I've done to add sweetness to the bitter circumstances of my life.

"I'm going to be Mrs. Eden Taylor," I say excitedly, adrenaline and nerves combining to make the words sound like bubbles floating up in the air between us. The thought makes Chase's amber eyes crinkle at the edges as he plants another kiss on my temple.

"Mrs. Taylor," he says, more to himself than to me. His gaze travels over the horizon, focusing on something far in the distance. "You wouldn't believe how excited my mom is to share the title with you."

His words are light, floating on the surface of the water. Just beneath this truth lies two people we both wish we could share this moment with. I can tell from the softening edges of his smile that he's thinking about his father. I lean my head into the crook of his neck, excitement mingling with the longing to pick up the phone and call my mother. To tell her I'm getting married.

This beautiful moment exists, like so much of my life since she and I last spoke, as a bittersweet reminder that life goes on, even when you don't think it can. The long days stretched into months and then into a year, each passing moment tipping the scales away from the bad in favor of the good. I've carved out this little piece of heaven from my less-than-ideal circumstances, and that has to be enough for me.

As Zoey and Aaron finally rush toward us to join in on the

group hug, Penny lets out a howl of joy. Chase tears his glassy stare away from that far-off point, returning his focus to me and the promise we've just made to each other. For better or worse, for my whole life. It's more than enough.

Thank you so much for taking the time to read Eden's story. If you liked THE END AND THEN, please leave a review at your favorite retailer and tell a friend!

The Loveless series continues with Zoey's story, *What's Left of Me*, available Summer 2023. Turn the page for a special preview.

Enjoy a Sneak Peek of WHAT'S
LEFT OF ME

What's Left of Me

A plume of smoke blurs my vision as the acrid scent of cigarettes stings my nostrils. My two less-than-dedicated line cooks and the tagalong dishwasher are relaxing against the brick wall to my right, unaware that they're being observed. I place one hand on my hip and make a disapproving clucking noise with my tongue, causing three pairs of eyes to spread wide in embarrassment as the heads they're attached to whip around to find out who has caught them.

"Santi has three tickets on the order wheel. It'd be a lot easier to fulfill them if he had anyone in there cooking," I say.

A chorus of, "Yes, Boss," and "Sorry, Jefa," rises up on the last tendril of smoke as Eric and Mateo put out the cigarettes under their restaurant-grade non-slip shoes. They trudge past me while Marcelin takes one last drag and then does the same.

"My apologies, miss," he mutters in his thick Haitian accent, ducking his head as he follows the other two inside. I pour a splash of water from my insulated bottle over the flickering butts to make sure no sparks remain. When I'm satisfied, I return to the kitchen, pulling the door shut behind me and arming the alarm.

"You guys gotta be careful; you could start a fire," I say. They keep their heads low while they each scrub their hands before getting back to work. Santi winks at me as he doles out tasks, grateful I don't mind being the hard-ass so he doesn't have to be.

I push through the saloon doors as the sounds of the party reach me. It seems like the whole town is here, which probably still wouldn't be enough people to fill the bar considering Loveless's population after the summer tourists leave is laughable. It just goes to show how many people were rooting for Chase and Eden and want to celebrate their engagement.

My best friend saunters out of the crowd like Moses parting the Red Sea, holding an empty copper cup in the air and shaking it, the melting ice cubes singing the siren call of someone needing a refill. I reach for the mug, but Eden dances past me with a smirk, clinking it against the already made whiskey sour Maddie is garnishing for Chase's mother.

"Ed*en*," Maddie whines. "If I make a mess, it'll be your fault."

She tucks a bar napkin under the sweating glass and passes it to Laura before gathering the ingredients for the Honeybee Mule I created specifically for Eden's engagement party. Eden just rolls her eyes at Maddie, pinching her elbow affectionately.

"If I recall correctly, you once caused me to douse myself with an entire beer keg. Seems like I'm overdue for some revenge," Eden says, wriggling her eyebrows.

"That one was also your fault," Maddie reminds her. She curls her nose at the memory, the diamond stud nestled there winking in the low light of the bar.

"Touché," Eden replies. "I'm sorry, I just wanted to give Zo a chance to stop working for just a second and actually enjoy the party she worked so hard to put together."

"Zoey never stops working," Gary chimes in, his grumbly

voice cutting through the noise of the crowd. "But I don't have to tell you that."

Eden smiles, taking the refilled copper mug from Maddie's outstretched hand and sidling up to me, her free arm looping through mine. "But we love her for that."

"That we do," Gary agrees, stroking at his white beard, which looks more like a puffy cloud with every inch it grows. He drops his empty glass over the bar, refilling it with Sprite from the soda gun Maddie passes to him. Only she could be working as a bartender and somehow still have the patrons pour their own drinks.

She waltzes to the other end of the bar where Eden's brother-in-law, Jarrett, has his arm outstretched to get her attention. I haven't seen him in several years, with how busy his patients keep him. Gray is beginning to creep up his hairline, turning his temples more salt than pepper, though it makes him look distinguished rather than aged. He ducks his head in to calmly request another beer for himself and a margarita for Ella, who's no doubt locked in an emotional discussion somewhere with Rose. He catches my eye, and I nod at him with a smile, my thousandth time thanking him for taking the weekend off to be here for Eden.

"Seriously, Zo," Eden says, her voice low as her eyebrows pull together. "I can never thank you enough for putting this together."

Her emerald eyes shimmer with a fresh set of happy tears threatening to spill over, and I swallow back the lump rising in my throat. I pat her hand where it rests against my bicep, feeling the rough edges of a diamond ring scraping against my palm. The gratitude I feel for her happiness after so much undeserved pain is almost enough to overwhelm me.

Instead I clear my throat, and she shakes her head with a

laugh, looking skyward to encourage the tears to retreat. "Anything for you," I say.

She smirks as her gaze flickers over my shoulder, and I turn to see Aaron and Chase approaching. With chilly fall nights making their way into the valley, Aaron's dressed in a cream-colored Henley tee that he's left unbuttoned. It hugs the contours of his body, each ridge of lean muscle pressing against the fabric. His dark wash jeans sit low on his hips, and I know if he turned around, I'd see them conform to an ass that looks like it was sculpted from marble. A cocky grin tugs at his lips when he catches me checking him out, and I pull my gaze from his to leave him wanting more.

Not that that's ever a problem with Aaron. He always wants more. More than I'm capable of giving.

"It'll be your turn soon enough," Eden says. My head snaps around so fast it almost gives me whiplash. She's smiling even wider, and I know for her she's just offered me the best outcome she could imagine. But it's not in the cards for me, and I don't know how to explain that to her.

"I keep telling Aaron to lock her down before she wises up," Chase adds. He cuts behind me and tucks his head between ours, planting a friendly kiss on my cheek before locking his lips with Eden's. It's so much unadulterated love that I have to step away for fear it might burn me up from being too close.

A smile tugs at Aaron's tantalizingly full lips, but he doesn't correct his friend. It's one of my favorite things about him. He knows it's not him that's holding us back from that step, yet he takes the blame anyway, shielding me from having to produce an explanation for them when I haven't even found a way to give one to him.

Chase calls an order out to Maddie as Eden sips her drink, the alcohol filling her lily-white skin with a flush of color.

Maddie nods a quick acknowledgment before muttering, "Can't wait for Zander to be back."

"You've got about a month left," Eden says.

Chase nips at her earlobe, making her laugh. She leans into his side so easily, unaware that for every inch he moves, she mirrors him, and he does the same to her. It is a deep tie between them, one that tugs the other in the direction they are going without a second thought. I let myself envy it for just a moment before patching that wall back up.

Aaron slides an arm around my waist, pressing a kiss against the pulse point at the base of my neck and sending the rhythm skyrocketing. His breath disturbs the tangle of blonde curls escaping from my clip, bringing with it the familiar scent of whiskey and ginger ale. How many nights have I poured him that very drink and then licked it from his lips in the dark parking lot behind the bar, away from prying eyes?

The pleasure of that thought is so rich, so velvety soft in my mind, that when Aaron pinches the roll of fat at the base of my stomach and a memory like a sharp knife cuts through the moment, the juxtaposition is shocking. I go perfectly still, waiting for him to admonish me for the weight I've gained. I prepare myself to go on defense. *I've been working so much lately. It'll come off so easily, I promise.*

But it's not Aaron in my memory, nor his harsh words invading my mind, and just as quickly as I found myself a decade in the past, I come back to the present. I look up to meet his concerned gaze, his eyes two pools of jade green so beautiful that just looking at them feels like slipping into a cool lagoon. His playful pinch was meant to elicit a laugh or a squirm or a shriek like most women would react with, not the rigid spine and clammy skin he now feels underneath his touch. A wrinkle forms between his scrunched-up eyebrows. I smooth the crease out with my finger, shaking my head as I pull away from the embrace. I couldn't explain it even if I tried, so I don't.

"Okay, enough relaxing for me," I say. "Back to work."

———

I tug the gold *Engaged* banner from the last remaining hook where it was secured, letting it fall to the ground in front of the barstools. While I'm up here, I check the leaves of my ivy plant running wild across the wooden beam over the counter. All free and clear of any pests. Perfect.

"Kitchen is back in order," Santi grumbles as he crosses beneath my ladder. "Guys are all gone home. They're a mess."

"I know, but aren't you glad we have them? We'd never have survived a night like tonight with just you and me cooking," I reply.

Santi blows a shrill whistle out, wiping imaginary sweat from his brow. "Things were definitely less busy when Gary was running the place."

"That's what good marketing will do for you," I say, wiping my hands off on my sweater. "You keep making the magic and I'll sell it."

He smiles up at me and tugs on the leg of my flared jeans.

"Good night, Zoey," he says. "And you, Aaron."

"Night, Santi," Aaron calls from the other side of the room, where he is meticulously disassembling a rather impressive balloon arch by cutting a small hole in the base of each balloon to let the air slowly leak out.

"Why don't you just pop those?" Santi asks, pulling a headphone out of one ear.

Aaron glances up at me, and I press my lips together to fight back the smile trying to form. "Zoey hates the sound."

I mouth, *Thank you*, to him over Santi's shoulder as I finally plant my feet firmly on the ground, folding up my stepladder and gathering the rumpled banner. Santi scoffs, looking from Aaron to me and back.

"You got it bad, man," he says before shaking his head and turning to leave, waving a hand over his head in a final farewell.

"Don't I know it," Aaron replies, more to me than to Santi, who is already closing the door behind him. He holds my gaze, a dare in his eyes that I shy away from even as it causes goose bumps to stand at attention on my forearms. I'm grateful for the long sleeves covering the evidence.

I busy myself with disposing of the remaining decorations as he slits the throat of the last gold balloon. When they've all been reduced to a depressing puddle of latex, he heaps them into the waiting garbage bag and brings it over to its rightful place next to mine.

"I've been thinking," he says, reaching for the claw clip at the back of my head and releasing what little of my mane has managed to stay contained in its grasp. He tangles his hands in my hair, massaging my scalp. My eyelids flutter closed as a moan climbs up my throat.

"About what?" I hum, wrapping my hands around his waist and tugging him closer. I slip a hand under his shirt, searching for the comfort of his scorching-hot skin and tightly coiled muscles.

"About what Eden said."

My hands freeze in place, nails inadvertently digging into his skin a little too hard, but he doesn't say a word. He ceases his massage but keeps my curls tangled in his fingers, cradling my head a breath away from his face. I open my eyes and lock my gaze with his. We are in a standoff, neither of us one to back down from a challenge.

"Aaron, I told you—"

"I know, I know. 'We're nothing serious.'" He cocks his

head, a sad smile distorting his otherwise perfect face. "The problem is, you've been saying that for a year and a half. That timeline alone would suggest otherwise."

"It's what we agreed on," I say, stepping backward. He releases his hold, letting his hands fall but capturing one of mine on its retreat from his waist. "This is what we both wanted, remember? No strings."

"That was before, Zoey." He looks down at our joined hands, his dark skin in direct contrast to my pale knuckles. "I think I've proven to you how I feel, but in case I haven't made it clear enough, I'd marry you tomorrow if you'd let me."

I fight the urge to run away, forcing myself to study the familiar planes of his face. His smooth jaw free of stubble, his perfect nose and downturned eyes. Gone is the carefree guy who wanted nothing more than to sneak around with me and flirt under the noses of everyone else. He's been replaced by a man as serious as the relationship he's asking me for, the one I can't give him.

I can't take the desperate hope in his expression. I lean forward, pressing my forehead against his collarbone. I listen to his familiar heartbeat, quickened as it is when we summit a mountain, or when I sink my teeth into his shoulder as he buries himself inside of me.

"I just don't want the same things," I say. "I don't know that I ever will."

He scoffs, stepping away from me completely, leaving me so suddenly cold I cross my arms to insulate myself. "Bullshit, Zo. I see the way you look at me. I feel the way you respond to my touch. I know I'm not alone in this."

His anger flips some switch inside me, hot flames of indignance lapping at the tendrils of sadness. I bristle, glaring at him with what I hope is an intimidating amount of rage despite the five-foot-tall, blonde-hair, blue-eyed package it's being delivered in.

"I have never been anything but honest with you," I say through gritted teeth. "About where I stand and what I want. If you misread anything, that's on you. I am who I am, and you can take it or leave it."

"Zo, please—"

"No." I have to say these next words clearly so he will understand their weight. I can't let him have any false hope, because I've had it before and it's soul crushing. "No talk of forever. No commitments. I'm not ready. I don't know if I'll ever be ready. And if you insist on demanding a final answer, the answer will be no."

I can't stand here one moment longer; my skin feels like it is too tight for my body and any second I'm going to break free of it. I grab the ties of the two garbage bags and march toward the back door, leaving Aaron standing there with the muscle in his jaw twitching, hands flexing and unflexing in a rhythm all their own. What he doesn't know is that he's clenching around the remnants of my heart, which I've torn to shreds and left tucked into his fists.

Acknowledgments

First and foremost, to Andrew. I was only able to write about the love of a good man because you showed me what that looked like. Thank you for loving me so well. For being a warm beam of sunlight that reaches the darkest corners of my soul. I will never stop pinching myself to make sure this beautiful life we've built is for real.

A hundred thousand thank-yous are owed to Lea Ann, editor-in-chief, professional encourager, late-night-text reader, semi-professional therapist and big sister to boot. Thank you for believing in this story and, more importantly, in my ability to tell it. I couldn't have done it without you.

To my amazing team of beta readers: Amanda, Patrice, Avery, Alexis, and Savannah. Thank you for putting eyes on these characters and helping them grow to their full potential. From fleshing out the therapy scenes with Alexis to Amanda's reaction texts while reading the spicy scenes to Patrice troubleshooting Zander's accent, I owe you all my endless gratitude.

I'd be remiss if I didn't mention Lauren, who has become a fast friend and fantastic cheerleader as I navigate all things Bookstagram and website related. Thank you for loving and being genuinely excited for this book. Nicole, my writing soul sister, thank you for always knowing what word I'm trying to think of and for staring at the wall right alongside me.

A special shout-out to Noah Gundersen, whose music was the soundtrack of my college years and the rough ones that followed. Thank you for writing an anthem to every heartbreak, change of life, and beautiful moment I've experienced.

To each and every reader, I don't know that I'll ever be able to adequately explain to you what it means to me that you've read my book. This story is, first and foremost, Eden's, a character I admire for her strength and resilience. Something I hope you love about her, too. But at its core, the hardest parts of Eden's story are those that I borrowed from my own.

In a way, this book is my trauma narrative, one that I wrote with a very specific purpose. I wanted to make the message clear for whoever needs to hear it that you own what has happened to you and there is power when you tell that story, even if it's just to yourself. You owe no one an explanation or apology for the boundaries you create in order to heal. There is no right way to move past trauma, but know that whatever path you choose, somewhere in the world I am rooting for you with all my heart. You are worthy of good love, especially the kind you give to yourself. This story, dear reader, is for you.

If you have been the victim of sexual violence, help is available. The National Sexual Assault Hotline can be reached at 1-800-656-4673 (US) and more resources are available at www.rainn.org and www.NAMI.org for mental health assistance.

About Hannah Bird

Hannah's accolades include a second grade teacher who said her story about bats had "very good potential" and enough accelerated reading medals to sink a body at sea. Her goals in life are to write Contemporary Women's and New Adult Fiction novels that will make you cry, and to check everything off the bucket list she wrote at seventeen.

Hannah resides among the rolling hills of Tennessee with her other half and their clingy golden retriever. When she is not writing, she is trying to outrun her sweet tooth in the gym.

You can travel along with Hannah on her writing journey at her website, hannahbirdauthor.com, and at all the bookish destinations below:

 facebook.com/hannahbirdauthor

instagram.com/hannahbirdauthor

9 798987 266601